LORD MARTIN'S SCANDALOUS BLUESTOCKING

Elizabeth Rolls

MILLS & BOON

First published in Great Britain 2022
by Mills & Boon, an imprint of HarperCollins*Publishers* Ltd,
1 London Bridge Street, London, SE1 9GF

www.harpercollins.co.uk

HarperCollins*Publishers*
1st Floor, Watermarque Building,
Ringsend Road, Dublin 4, Ireland

Lord Martin's Scandalous Bluestocking © 2022 Elizabeth Rolls

ISBN: 978-0-263-30204-2

12/22

This book is produced from independently certified FSC™ paper
to ensure responsible forest management.
For more information visit: www.harpercollins.co.uk/green.

Printed and Bound in Spain using 100% Renewable Electricity
at CPI Black Print, Barcelona

For my two editors.

Linda, who worked with me for over twenty years and started this book with me. And Sheila, who has taken me on with her eyes wide open and helped me finish it.

Thanks to both of you for your patience, expertise and good humour.

Prologue

Bloomsbury Square, London—
Christmas Eve 1803

Catherine Carshalton rested her forehead on the cold window of her bedchamber. Outside soft, fat snowflakes whirled down into the garden of her father's Bloomsbury Square mansion. It was generally considered a very fine house. Luxurious, with every modern convenience that a man of wealth and standing in the City could desire. Everything of the best and no expense spared. Even the servants' livery dripped gold braid. Kit considered it the gaudiest in London. Her own bedchamber was enormous. Painted white and the palest of pale eggshell-blue, the plaster mouldings glinted gold in the lamplight. A fine Axminster carpet covered the floor and damask silk hangings of the same eggshell-blue, trimmed with gold braid to rival the footmen, shrouded the bed.

It was a gilded cage.

A month ago she had believed she would be escaping the cage for ever. She had accepted the necessity of a marriage of convenience to Lord Martin Lacy as a means to that end. But now her betrothal was broken and her heart along with it. She wasn't quite sure how it had happened. Love had never been part of the bargain struck by their parents for Lord Martin Lacy, youngest son of a duke, and the slave trader's daughter. She blinked back the stupid, useless tears welling up. She had done the only possible thing in breaking the betrothal. Martin was lost to her and tears wouldn't bring him back, or ease the raw ache of her heart.

She stared out at the snow. Her fingers went to the fading bruise on her cheek, legacy of her father's fury when she told him her betrothal was ended. She had barely been permitted to leave her apartments in the last three weeks, let alone the house. This wasn't the first time she'd felt the restrictions of being a mere female, but now those restrictions bit deep.

When I win free of this coil, I swear on Mama's grave, I'll never submit to a man again!

In less than three months she turned twenty-one, legally free of her father's authority. She would no longer be his property to dispose of or discipline as he saw fit.

She needed a plan. Even once she was twenty-one, none of the servants would dare help, or turn a blind eye if she attempted to leave. She needed to act sooner rather than later. Tomorrow morning, after church. That was her chance to reach the one person who could help her when the time came. If she could slip away in the crowd as the congregation left, a few minutes' head start would suffice. She would accept the inevitable whipping afterwards.

For the first time ever she was grateful for the presence of her father's friend and business associate Mr Lucius Winthrop at dinner. She loathed Winthrop. According to Mr Winthrop a woman should think only what her male relatives told her to think, if think she must. She knew the litany of what was expected of a proper woman: subordinate, meek, submissive, unheard. Exactly as her father demanded.

So she hid behind a mask of compliance and gritted her teeth.

When Winthrop had commended piety in a young lady she had smiled demurely.

'Shall you be attending divine service with us tomorrow, sir?'

Winthrop had preened.

'Why certainly, my dear Catherine. A very proper day of observance for a young woman, if I may say so.'

She'd resisted the urge to throw her soup at him

and disguised her triumph under the cloak of passivity, not daring to look at her father. He wouldn't want to offend Winthrop, but if he suspected she had manipulated them, he would block her.

But her father merely nodded, barely glancing up from his soup bowl.

Check.

Winthrop and her father were, at bottom, two bullying, domineering peas in a pod. Only Winthrop's darkness hid beneath a veneer of aristocratic sophistication. But this evening, as she forced herself to eat and hid herself within the submissive demeanour her father demanded, her skin had crawled.

Three months. That was all.

Now, hours later, she shivered. Winthrop's eyes had been constantly on her, although rarely on her face. She understood his expression. It had often been on her father's face when he eyed a new housemaid. Although, she mused, not so much this last year or two. Nor had any housemaids been dismissed—the usual fate of housemaids who caught his eye.

Winthrop had not troubled her in the past. He could not possibly think to seduce her. Nor could her father be unaware of his interest, but he had been after a bigger catch than the heir presumptive to a mere viscount—to wit, Lord Martin Lacy. And even she had not understood exactly how big Carshalton had intended the catch to be. But with the betrothal broken, its protection was gone. A broken betrothal cast a slur on a girl—Carshalton was forced to look lower than a duke's son for his daughter. And although Winthrop was merely heir presumptive to his great-uncle, Viscount Staverton, given that Staverton was a widower in his eighties, Lucius Winthrop's accession to the title was almost guaranteed.

He wanted an ally in the Lords, not merely a duke's younger son.

She had to talk to her great-uncle, Ignatius Selbourne.

Would her father attend church in the morning, or would Winthrop escort her alone? If Carshalton came, slipping away might be impossible. She needed to know and she was fairly sure the pair of them were still downstairs quaffing brandy in what her father fondly thought of as his library. The clock on her dressing table chimed midnight. Drawing a deep breath, she went to the servants' door that led to the backstairs. The servants would be abed now except for her father's valet and whichever footman was waiting on Winthrop. And they would be waiting in those respective bedchambers.

Not needing a candle, she slipped into the darkness beyond.

'Stupid little bitch.'

Her father's voice. No need to wonder who the

stupid little bitch was—he called her that with great regularity. Along with the hurt, her guilt over eavesdropping had long since died. Information was the currency of survival in this house.

'She's still moping over that bloody fool Lacy.'

'No matter, Carshalton.' Winthrop sounded dismissive. 'I trust I know how to give a feckless girl's thoughts a better direction.'

She gritted her teeth. Feckless? For an enduring affection?

'I'll warrant you do. She'll come around quick enough once you've got her to wife.'

Catherine's stomach executed a slow roll. She might not have until her birthday if it had gone this far...

'You've got the licence?'

She barely stifled her gasp.

'Certainly.'

'Good. Bring it to church in the morning. She's played into our hands, suggesting you attend church with us. I've spoken to the parson. You can be married directly after the service.'

Fear crawled over her in the darkness, sinking poisoned claws deep, paralysing her.

'Excellent!' Winthrop sounded delighted. 'As you say, the chit will come around soon enough.'

Something about his smug assurance shattered her choking fear.

Like hell she would!

'You'll want to make quite sure of her.' Her father's voice. 'I told you. She fancies herself in love.'

'You think she might refuse to do as she's bidden?'

Nothing was more certain!

'Oh, she'll do as she's bid. When she's boxed in right. When she's got no choice.' His words fell cold and heavy. 'I suggest you see to that tonight.'

There was a long silence while ice deepened and twisted in her belly.

Carshalton spoke again. 'Aye. I see you take my meaning. Once you've had her, the game's over. Just make sure you don't mark her where it will show. Another brandy? There's no rush.'

Ten minutes later, clutching a small valise and huddled in her mother's old ermine cloak, Catherine slipped into the dining room by the servants' door. Winthrop and her father were still next door in the library, but she dared not wait. A glass of brandy didn't take long to drink and once they found her missing...

They might search quietly at first, not wanting the servants to gossip, but the hunt would be raised eventually. She had to be long gone by then. Her throat still burned from throwing up uncontrollably in her chamber pot when she reached her room. Hopefully they would think at first she was unwell and had sought out the housekeeper. But when they realised she was gone...well, she'd done her best to misdirect the hunt. Please God, it would buy her enough time.

Pushing the curtains aside, she slipped the catch on the dining room window, opened it and stepped over the sill into the snowstorm. The wind whipped in, nearly tugging the window from her grip, and she gasped, pulling the casement shut. How to secure it from outside? She dropped the valise, fished in her pocket with one hand and found her handkerchief. Wadding it up, she opened the casement a fraction and stuffed the handkerchief in the gap, pulling hard. Holding her breath, she released the window. It held.

The cold slashed at her, but she wrapped the cloak tighter around her. The snow was a blessing. It would shield her and cover her escape if anyone should chance to look out a window.

A single muffled chime came from the tower of St George's Church around the corner. Christmas morning and she was fleeing into a snowstorm.

Five minutes later she was astride the garden wall, courtesy of a gardener's ladder left handy for clearing gutters. The snow drifted down, shrouding the world in white silence. With a deep breath she pushed the ladder away from the wall and it fell with a soft *whump*, immediately beginning to disappear beneath the blanketing snow.

She glanced back at the house, barely a ghostly outline in the veiling snow. There Catherine Carshalton had been a cipher, a prisoner with no future beyond what her father decreed.

Catherine and the past were dead.

Kit drew another deep breath, swung her leg over and jumped.

Chapter One

Soho—March 1805

*T*he grey, wintry wind whipped around the curricle, sneaking through a gap in the hood, but snuggled in the heavy fur cloak she felt nothing beyond the lash of it on her cheek. Everything faded away as she stared at the ring Martin had just placed on her finger and slowly looked up.

His eyes. She had always loved those bright tawny eyes. Eyes that could snap with anger or laugh uproariously into hers. But surely they had never gazed at her quite like this?

As though...as though...

'You like it?'

She couldn't speak, only nod. Words were an impossibility, blocked by a choking lump compounded of everything she did not dare to say.

'Sweetheart?'

*And when he called her that? She knew better,
but yet she believed.*

*'I had it engraved for you, but if you are not
quite sure, we can—'*

*She fumbled the ring off and read the tiny in-
scription inside the shank:* The star to ev'ry
wand'ring barque.

*She slid the ring back on to her finger as his
arms closed around her, drew her close, and a
gentle hand under her chin lifted her face for his
kiss. But at the first seeking touch of his lips the
wind rose to a howl and everything tumbled away
in a shriek of accusations and shame, bitterness
and grief, and galloping hooves...*

She woke in a rush, tears still wet on her cheeks,
to the real rattle of hooves. Outside the light was
growing, flinging a bright banner through the gap
in her curtains on to the opposite wall.

The light always comes back.

Kit pushed back the night's dreams with the
bedcovers and rose.

The woman who had been Catherine Carshalton hurried downstairs, her dog at her heels. Her
only jewellery was the little anti-slavery medallion
that had belonged to her aunt. The bookshop below
the apartment she shared with her great-uncle was
still shuttered, but she knew where everything was
and made her way unerringly in the dimness to the
kitchen and storage area behind the shop.

Dragging back the bolts and unlocking the door, Kit let the dog out into the yard and wondered who the early rider had been. No doubt she'd know by mid-morning. News travelled up, down and across the busy Soho streets faster than a pickpocket could make his getaway. Moth trotted straight over to her preferred corner and squatted to do what a dog needed to do. Kit pushed her short curls back from her face as the dog sniffed around the yard to investigate any evidence of overnight visitors of the feline persuasion. Later, she would need a proper walk, but this would do for now. Used to the routine—after all, it involved breakfast—Moth came back, wagging her tail.

A few moments later Kit had bread and cheese cut, the fire stirred up and the kettle on to make tea. While Moth wolfed down breakfast in the kitchen, Kit folded back the shutters on the front windows of her uncle's bookshop while a sharp breeze frisked down the street, banishing tendrils of fog, and whipped her skirts about her ankles. It was *her* bookshop, too, she reminded herself, as she latched a shutter back. Uncle Ignatius had taken her into partnership last spring after she turned twenty-one.

Up and down the narrow street shopkeepers were opening for the day. Soon the street would rumble with wagons and hooves, the air shrill with the voices of delivery boys. But it was quiet yet, although somewhere around the corner a cow lowed.

Kit made a mental note to watch for the dairymaid who milked her charges right at the door for you.

Over the road her closest friend Psyché, the proprietor of the Phoenix Rising coffee house, was out on the pavement opening her own shutters. A large, glossy orange and white cat wound about the Black woman's ankles, mewing in what sounded like the final stages of starvation.

'Good morning, Kit.'

'Psyché. Good morning.'

Kit latched the last shutter and they smiled across at each other. Two women who ought not, according to the dictates of society, have ever met, let alone become friends.

'Is Ignatius ready for his coffee?'

'I hope he's still asleep.'

She had finally persuaded her great-uncle to sleep longer in the mornings while she readied the shop for the day. It was a small thing, but he became so weary and short of breath by the end of the afternoon that she did as much as she possibly could to spare the man who had braved Carshalton's wrath, taking her in and protecting her when she fled. She owed him a debt she could never repay.

'How is he?' Psyché reached down to rub her cat's head.

'He won't admit it, but he's tiring more and more.' Ignatius had confessed last November that his doctor thought he was dying.

Old age, Kit. Finally caught up with me. I'll be sorry not to have more time here with you, but you're safe enough now.

Psyché nodded slowly as she straightened. 'I'll miss him.'

Ignatius had been Psyché's business mentor, too, when she took over the coffee house some years earlier. And she had repaid the debt—although Ignatius never thought of it in those terms—by hiding Kit when she fled her father's house fifteen months ago. Kit still wondered at the risk Psyché had taken for her when they barely knew each other. The daughter of a slave and the slave trader's daughter—an unlikely pairing if ever there was one.

But then Psyché, thought Kit, had more courage in her little finger than she had ever had.

Psyché went on. 'Caleb will bring coffee over later. I… I have to go out to Hampstead immediately.'

Kit's gut iced. 'Your cousin—the rider earlier was for you?' She noticed the valise sitting by the open front door of the coffee house.

Taking advantage of a break in the traffic, she clicked her fingers for Moth and hurried across the road.

Moth, keeping a wary eye on the cat, sat in front of Psyché and offered a paw, something she only did for those she knew and liked. Psyché laughed and shook the paw just as her husband, Will, came out of the Phoenix dressed for riding and carrying his hat along with a bulging satchel.

He gave Kit a worried smile and nod. 'Good morning, Kit.'

He bent to his wife, kissed her. 'I'll reach Hampstead by late afternoon. I promise.'

'There's no need, Will.' She returned the kiss. 'You have your work to do and—'

'Don't waste your breath. Give Hetty my love and assure her we'll stand by her.'

Will slung the satchel across his body. 'Caleb is bringing your trunk. It's got my clothes in it, too.'

The cat meowed piteously and stood up to bat at Will's hand. He petted the creature absentmindedly. 'Promise me you'll have a rest after lunch?'

'Damn it—'

He silenced her with the simple expedience of another kiss. 'I love you.'

'Oh, very well. I'll rest.'

He kissed her again. 'Thank you. Sure you won't be carriage sick?'

'I've enough ginger root to chew my way to Land's End.'

Kit stared—unlike herself, Psyché was never carriage sick.

Psyché patted her arm. 'I'm increasing. He hasn't stopped fussing since I told him.'

Even as Kit blinked, Will kissed his wife again. 'Learn to live with it.'

Kit's heart melted at Will's tender concern so

the crack in it ached. She pushed the feeling down firmly. She couldn't help her dreams, but she must not live in them. She had her whole *independent* life ahead of her. And if a little voice whispered to her that Psyché had her independence *and* a loving husband to boot, then exceptions always proved the rule. She, Kit Selbourne—she would *never* use the Carshalton name again—was building her life and happiness on her own terms.

She watched as Will strode off down the pavement to the Red Lion where he stabled his horse. Until his marriage to Psyché he'd been employed by the Marquess of Huntercombe as his private secretary. He was still employed by the Marquess, but as His Lordship's London agent, overseeing all properties belonging to Huntercombe within a fifty-mile radius of London. Also, he continued to carry particularly sensitive letters for the Marquess if they needed to go beyond London.

'Is Hetty unwell? Must you go?' Henrietta, Lady Harbury, was Psyché's much loved cousin. She had inherited their great-uncle's house above Hampstead Heath and lived there, estranged from her husband. But Psyché—Kit risked a glance at her friends as-yet flat belly—now had a new someone to think about.

Psyché turned from watching after Will, worry in her dark eyes. 'I must. Harbury is dead.'

'*Dead?* How?'

Psyché let out a shaky breath. 'A highway man two nights ago—on the Heath.'

Kit's mind raced. 'On the Heath? What was he doing there? Surely he wasn't visiting Hetty?'

Psyché shut her eyes for a moment. 'That's the bad bit. Apparently he showed up at the front door just after sunset with Lucius, demanding dinner and accommodation for the night. Hetty refused and the servants barred the doors.'

'With Lucius.' Kit's stomach churned. Lucius Winthrop, the man who had intended to force her into marriage—now Viscount Staverton—was Hetty's father.

'Is he dead, too?'

Psyché grimaced. 'I'm afraid not. Just Harbury. I must go to her. Lucius is making noises about assuming guardianship of her children.'

Kit hugged her. 'She's your family.'

'I'm leaving Caleb in charge as usual. You'll keep an eye on things a bit, won't you? There's always the possibility of some idiot stranger who thinks to take advantage of his youth.'

'You don't have to ask.'

A young Black man came out of the Phoenix, hefting a trunk. 'Here's your luggage, Miss Psyché. Anything else?'

'No, Caleb. You're in charge, remember. Any trouble, though and Kit and Ignatius will back you up.'

'Aye, Miss Psyché.' He gave his employer a patient we've-been-through-this-before sort of look.

Kit grinned. She didn't think there would be any trouble at all. It wasn't the first time in the past several months that Caleb had been in charge for a few days—he'd managed perfectly well, only coming over to the bookshop to deliver coffee, or for company at the end of the day.

An expensive-looking carriage, drawn by two horses and followed by an outrider, swung out of the yard of the Red Lion.

'Here's the carriage.' Psyché gave Kit a quick hug. 'They were just going to change the horses and come back, but Will gave them some money for breakfast and said it would give us time to pack. Take care.'

Kit returned the hug. 'You too. And give my—' *Condolences?* After Harbury's involvement in an attempt to kidnap Psyché a year ago Hetty had flatly refused to see him. Hetty's friends had used the threat of scandal to secure Harbury's agreement to the separation and to leave the children with her.

'Give my best regards to Lady Harbury.' She had no idea how Psyché's cousin would feel about Harbury's death.

They waited as the carriage rumbled off doing a circuit of the streets to finally pull up in front of the Phoenix. A footman leapt down from the back and he and Caleb heaved the trunk into the boot.

'All ready, Mistress Psyché?'

'Yes. Thank you.' Psyché permitted him to hand her into the carriage and leaned out the window once he'd shut the door. 'Will is only remaining a couple of nights at the most and I'll be back in a few days. Give my love to Ignatius. Caleb, you'll remember to—'

'Feed the cat?' He rolled his eyes. 'You think he'll let me forget?'

She laughed. 'Probably not. Now, don't forget—'

But whatever she thought he might have forgotten was lost in a clatter of hooves and a rumble of wheels as the coachman took advantage of a gap to pull away from the curb.

Kit tried to stifle her laughter as she turned to Caleb. 'Whatever she thinks you've forgotten, I'm sure you'll remember it.'

Caleb snorted. 'She's been like a cat on hot bricks since the groom brought the message. Worrying about this and fussing about that—probably because she didn't have time to think about it all.' He scowled. 'I'm not going to pretend I'm sorry—' he paused, cleared his throat, 'Lord Harbury's dead. Not after what he and Staverton got away with last year. Not very Christian of me, but neither's lying.'

Kit patted his shoulder. 'I can't blame you.' Being shot at as you leapt from a moving coach and ran to raise the alarm that your mistress was being kidnapped was the sort of thing one neither forgot nor forgave quickly. If Staverton and Harbury weren't wealthy members of the House of Lords, they would have faced charges. Instead the threat of the scandal had been used against them to help Lady Harbury negotiate a deed of separation while keeping her children. Caleb had accepted that, but she knew it rankled.

He gave her his lopsided grin. 'Mr Will saw Lord Staverton not far from here the other day. Warned me to be on the lookout. He doesn't trust that one as far as I can spit. I'd best get on, Miss Kit. Rest of the staff will be along soon and—'

He broke off as a hackney pulled up in front of the Phoenix and two men, their red waistcoats marking them as Bow Street Runners, leapt out. Another mounted Runner following pulled up and dismounted.

'Caleb Wright?'

His face became wary. 'Aye.'

'Caleb Wright, you are under arrest in the King's name.'

He stared. 'What? What for?'

The two Runners from the hackney had already seized his arms.

'Attempted highway robbery and the murder of Lord Harbury.'

'What?' Kit rounded on the Runner. 'Are you mad?'

'He's been identified, miss.' The Runner adopted a patronising tone. 'Now you take yourself off. You don't want to be interfering.'

The hell she didn't!

'Who identified him?' The moment the question was out of her mouth she knew the answer—Lucius had been with Harbury. It could only be him.

'He'll hear all the charges at Bow Street. Get him in the coach, men.'

'Wait a moment.' Caleb baulked. 'I can't leave the shop open! I've got to lock up for the mistress.'

The Runner hesitated.

Kit stepped in. 'He must lock up, Officer. He's trying to do his job.'

The man scowled. 'Right.' He pulled out a pistol. 'No tricks though, lad. We'll be with you every step of the way.'

It didn't take long. When they came out again Caleb locked the front door and turned to Kit.

'Miss Kit, I—'

'I know you didn't do it, Caleb.'

One of the Runners sniggered. 'Have a hard time talking his way out of it with a lord's word to say he did it.'

Kit's stomach churned greasily. She knew exactly how untrustworthy Lucius Staverton was.

'You'll take the keys, Miss Kit?' Caleb's voice shook slightly. 'And, you know, feed the cat. Tell the other staff.'

She nodded, and he gave her the heavy keys.

'Back door's bolted and barred.' He grimaced. 'Can't bar the front, but it can't be helped.' He swallowed.

She pulled herself together. 'Caleb, I'll get help. Do you hear me? Ignatius will know what to do.' She looked at the Runner in charge. 'You are taking him to Bow Street, are you not?'

The Runner nodded. 'Aye. Sir Richard Ford will be dealing with this himself.'

She looked back at Caleb. 'That's a good thing. Ignatius knows Sir Richard—he's the chief magistrate.'

'Miss Kit? Is something wrong?'

The puzzled voice had them all looking up to where Morgan, Ignatius Selbourne's manservant, peered from his window, just below the roof.

Kit breathed a sigh of relief. 'Morgan, is my uncle awake?'

The manservant shook his head. 'I've not been down to him yet, miss. I don't want—where's young Caleb going?'

'They're arresting him.' Kit shaded her eyes. 'Lord Staverton has accused him of murdering Lord Harbury! Please let my uncle know immediately.'

Morgan's eyes widened. 'Good heavens!' He disappeared, closing the window.

Kit hesitated, glancing back up at her uncle's window. If Morgan hadn't been in yet, Ignatius would not be down quickly… Biting her lip, she clicked her fingers at Moth and took advantage of a break in the increasing traffic to dash back across the road.

When Morgan came down a few minutes later Kit had scribbled a note for Ignatius and donned her cloak and bonnet.

'Miss Kit, I went in. He's up and getting dressed. He'll be as quick as he can, but—where are you going?'

'Bow Street. There's no time.' She fumbled with her bonnet ribbons.

'Miss Kit, Bow Street is no place for a lady! Please, at least wait for Mr Selbourne.'

If Psyché were here she would have gone to Bow Street to speak for Caleb. He was her employee; she would see it as her duty. But Psyché was on her way to Hampstead.

Kit drew a deep breath. 'I have to go, Morgan. When the staff of the Phoenix arrive, let them know what has happened, please.'

Psyché and Will had risked everything to help her when she fled from her father and Lucius Staverton. Psyché had hidden her above the Phoenix and Kit knew what the charge would have been had they been caught—abduction of an heiress. Will had actually been shot as he and Psyché created a diversion to allow her to escape London with other friends.

Even more, Psyché had offered unconditional

friendship. She hadn't cared that Kit's father, Carshalton, was a slave trader—well, she had, but she hadn't blamed Kit. She had acknowledged Kit's rejection of Carshalton and taught her how to manage business accounts.

The debt she owed Psyché and Will was immense. She knew they didn't agree. Psyché had once told her the boot was on the other foot…

Don't be idiotish, Kit. Helping you brought me Will. That's recompense enough.

That was one way of looking at it, but Psyché and Will's intervention on her behalf had put them in danger. If she had a chance to do something deliberately to redress the balance, she would take it.

'Miss Kit—think!' Morgan wrung his hands. 'You said Lord Staverton is the accuser—he's likely to be there as a witness!'

For an instant Kit's stomach twisted. Then she steadied herself. Lucius Winthrop, now Viscount Staverton. Psyché's uncle. The man who had been prepared to sell his niece back into slavery. The man who had been prepared to rape *her* to force a marriage.

She had run from Lucius and he had struck out at her rescuers.

The girl who had run in terror was gone, lost in the snowstorm that had veiled her escape. Instead, there was Kit. Kit, who was dependent on no one, who had charted her own course and learned to manage a business. Kit, who could stand up for herself now and someone else as well.

She took a deep breath, steadied her roiling gut and spoke in a voice like winter itself. 'He'll be in for a shock when he faces me then. Besides—' she clicked her fingers at the dog '—I'll wager Moth won't like him at all.'

Chapter Two

Martin Lacy turned back to the first page of the magistrate's report of the murder of Lord Harbury and began reading again, slowly, while he jotted notes and occasionally gazed unseeingly at the pigeons on the opposite rooftops.

The shooting fitted the pattern he was looking for, as had others in the past few months since he'd returned to London and been assigned to this battered desk. Tucked away in an unassuming building run by the Home Office on a lost square in Whitehall, he had found something akin to peace. Very few outside the Home Office knew he was there at all and within the Home Office very few knew what he did. Outside no one knew what he did. They didn't even know the building was there. Or the square for that matter. His invariable answer whenever he ran across an acquaintance who asked what he was doing with himself these days, was, *'Oh, just pottering for the Home Office'*. Everyone assumed the Duke of Keswick had applied pressure to gain a government position for his scandal-ridden third son and left it at that. No one invited him for a game of cards, to dine, or to *'meet at the club'*.

At least that meant he didn't have to dance around the answers to awkward questions.

Occasionally Martin himself wondered what the devil he was doing and if it made a ha'porth of difference to the safety of the realm. He wasn't entirely sure he cared very much. He was earning a living, every so often he found something he was looking for, and, given his father's reaction to the position, he at least knew the duke had not had anything to do with his appointment.

The duke considered employment, actual paid employment beyond the military or possibly the church, to be beneath contempt for any son of his. Unfortunately neither Keswick nor the duchess had any other feasible suggestions about how a third son might support himself beyond marriage to an heiress, and Martin's brief betrothal to Catherine Carshalton had ended in scandal fifteen months ago.

He was done with heiresses and their scheming fathers and he needed to do something with his life. The military didn't appeal in the slightest and the church even less.

So he sat here in this quiet, sparsely furnished room largely hidden from the world, not far from his very unfashionable lodgings, and looked for patterns that might indicate a plot which could destabilise the government or the Crown. Patterns in behaviour, patterns in what people said, in what they wrote. And he looked for inconsistencies in patterns he'd already found. Oddities could show where someone or something had strayed from the usual pattern. Like a horse breaking stride could show you when something was wrong with the road.

Like Kit... No, Catherine. Safer to remember her only as Catherine. Only the façade of quiet, compliant Catherine had cracked and he'd seen the truth behind it...

Irrelevant now, except as an example—once you understood the pattern, you had a chance to predict, even control what came next—unless something else broke stride. He rose abruptly, went to stir up the fire and add some coals. The room was peaceful, but little light found its way through the narrow window and it was damn cold at times.

For a moment he stared at the leaping fire. He didn't often investigate murder, but this one felt like a break in stride.

Martin went back to his desk.

Who gains from this?

He stared at the simple question he'd written.

The widow?

He scored a line through it. Wrong question. Several persons besides Lady Harbury would gain from this murder. More useful to ask who had an opportunity…

Who knew where he'd be that evening? Not the widow. All the evidence suggested Harbury's visit had been an unwelcome surprise.

Because despite surface appearances, this murder did not smell like a robbery gone horribly wrong.

It's like the others. It fits the pattern.

Because of Bow Street's vigilance, mounted highway robbery in and around London was no longer common. Oh, it still happened, but not often. And with violence? Even less common, although those were the attacks everyone remembered. Martin drummed his fingers on the desk.

And he knew of three others in a relatively short period.

So, the shootings might be a break in stride amounting to a separate pattern.

Only his search for this pattern now verged on obsession according to his commander's pithy observation.

'*Lacy, sometimes highway robbery does go wrong. The fellow is nervous and the pistol discharges, or his horse shies. Someone is shot and the miscreant panics. He bolts without the money or jewellery. It happens.*'

He knew that. But in two instances—one definitely and another suspected—killing a specific individual had been the whole purpose of the robbery. A supposedly botched robbery had effectively disguised the real motive. No one had looked for anything beyond a convenient highway man to hang.

Martin pulled another set of documents from the file on his desk. Two months ago a prominent Abolitionist had died in a highway robbery near Bromley.

Martin read the report yet again. Sir John Beechworth, MP, had been returning home from a dinner with political friends. Upon his coach being halted with shouts of *'Stand and deliver!'*, followed by a further demand for *his nibs* to hand over the goods, Beechworth had descended to comply according to the coachman and footman.

'The master didn't make a fuss, just got down and took his watch out, and took a ring off his finger. He didn't have any money with him. 'Twas just a dinner we'd driven him to.'

Despite compliance the highwayman had shot Beechworth at close range and fled without the watch and ring.

Exactly like Beck.

Martin gritted his teeth. Thirlbeck, not *Beck*. He couldn't think of him as Beck, his eldest brother, and also be objective. He had to think of him as Viscount Thirlbeck, heir to the Duke of Keswick, murdered in what had also looked like attempted robbery two years ago. And like Beechworth's coachman, Thirlbeck's secretary, Maitland, had insisted the highway man had not been interested in robbery.

'He didn't even try to take the money, Lacy. He waited until Beck was close enough and fired. He wanted Beck.'

Maitland had been utterly sure.

He had to be objective. He had to think of justice, not revenge. Above all he could not think about the whispers that had followed Beck's murder. Who benefited from the death of the unmarried heir to a dukedom? Why! His sole surviving brother, of course!

Because at first no one had remembered Martin wasn't the heir.

No one had forgotten Keswick's second son Lord Peter and his scandalous elopement ten years earlier with Lady Emma Brandon-Smythe. What they had forgotten was that the elopement had involved a marriage. And that although Lord Peter had died, there was a son of the marriage.

Martin brought his gaze back from the pigeons and focused on the miniature on his desk. Two children, a dark-haired, blue-eyed boy who looked out at him with Peter's grin, his arm around a small girl with her father's tawny eyes. Peter's children.

Their mother, Emma, and her second husband, the Marquess of Huntercombe, had sent it to him for Christmas…

'*Harry and Georgie wished to send you something. A puppy was suggested, but Huntercombe and I thought this rather less disruptive. They also wish very much to see you...*'

Martin let out a breath. He'd like to see them, too. But it was safer if he went nowhere near Peter's children. If word reached Carshalton that he was being hunted, any suggestion that Martin's nephew and niece were important to him could put them in danger.

Josiah Carshalton, slave trader and vocal opponent to Abolition, would stop at very little to bolster his cause politically. Including dangling his daughter before a man he intended to inherit a dukedom.

Up to and including staging a robbery to effect Harry's murder so Martin could inherit. All to give Carshalton a son-in-law he could control. A son-in-law who would, sooner or later, sit in the House of Lords.

And Martin had sprung the trap by offering for Carshalton's daughter in a moment of chivalry.

Emma's courage had saved Harry, but the only evidence against Carshalton had been the word of the highwayman who had died with a knife in the belly awaiting transportation in Newgate. Carshalton was safe—most of the murmurs had been directed at Martin himself. The rumour that Carshalton's daughter had broken their betrothal had been the final damning factor in society's eyes. In a world where wealth and status depended largely on primogeniture, who would believe a duke's third son did not dream of the title? Especially after Beck's murder nine months earlier.

Holford didn't believe it. Even when he was pressured to dismiss you, he persuaded the Admiralty to assign you to the Channel Fleet—he gave you this position when you returned.

Martin shoved all that aside. While Harbury's death fitted the pattern of robbery ending in violence, he couldn't for the life of him see how the viscount's death benefited Carshalton. Harbury, with significant holdings in the West Indies, had been strongly pro-slavery. Why have him killed, thus removing a pro-slavery vote when Wilberforce and his allies eventually brought another Abolition Bill before Parliament? With Harbury's heir scarcely out of leading strings, the seat would remain vacant until he reached his majority. It had to be coincidence. He owed it to Holford to put all this aside and focus on other matters.

Yet all his instincts itched, insisted he look beyond the obvious. Or was that obsession? Had he really crossed the line between doing his job and seeking private revenge? If the latter, he needed—

The peremptory knock on his door jolted him out of his thoughts. And he blinked as the door opened and his immediate superior gestured another man into the room.

'Sir.' He rose at once.

Lord Holford was a thin, middle-aged man with a hawkish face. Bright, hard eyes and a beak of a nose. While rank as such was usually in abeyance in this dusty, forgotten building, Holford was more likely to send someone to fetch him.

Holford shut the door. 'You're needed at Bow Street, Lacy. Ford won't be happy, but I'll smooth that over later.'

'Yes, sir.'

Then he looked properly at the elderly man unwinding his muffler and ice formed in his gut.

Ignatius Selbourne looked straight at him. 'I'm calling in that favour, boy.'

'Kit.' Martin forced words past choking fear. 'Has that bastard Carshalton hurt Kit?'

Kit reached Bow Street before the morning session opened. She read the papers and followed the court proceedings, and several magistrates apart from Sir Richard patronised the shop—she understood how the courts worked. After the Runners had hunted for her last year, she had wanted to understand how Bow Street worked.

Paying off the hackney, Kit glanced about. Directly over the road from the courthouse was the Brown Bear Tavern. Ignatius had told her Sir John Fielding had often breakfasted there and examined prisoners at the same time. She hoped Sir Richard was going to be a little more formal about things this morning.

The examining magistrate would hear the evidence brought by accusers and decide if it warranted a trial. With Staverton as his accuser, it was vital Caleb had someone there to speak for him. He wouldn't stand a chance otherwise.

He might not stand much of a chance even with you.

She could slow things down. Ignatius wouldn't be far behind her. Ignatius attended when a case interested him and he had described the process to her...

'It's a great deal fairer than before Fielding's reforms. Gives the accused a chance to mount a defence, find an alibi, character witnesses, that sort of thing. Of course, the accusers don't always like it. Plenty of them think their word should be sufficient for the magistrate to convict on the spot.'

She trod up the steps to the door, heart pounding, Moth close at her side. What if they didn't let her in? What if they said she had no business here and—?

Character witnesses, Ignatius said.

She steadied herself, lifted her chin. As a character witness she had every right to be there and to be heard.

People glanced at her with no more than casual curiosity and, quelling her nerves, Kit looked around, fascinated. Men and women—although not many of the latter and none alone—waited quietly in groups. Some looked prosperous, scowl-

ing indignantly as they discussed the case they
were bringing. Others looked sick with fear—Kit
wondered if they were there waiting to hear the
evidence against a loved one. The penal code was
brutal, with hanging or transportation not uncommon.

Several people gave her, and Moth, sideways
glances, but no one challenged her or the dog's
presence.

Staverton was nowhere to be seen. Hardly surprising. The great Staverton to wait in a public
room with the common herd? No doubt his rank
entitled him to a private room.

A door behind the magistrate's desk opened to
admit Sir Richard Ford.

He had been in the shop a number of times in
the past year. At first he'd been stiffly polite to
her—after all, when she'd run away fifteen months
earlier Carshalton had hired the Runners to find
her, claiming she had been abducted. She couldn't
blame Sir Richard for being annoyed when she reappeared after turning twenty-one and refused to
return to her father's house.

Sir Richard had called on Ignatius, demanding
an explanation, and she had told him straight out
why she had fled. Not being sure what he might
or might not tell Carshalton she had flatly refused
to tell him where she had been, or who had sheltered her.

'*I was with friends, sir. Friends with whom I was safe.*'

Those friends had protected her: she would protect them from her father's fury.

Sir Richard had considered her behaviour both unladylike and unfilial; daughters ought not to question their father's edicts. Certainly not on the subject of an advantageous marriage. He had made it clear he thought Ignatius very much in the wrong to intervene between father and daughter, but over the past few months he'd thawed slightly, no longer calling her *Miss Carshalton*, but accepting her legal name change to Selbourne, even calling her *Mistress Kit* occasionally.

She crossed her fingers in the folds of her skirts. She knew Sir Richard liked Ignatius and respected his judgement. Please God, it would be enough to secure Caleb a fair hearing.

Sir Richard took his seat behind the bench, frowning heavily.

'A most serious case is come before us this morning. Have Caleb Wright brought in, if you please.'

In a corner a man scribbled at a small desk.

A news reporter, perhaps. Ignatius said they were usually there. Now when she read the Bow Street proceedings she would see this fiercely concentrating little man working away at his desk.

'And I would ask Jonas Bragg to come forward.'

The murmurs started up again as people exchanged glances and comments. A liveried servant began to work his way to the front.

Murmurs rose. *'That's the coachman was driving the carriage.'*

Ignoring grumbles, she pushed her way through in the coachman's wake, giving a brief *sorry* and *excuse me* as she wriggled through the press of bodies. They had made way willingly enough for Bragg, far more grudgingly for herself.

She was nearly to the front when the murmurs rose sharply as Caleb was brought in between two Runners. Standing on tiptoe, she could just see over the shoulder of a plump man in front of her. He blocked her attempt to get past with an elbow, moving closer to the man beside him.

Gritting her teeth, Kit waited.

'You are Caleb Wright, of no fixed address?'

'No, Your Honour.' Caleb sounded puzzled.

'What the devil do you mean?' demanded Sir Richard. 'You aren't Caleb Wright?'

Murmurs riffled through the crowd and Kit stood on tiptoe again, straining to see as well as hear.

Caleb shook his head. 'No, I mean, yes. I'm Caleb Wright, but I've got an address. I live at the Phoenix Rising on Compton Street. Before that I lodged nearby with a Mrs Archer, but I've been living at the Phoenix for over a year now. I work there.'

Sir Richard consulted his notes. 'Can this be confirmed?'

'Yes.' Kit pitched her voice to be heard over the crowd.

Sir Richard looked up. 'Whoever spoke, come forward.'

Kit pushed past the man who had blocked her.

A clerk of the court rushed forward. 'I'm sorry, miss, but you can't have that dog in here!'

'It's all right, Sutherland.' Sir Richard's voice held resignation. 'I am familiar with the young lady. And her dog. Under the circumstances, I'll hold this examination in my office.'

He rose, taking no notice of the disappointed mutters from the crowd. 'Have the accused and all witnesses brought through.' He rose and went back through the door behind the desk.

The clerk inclined his head to her. 'Follow me, if you please.' He glanced around at the liveried servant. 'And you, Mr Bragg. This way.'

Sir Richard's office was commodious enough to hold all of them. He sat behind the desk and the clerk set a chair for Kit and one for Bragg.

Sir Richard looked at Kit. 'Please be seated, Miss Selbourne. And you, if you please, Bragg.'

Kit sat, then spoke quietly to Moth who settled by the chair, nose on her paws.

There was one more chair and a moment later

the door opened to admit a man Kit had wanted never to lay eyes on again.

Lucius, Viscount Staverton.

For a moment he looked at her in frowning incomprehension. Then outraged recognition flared. 'What the devil is *she* doing here?' He strode forward. 'She is to be removed immediately, Ford. I'm damned if I'll put up with—'

Moth rose slowly and uttered a warning growl.

Kit laid a hand on her head. 'Sit.'

Moth sat, but her amber gaze remained focused on Staverton and the low rumble continued.

'Staverton, sit down.' Sir Richard's voice brooked no argument. 'This is *my* courtroom. Whatever the history between you and Miss Selbourne, it is irrelevant here.'

To Kit's amazement, Staverton adopted a pious expression. 'Ford, you cannot possibly consider a court of law an appropriate setting for a delicately bred young lady. Every feeling revolts. My shattered hopes aside, as a friend of her father—'

'Hence my decision to hear the evidence in here.' Sir Richard gestured to a chair. 'Sit. It is the practice of this office to hear from witnesses who may be able to offer an alibi or other useful information.' He shot Lucius a quelling glare. 'Assuming they show all due respect for this office.'

'That dog is dangerous!'

Sir Richard shrugged. 'I've met the creature on several occasions. Interestingly this is the first time I've known her to object to anyone. While she remains under Miss Selbourne's control I have no issue with her presence. I suggest you sit down, Staverton, before she objects again.'

His jaw rigid, Staverton sat on the chair next to the servant.

At Kit's signal Moth lowered to the ground and the growling subsided.

Kit sat quietly in complete ladylike decorum even if a very faint smile flickered at the corner of her mouth. No doubt it had been a very long time since anyone had come close to telling Staverton to sit down and shut up.

Sir Richard looked at his notes. 'Very well, Wright. You say you live at the Phoenix.'

'Yes, Your Honour.'

Sir Richard looked at Kit. 'Miss Selbourne, you can corroborate?'

She inclined her head. 'Certainly, Sir Richard. I understand from my friend, Mrs Barclay, that Caleb has been employed there for well over two years now. Initially he lodged at a nearby boarding house, but after some trouble last year with an attempt to break into the Phoenix, Mrs Barclay suggested he might like to live behind the shop.'

'I scarcely see how all this is relevant!'

The magistrate raised his brows. 'That would be why I am in this chair and not you, Staverton.' He looked again at Kit. 'May I ask, where *is* Mrs Barclay?'

'Playing least in sight if she knows what's good for her!'

Kit ignored Staverton. 'Mrs Barclay received a message summoning her to Hampstead this morning. She had left before your Runners arrived.'

She swallowed. If only Sir Richard didn't decide she could have nothing to add and toss her out.

'I see. Very well. You have come in her place to speak for Wright.'

'Yes, Your Honour.'

Staverton snorted. 'Putting herself forward. Really, Ford! This is—'

'Miss Selbourne—' Ford cut him off '—are you able to vouch for Wright's general character?'

'I am, Sir Richard, and my uncle will do the same. And, of course, Mr and Mrs Barclay. They would hardly have him living in their home if he were not trustworthy.'

'Thank you, ma'am.' Ford turned his attention to the servant. 'I understand you to be one Jonas Bragg. You are…*were*, I should say, Lord Harbury's coachman?'

The man puffed up a little. 'Yes, Your Honour. Working for Lord Staverton now—and that's the young vermin who—'

'We'll get to that in due course, Bragg. I am merely ensuring everyone's particulars are correct.'

Despite Sir Richard's mild tone Bragg subsided.

Staverton sniffed. 'Well, I for one wish to know

how a young *female* has been permitted to spend so much time with the prisoner that she *can* vouch for his character? Most unseemly. Catherine's dear father would be horrified!'

Ignoring the coachman's snigger, Kit turned an enquiring gaze on Sir Richard. 'Do you wish me to respond, Your Honour?'

Respect flickered in his eyes. 'Thank you, Miss Selbourne.'

'Very well. My uncle has been teaching Caleb two or three evenings each week for the past year or more. I am usually in the room and have seen the liking and respect in which he holds Caleb.'

Another snigger from the coachman and a disbelieving snort from Lucius.

Kit turned her head. 'Do you require a handkerchief, Staverton?' She proffered her lace-edged handkerchief, neatly embroidered with her initials and an open book.

He stared, patently outraged. 'What?'

'I thought you sneezed.' She shrugged. 'No matter.' And tucked the handkerchief away.

'And where *is* Selbourne?' asked Sir Richard.

'Delayed.' Kit stopped short of further explanation. Sir Richard knew well enough that Ignatius was not in good health. 'However, as his business partner, I believe I can speak for him to an extent.'

The noise Staverton made now was more a grinding of teeth, but Sir Richard merely nodded.

He might not approve, but he was known for dealing with things as they were.

'We come now to the charges that on the night of Monday last—'

Kit let out a stifled gasp, echoed by Caleb, but at a warning glance from Ford held her silence as he continued with the charge.

'Caleb Wright, you did hold up a coach outside Hampstead driven by Bragg and containing Viscounts Staverton and Harbury. When their lordships obeyed your demand to descend from the coach and hand over all money and valuables—'

'Monday last, did you say, Your Honour?' Caleb said carefully.

Ford lowered his notes and glared. 'Hold your tongue until I have completed reading the charge.'

Caleb's face was mutinous, but he said nothing more.

'Despite them being willing to do so, you fired on them, hitting and killing Lord Harbury. Whereupon you galloped away towards London. Do you understand the charge against you, Wright?'

'No, Your Honour, I don't.'

Lucius snorted again. 'What did I say? Boy's a halfwit. Exactly the sort to be suborned and used by those more cunning to—'

'Staverton, either hold your silence or leave.' Again, Ford lowered his papers to address Caleb. 'You don't understand that you are charged with the wilful and violent murder of Lord Harbury?'

'I understand that, Your Honour.' Caleb's voice was polite, utterly respectful and yet determined. 'What I don't understand is *why* you're charging me. I was nowhere near Hampstead last Monday.'

Ford's mouth hardened. 'You were recognised, Wright. Both Lord Staverton and Bragg have identified you as the horseman. Now, if you please—'

The door opened and Kit turned in her chair, relief flooding through her. Ignatius would sort everything… But Ford rose slightly from his seat and stared, as the last man Kit had expected to see strolled in.

She had last seen Lord Martin Lacy when she broke their betrothal.

Tall, his dark hair untidy as usual and those bright tawny eyes utterly unreadable as they rested on her. The very slightest inclination of his head towards her in acknowledgement and only the tightness about his mouth to hint at emotion.

Was *his* stomach flopping about like a landed fish? It was all she could do to pull her scattered wits together.

What on earth is he doing here? And where is Ignatius?

Beside her Moth's tail thumped and, before Kit could grab her collar, she stood up, uttering a short bark, and trotted forward.

Chapter Three

Strolling into Ford's office, Martin reminded himself that grabbing Staverton by the throat and choking the life out of him ranked as a Truly Bad Idea because it would flag to the bastard that Martin knew more than he ought to about the Viscount's attempt to marry Kit. And, while he couldn't be sure how Kit would react to his arrival, Staverton was going to be furious with any interference, let alone his. And the more arrogant and at his ease *he* was, the angrier Staverton would—

He blinked at the dog trotting up to him. Good God! Surely that wasn't—

The dog sat and offered an enormous paw.

'More like a bear. Look at the size of the paws.'

He took the paw and bent down, speaking softly. 'He wasn't wrong about the paws, was he?'

'What will you call her?'

'I'll let Kit name her.'

The tail thumped.

Charmed, he glanced up, found Kit's startled gaze on him. At the sight of those familiar, smoky eyes his world lurched.

'What did you call her in the—?' He caught himself. 'I mean, what's her name?'

'Moth. Short for—'

'Behemoth?'

Kit stared. 'Well, yes.' She clicked her fingers and the dog returned to her.

He'd always enjoyed the way her mind worked. Suppressing a smile, he turned to Sir Richard.

'Good morning, Ford. I hope you don't mind if I join you?'

The magistrate looked him up and down, res-ignation writ large on his face. 'If the dog doesn't, how should I, Lacy? Dare I ask what Whitehall is doing in this?'

Aware of Kit's startled expression, Martin shrugged. 'Obviously Whitehall is concerned when a member of the Lords is murdered.'

'I see.' Ford's tone suggested he saw rather more than his bland response revealed. His next words confirmed it.

'I believe you are acquainted with Miss Sel-bourne?'

'I am, sir.'

Steeling himself, he faced Kit again. The girl he had intended to marry. The girl he had aban-doned to the scandal of a broken betrothal. The girl he had—

He turned to her. 'Miss Selbourne. I hope I see you well?'

A steely grip on his control, he held out his hand.

'Thank you, my lord. Very well.'

She placed her gloved hand in his and his world tilted again as he felt the tremor in those slight fingers.

But her light, cool voice betrayed nothing of that. The frightened girl who had broken their betrothal, finally fleeing her father's house in the teeth of a blizzard fifteen months ago, had grown up.

Staverton stood up. 'I don't know what business you imagine you have here, Lacy, just because you indulge in some jobbery for Whitehall, but for my part—'

'Justice, Staverton. Justice.' Releasing Kit's hand, Martin controlled his temper. Angry men made mistakes. It was no part of his brief to enlighten Staverton on his position with the Home Office. 'Naturally you want justice for your son-in-law.'

'Of course I want to see the young brute swing!'

Martin raised his brows. 'Not necessarily the same thing, but I'm sure you do.' He inclined his head to the magistrate. 'My apologies for interrupting, Ford.' He reached into his satchel. 'I've information that may be of assistance.'

'Waste of time!' Lucius snapped. 'Bragg recognised the miscreant and so—'

Sir Richard cleared his throat. 'Wright has been identified, Lacy, so—'

'He's mistaken!'

Martin turned to look at Kit. 'How so, ma'am?'

'Because Caleb was nowhere near Hampstead on Monday night.'

'My dear girl!' Staverton bestowed a pitying glance on Kit. 'You can't possibly know such a thing. Even if he *is* lodging in that rubbishing coffee house—'

'Staverton—sit down!'

The dog issued the faintest of growls and Martin repressed a grin as Staverton sat down, shooting Moth a wary look.

Ford looked as though his patience teetered on a very thin edge. 'Miss Selbourne, you have averred Wright was nowhere near Hampstead on Monday night. Are you able, from your personal knowledge, to state precisely where he was?'

And there it was. That tilt to her head as she listened to a question—to the *exact* wording—and considered her answer.

'Not *precisely*, Sir Richard. But—'

'There! You see? The poor child has no idea—'

'Staverton—no gentleman interrupts a lady. Kindly hold your tongue.' Martin's veneer cracked and Staverton subsided.

Ford clenched his fists on the desk, but spoke calmly. 'Continue, Miss Selbourne.'

'I know where Caleb was going and with whom.

But surely—' she gestured to the boy '—he should tell you himself? Then I should corroborate.'

Oh, brava! He wanted to clap. The shy girl he'd known would never have dared speak up like this.

Ford's faint smile suggested he appreciated it, too. 'Quite correct, Miss Selbourne.'

'Ford?'

'Yes, Lacy?'

Knowing he was skating a very fine line with the magistrate, Martin eased into the request. 'This is your court, your jurisdiction, but—would you permit me to question the accused and witnesses?'

Ford stared. 'Are you pulling Whitehall *rank* on me, Lacy? In *here*?'

'No, sir.' The magistrate knew perfectly well what he did, but he could hear, *feel*, the ice cracking under him and put as much deference into his voice as possible. 'Naturally if you prefer to conduct the examination, I must abide by that.'

He was fiercely aware of Kit staring at him, the questioning tilt to her head. He turned, murmuring, 'Trust me…'

She gave a barely perceptible nod, lifting her chin. He remembered that gesture, too—reluctant acquiescence incarnate.

'It's a damn funny thing,' snarled Staverton, 'when a gentleman's word is not good enough—'

'Do you know,' Martin cut in mercilessly, 'I heard of a shocking case last year, where two *gentlemen* forced a young Black woman into a coach in order to take her to a ship leaving from the West India Docks.' He didn't need Kit's startled gasp to know she knew of the attempted abduction of Psyché Barclay and understood the significance of raising it now.

He continued. 'The coachman—' he favoured Bragg with flat stare '—fired on her when she managed to escape. Naturally they had a very different story and it was hushed up, but there you are. Did you hear that story, Staverton?'

Staverton flushed, then paled. 'I've no time for idle gossip!'

'No?' Martin smiled. 'There was a young Black lad in the story, too. He escaped and raised the alarm. Most inconvenient for the kidnappers.' He glanced at Ford. 'Perhaps you heard something of this?'

The magistrate's eyes narrowed. 'In an unofficial capacity, although no charges were brought. You may continue, Lacy, but I reserve the right to ask my own questions.'

Martin smiled. 'Of course, Ford.' Unofficial capacity or not, the magistrate was alert to the problem now. He turned to the boy standing quietly in his shackles. Even with the ebony skin he could see the bruising on the boy's face, the cut lip.

'Caleb Wright?'

The boy faced him, chin up, despite the fear living in his eyes. 'Yes, sir.'

Staverton snorted. 'There! You see? Can't even address his betters!'

Martin turned to him. 'Really, Staverton? Wright has never before laid eyes on me. I'm reasonably certain there's no sign over my head announcing, *Duke's Youngest Son*.'

Caleb cleared his throat. 'Right. Beg pardon, my lord.'

Martin nodded. 'Never mind that. What happened to your face?'

Caleb shrugged. 'I must have bumped it, my lord. Getting out of the hackney.'

'Really?' Ford directed a hard glance at the guards who shifted uneasily. 'Hmm. You will answer Lord Martin's questions truthfully, Wright.'

Martin smiled at Caleb. 'Let's clear a few things up first. You live at the Phoenix Rising?'

The boy nodded. 'Yes, my lord.'

'Could you get out at night if you wanted to?'

'Yes, but—'

'Just yes or no will suffice. What do you do in the evenings?'

He shrugged. 'My time's my own once I clean up the shop and I have a key. But I have to be up early and most nights I have a lesson with Mr Will, or with Mr Selbourne across the road.'

'Lessons?' Staverton scoffed. 'What *lessons* does an ignorant street rat require?'

Caleb responded literally. 'Mr Will or Miss Kit teach me mathematics a couple of nights, my lord, and Mr Selbourne helps me with my reading. And Miss Psyché is showing me how to keep the books proper. She's training me to manage the shop.'

Staverton looked affronted, but Ford spoke up. 'You did ask, Staverton.' He spoke to Caleb. 'But you could get out if you wished to do so?'

'What are you doing?' Kit spoke softly under cover of Ford's question, her fingers clenched on the arms of her chair. 'If you just *ask*, he was—'

He shook his head. 'I know where he was.' He fought the urge to lay a reassuring hand over hers, feel those slight fingers under his once again.

Caleb was speaking politely. 'Yes, Your Honour. But I always tell Mr Will or Miss Psyché so they know if a door is unbolted.'

Martin gave Kit a quick glance. He didn't want merely to prove Caleb's innocence. They had to bring Staverton's testimony not just into doubt, but into disrepute. 'We're digging a hole for Staverton,' he murmured.

'It had better be a deep one.'

Compulsion won and he laid his hand lightly on hers. 'Believe me.'

A slight smile flickered and as his world danced, he had to force his attention back to the situation at hand.

'Easy enough, though, for you *not* to tell them?' Ford was suggesting.

'I wouldn't do that, Your Honour.' Caleb shook his head. 'Miss Psyché had trouble with—' he cleared his throat and his gaze drifted to Staverton, hardened there '—ah…with someone stealing a key last year.'

Sir Richard frowned. 'I see.'

It sounded to Martin as though the magistrate now saw a great deal.

It seemed Staverton thought so, too. 'This is ridiculous!' His face scarlet, he waved dismissively. 'The boy has been identified. He should be made to confess! Poor Catherine should never have been dragged into this disgraceful situation.'

Martin ignored him, shifted his attention to the coachman. 'You are Jonas Bragg?'

'Aye.'

At the insolent tone Martin levelled an icy glare. Bragg lost the sneer. 'Yes, my lord.'

'You have positively identified Caleb Wright as the assailant?'

'Yes, my lord.'

'How?'

Bragg sniggered. 'Hard to miss *that* face, I'd say.'

Martin raised his brows. 'Really?' He drew a sheaf of papers out of his satchel. 'This is a copy of the local magistrate's report and your initial statement—'

'How the *devil* did you get that?' Ford demanded.

Adjudging that as mere rhetoric, Martin didn't answer. 'Bragg—Sir Lawrence Mapplethorpe asked you that night if you could describe the assailant. To quote your reply: *"No, Your Honour. It was too dark and he wore a mask with his hat pulled right down."* So, how, Bragg, can you identify Caleb Wright so positively now?'

Bragg looked to Staverton.

Staverton scowled. 'Bragg, you must—'

'Ford.' Martin smiled at the magistrate. 'Don't you agree the witness ought to speak from his own knowledge without the prompting of Lord Staverton?'

'How dare you, Lacy!' Staverton snarled. 'What are you insinuating?'

'That a witness ought not to refer to anything beyond his own memory of events?' suggested Kit in deceptively dulcet tones.

Martin shot her a sideways glance, saw the steely determination as she met Staverton's bluster with steady calm and the very faintest of smiles.

Oh, well done! Right between the ribs.

'Correct again, Miss Selbourne.' Ford glanced at Staverton. 'Any prompting of the witness, Staverton, and I'll have you removed. Proceed, Bragg. In your *own* words. However, I shall remind you that deliberately giving false testimony is in itself an indictable offence.'

'Perjury.' Kit's voice was the merest murmur, as if she spoke to herself.

Sir Richard inclined his head. 'Quite so.'

Martin managed not to look smug at the nervousness on the coachman's face. 'Come now, Bragg.'

Bragg swallowed. 'Well, as to that, it was his lordship—that is, Lord Staverton—who thought as *he* knew the murderer.'

'Thought?' Martin kept his smile friendly. Bragg was eager to exculpate himself and Martin suspected Kit's soft *perjury* had wound nasty, sticky doubts around his earlier smug certainty.

'Ah, he asked me later if I didn't think as the man was Black.'

'Black?'

'Yes, my lord.'

'And you hadn't noticed this?'

'No, my lord. He wore a mask, like I said.' Bragg gulped and added hurriedly, 'But when his lordship mentioned it afterwards I remembered what I *could* see of the fellow's face was mighty dark. And his lordship said as it was probably this Caleb Wright, being as he might have a bit of a grudge against my lord, which I remembered him from last year being very uppish.'

Martin raised his brows. 'You remembered him? Under what circumstances did you meet Wright? When he was leaping from the box of a carriage you were driving? To raise the alarm about a kidnapping attempt?'

Bragg flushed. 'Ah, that was a…a misunderstanding.'

Martin flicked a brief glance at Staverton. 'Quite

a significant misunderstanding—however, let us keep to the current crime.

'On the basis of Staverton's *suggestion*, Bragg, you identified Wright, a boy you had met briefly once, as the murderer.' Martin didn't bother to disguise his scepticism.

Bragg swallowed. 'It *was* him. I… I remembered things afterwards, when I thought about it proper.'

'Or when you were told what to think,' Kit muttered.

'Miss Selbourne!' Sir Richard frowned at her.

'I apologise, Your Honour. Stating the obvious is so annoying.'

Martin disguised a snort of laughter as a cough.

But Bragg was stung. He glared at Kit. 'Weren't like that. It was more like when his lordship here talked to me about it, it jogged me memory like.' He pointed at Caleb. 'It was him. On me mother's grave, I'd swear it!'

'And I!' Staverton backed the coachman up at once.

Martin turned to Caleb, who was now looking at him with something approaching hope.

'Something else we should clear up, Wright,' he said. 'Where were you in fact on Monday night when Lord Staverton and Bragg claim you were holding up Lord Harbury's coach and shooting him?'

Caleb's bruised and tired face broke into a grin.

'Monday afternoon I rode out to Isleworth with Mr Will, my lord. That is, Mr Will Barclay. We left… two o'clock? I think. I don't have a watch, but Mr Will would know. About then. He had a meeting with his lordship and asked me if I'd like to go along. It was my afternoon off and he thought I'd like the ride, being as I used to work as a groom.'

'What?'

Martin really couldn't blame Ford for his reaction. And judging by Staverton's sharp intake of breath, it was the last thing he'd expected. Which lined up precisely with the information he had been given.

'Which *his lordship*, Caleb?' Martin asked. 'Be specific, if you please. There are two of us in this room alone.'

'Sorry, my lord. Lord Huntercombe. The marquess, you know. Mr Will looks after his rents and such here in London and roundabouts.'

Ford drew in an audible breath. 'What time did you return, lad?'

Caleb looked straight at Ford, his chin up. 'We didn't, Your Honour. We stayed the night, had supper and all. I'm off Tuesday mornings, too, so I didn't need to be back early. Not that it mattered, being as Miss Psyché knew where I was.'

Martin turned to Ford. 'Puts quite a hole in the case, doesn't it?'

'Nonsense!' Staverton waved dismissively. 'The boy said they *rode* to Isleworth. He had access to a horse. May I remind you that we were held up? By a mounted man! Easy enough to ride from Isleworth to Hampstead and back. Why, I could do it myself!'

Martin opened his mouth.

'Across country? In the dark?' Caleb stared at Staverton as if the Viscount had grown a second head.

Martin drew breath to intervene and take back the reins, but, catching the slight shake of Sir Richard's head, he sat back. Let the boy speak for himself and prove his mettle.

Caleb continued. 'Suppose I *could* have, sir—'

'My lord…' Martin murmured.

Caleb flung him an impatient glance, before facing Staverton again. 'Supposing I could, *my lord*? I'd have near killed the horse getting it there and back in time. And why ride all that way just to hold up a coach? Plenty of coaches closer, I'd wager!'

Staverton glared at him, but deliberately spoke to Ford. 'The miscreant's grudge against Lord Harbury—'

'So, you admit the kidnapping attempt, Staverton?' Kit asked sweetly.

Staverton went white. 'I admit nothing,' he snarled.

Ford shot Kit a warning glance, but said, 'Then what grudge are you talking about, Staverton?'

Under cover of Staverton's confusion, Martin leaned close to Kit. 'That was a masterstroke.'

Finally, Staverton spoke. 'It was all a misunderstanding.'

Martin stepped into the breach. 'Staverton, even if the boy *had* deliberately targeted Harbury, how did he know what time that specific coach would be on the road?' Martin asked.

Caleb spoke again. 'And how'd I get myself out of the house, leave alone take a horse out of his lordship's stables, without being caught?'

Staverton shrugged. 'A venal servant in the stables, no doubt. The distance? A mere nothing! As the crow flies—'

'Leaving aside the very pertinent question posed by Lacy, the boy would have been riding a horse, not a crow, Staverton,' said Ford irritably. 'Miss Selbourne, are you able to corroborate this?'

'Yes, Sir Richard. I saw Mr Barclay and Caleb leave on Monday afternoon and return late Tuesday morning. On horseback.' She let a beat of silence fall. 'Speaking for myself, I've never seen anyone riding a crow. Perhaps Staverton has.' Her voice was dry enough to turn Hyde Park into a desert.

Martin let out a crack of laughter and Ford appeared to have lost something under his desk.

He emerged red in the face. 'Thank you, Miss Selbourne. Ah, can you confirm the time they left for Isleworth?'

If there was a wobble in his voice, no one was fool enough to remark on it.

Kit nodded. 'Yes. Although I believe they left closer to two thirty. I remember waving to them. And I knew where they were going because the message from Lord Huntercombe requesting the meeting arrived while I was in the Phoenix fetching coffee.'

Ford made a quick note. 'Wright, did you attend the meeting with the marquess?'

'Yes, Your Honour. I took notes for Mr Will during the meeting and we both had supper with the family. Her ladyship's son gave me a game of chess afterwards and I had a truckle bed in Mr Will's room for the night.'

'And when did you leave?' Martin asked.

'After taking breakfast with his lordship.' He frowned. 'A bit after eight o'clock, I think.'

Ford drummed his fingers on the desk. 'All of which can be confirmed with Huntercombe, his lady and Barclay.' He was silent for a moment, then glanced at the clerk by the door. 'Sutherland, I'll write a note to Huntercombe which you will have delivered directly into his hand. Or his lady since she can directly corroborate this information.'

'Damn it, Ford! Are you doubting my word?' Staverton demanded.

Martin waited; beside him Kit had taken a sharp breath. Caleb was cleared, but how far would Ford go in directly antagonising the Viscount?

'Staverton, I believe you have been mistaken in identifying the boy.' Ford's tone was uninflected, dispassionate. 'It happens all too frequently. Especially in the dark. There was no moon on Monday night until much later than the time of the hold up. Since the accused has proved he was elsewhere I have no choice but to assume mistaken identity on your part and that of Bragg.'

'This is outrageous!' Staverton glared at the magistrate. 'An absolute travesty of justice! I demand that you—'

'Conduct a public trial with the Marquess of Huntercombe as a witness for the defence?' Ford's voice remained even, but his eyes narrowed. 'I suggest you reconsider your position, Staverton. The outcome of such a trial could well be charges of perjury laid against yourself and Bragg.'

Martin held his silence. If Staverton were tried at all, it would be in the Lords—literally by his peers—who were unlikely to convict. But Bragg? He was another matter entirely.

Bragg swallowed audibly. 'It…it weren't like that, Your Honour. I just—'

'Thank you, Bragg.' Ford cut the man off mercilessly. 'Case dismissed.' He cleared his throat. 'I'll write to the marquess, but in the meantime, Wright, you are free to go. It is patently impossible for you to have murdered Lord Harbury.' He glared at Staverton. 'Unless Lord Staverton can provide evidence of an extraordinarily large crow, or, failing that, a winged horse!'

Kit didn't bother to disguise her snort of laughter.

Staverton rose abruptly. 'Bragg—with me.'

Bragg scrambled up and followed him from the room. The clerk sprang to open the door and closed it behind them.

Ford let out an irritated noise. 'Sutherland, have someone get those shackles off Wright.'

Chapter Four

Kit was fiercely aware of Martin following them
out into the brisk wind hunting down Bow Street.
Somewhere church bells chimed for midday. Usually she loved the bells, but now they seemed to
ring out a death knell for all she could not have.
Would her heart always ache for what she had
turned her back on with Martin?

*He offered marriage only to protect you from
Carshalton. It was never supposed to be a love
match—only a marriage of convenience.*

And how pathetic had she been to accept because she was too afraid of her father to refuse
Martin's offer. Had Carshalton appreciated the
irony of *that*? That she had been prepared to accept the grand match he had arranged because it
offered the only escape from *him*? Only to have
it fall apart when she discovered he had not been
content with her marriage to a mere younger son
after all, but had ordered the murder of Martin's

elder brother and attempted to have his nephew killed as well. A child. Carshalton had ordered the murder of a *child* to further his own ambition. If ever a woman was tainted goods, she was. She had to remember that, even if Martin's chivalry and kindness tempted her to forget.

And she had to face Martin, thank him for coming without her voice wobbling and without allowing herself to think of what might have been.

You found your place, your life. It can't include him. Just imagine if it had all come out after *the wedding.*

Martin would have been trapped in marriage to a woman he might well have suspected had been involved in the plot to kill his nephew, Harry. And she would have been trapped in marriage to a man she loved but couldn't blame for despising her. Even without that, he might have regretted a marriage he had only offered out of chivalry and pity.

Nevertheless, she had still to thank him and—

'My lord?' Caleb turned to Martin. 'I've to thank you for this.'

Kit took a steadying breath. Sometimes she forgot the thin boy was nearly a man who could speak for himself and that it was *his* place to thank Martin. It was Caleb Martin had helped this time. Not her.

Martin looked uncomfortable. 'Actually, you don't. I doubt I made any difference whatsoever to the outcome. Miss Selbourne's testimony would have cleared you without my presence.'

Caleb shook his head. 'Aye. I believe so, but you still came. And Staverton, he's a right—well.' He cleared his throat, shot Kit an apologetic look. 'So, thank you both.'

Martin's jaw hardened for a brief moment and then he smiled. 'You're very welcome. But it should not have been necessary at all. I'm sorry you had to be put through it. You spoke well. Set them all back on their heels.' He held out his hand. 'I doubt Staverton expected any sort of defence.'

Slowly Caleb set his hand in Martin's and they shook.

Then, the moment she was dreading. Martin turned to face her. 'Miss Selbourne. I'll bid you good day. You'll find Ignatius in the Brown Bear.'

He gestured to the tavern across the road.

Kit blinked. If Ignatius was in the tavern... 'Why didn't he come in himself then? He must have told you everything obviously. And if you knew I could clear—'

'Do you think I'd willingly let you face Staverton alone?' He spoke as though the words were wrenched from him, his hands balled into fists. 'Damn it, Kit! Do you know me so little?'

The hurt in his voice shocked her. How much did he know? He couldn't know everything—not *how* Staverton had planned to force her into marriage. Who would have told him?

She frowned, weighing his reaction. His face was impassive now, but his right thumb was rubbing against his forefinger. She doubted he even knew he was doing it. What Ignatius had called a *tell* when he'd taught her to play piquet.

Always watch your opponent for tells.

'I'll escort you across the road and fetch Selbourne out to you.'

Kit raised her brows. 'I'm no longer a young lady, Lord Martin.'

He stared. 'The deuce you aren't!'

She shook her head. 'I'm a shopkeeper these days. My reputation will survive walking across the road with Caleb and into a tavern to find Ignatius.'

He was still struggling with that and that Kit had been clearly surprised at his savage reaction over Staverton—*Selbourne kept his word and told her nothing*—when the boy spoke up.

'You needn't worry, my lord.' Wright gave him a reassuring smile. 'I'd never let anything happen to Miss Kit.'

'I don't doubt it. However...' he took a deep breath and offered Kit his arm '...if my escort is redundant, may I accompany you?'

She could refuse.

Would she?

Smoky grey eyes lifted to his, locked—the faint

questioning lift of her brows had always intrigued him. He waited…the world waited…

A gloved hand withdrew from the muff and she laid it lightly, so very lightly, on his sleeve. He wanted to cover it with his other hand, to hold it there, keep it forever. They couldn't have forever now. Just the finite space of crossing the road, the pavement, to the door of the tavern. If this was all he could have—

He laid his hand over hers. Did she tremble again, or was it just him? Eternity stretched between now and the day fifteen months ago when he'd won her—only to lose her within the hour to the dictates of honour, her own as well as his. And she had been the one to speak, breaking the betrothal, returning his ring.

He could have cursed the traffic. Usually so busy, now, when a throng of carriages and wagons would have been a blessing, there was a break allowing a swift, easy crossing. The door of the Brown Bear bore down on them and, with young Wright keeping pace, no chance to speak.

'Caleb—' his eyes didn't leave Kit's face '—would you be so kind as to find Mr Selbourne in there?'

'Miss Kit? That all right with you?'

He couldn't fault the boy's reluctance.

She flashed the boy a glance. 'Yes. Thank you, Caleb. I will be perfectly safe with Lord Martin.'

Perfectly safe? That she could say it and mean

it… He watched as Caleb disappeared into the tavern.

'You're very generous saying you'd be safe with me.'

Again that serious questioning look. Then— 'You followed me back to London.'

For a moment he was lost. And then he was back there again…the confrontation in Huntercombe's library where her father's henchman had admitted the attempts to murder Harry, to make *him* his father's heir. And, as it turned out, with his mother's connivance.

'I didn't realise you had noticed.' He had to say it. 'Kit, I'm sorry. For everything.' Useless, insufficient words for what he'd done—

'*Sorry?*'

He flinched. Worse than useless—

'What on earth *for*?'

He stared. 'Damn it, Kit! I abandoned you!'

She frowned. 'No, you didn't. *I* broke our betrothal and—'

'You tried to convince me that you, rather than my mother, told your father Emma was taking the children to Isleworth.' His gut roiled in shame at the memory of the sickening instant in which he'd believed her before his brain had reasserted itself and he'd seen the lie for what it was.

She flushed. 'I'm sorry about that. I thought—'

'That I'd rather believe *you* wanted Harry dead, than know it was my mother?' Faced with the appalling reality of her father's criminality, Kit had tried to protect him from a similar revelation.

'No, but I—oh, it doesn't matter now and you *didn't* abandon me.'

The hell he hadn't. Knowing what her father was, he'd let her walk back into that damned Bloomsbury mansion. Unable to marry her, he'd seen no other path then and now it was too late. But if he'd known what Carshalton would do…

'Kit, are you…? Are you—?' He had to know. 'Kit, are you happy?'

She didn't answer at once and his heart sank. If she was happy, he thought he could walk away, but if not—

'Happy? Yes. I'm happy. I've made a good life for myself.' Her mouth quirked. 'Well, Ignatius made a good life possible for me.'

He could only thank God she'd had Selbourne to protect her. It still shamed him he'd left her defenceless, that he hadn't protected her when she'd needed it most. What if Selbourne had been away for Christmas? What if—?

The question was out before he could stop it.

'Kit, if you had not had Selbourne to go to, if he had not been there, would you have come to me?'

She bit her lip in the way he remembered, scratching the bridge of her nose. 'I… I don't know.'

He let out a ragged breath. An unfair question. And this was unfair, too…

Slowly, giving her every chance to turn away, deny him, he bent his head. A kiss, chaste and gentle, on the cheek was all he could have in farewell and he should not even take that.

But she did not protest, stayed utterly still, her smoky eyes with those black rims steady on his face.

He was going to kiss her.

Her pulse kicked up, every nerve dancing under her skin.

Once before, just the once, he had kissed her. In the gig as they drove out to Isleworth on the day he had given her the betrothal ring. Only once, and now he was going to kiss her again.

On the cheek.

She didn't want a chaste peck on the cheek. She couldn't have what she *did* want—but she could have more than a kiss on the cheek. Even if they were standing on a public street outside a tavern.

With his lips a breath away from her cheek she turned, oh, so slightly, and their lips met. Worlds stilled, his mouth on hers unmoving… Time shimmered in stasis—then a sound, half-sigh, half-groan, broke from him and his lips moved in the sweetest of dances, a large, gloved hand cradling her cheek as she caught the rhythm and the kiss deepened. For a heart-shaking moment that encompassed an all too short eternity every planet, star and moon aligned. Everything danced together for one brief measure. Then, as sweetly and gently as it had begun, it was over.

He stepped back, his hand lingering on her cheek and jaw.

'Kit, I'm sorry. I should not—'

'You didn't.'

Slowly she lifted her hand to trace with one gloved finger the edge of his lower lip. 'I did. If I can't have what I once wanted, at least I could have that.'

She wasn't sure kissing Martin Lacy again wasn't the most stupid thing she'd ever done, but—

'What did you want, Kit?'

Very well, saying *that* was the most stupid. She should shut up now, but he deserved the truth. 'You, Martin. For all the wrong reasons.'

'There were wrong reasons?'

She had started to turn away, but glanced back and managed a smile. 'Yours were admirable. Mine weren't. You deserved better than a girl who accepted your offer from sheer desperation.'

'Kit.'

She disappeared into the tavern before he could catch his breath.

It wasn't any damn bloody consolation at all.

As Martin stalked back along Bow Street to the nearest hackney stand, he understood part of him would never cease to want her. Deep down he'd known it already, but he'd tried to persuade himself that if he didn't precisely forget her, he might at least live without this constant ache of *what if* in his heart.

He cut through the throng on the pavement, keeping a wary eye out for pickpockets.

He saw Staverton first, but not soon enough to evade. The viscount's eyes latched on to him and a singularly unconvincing smile plastered itself to the man's face.

Damn. The last thing he needed was to knock Staverton's teeth down his throat and for the morning to conclude with an invitation to pistols for two in Hyde Park at dawn.

He maintained a neutral expression as Staverton approached.

'Lacy.' The smile widened. 'Well met. No ill feelings about that little fuss, I hope.'

'Ill feelings?' Martin had learned from a master to disguise his true thoughts by reflecting the other fellow's assumptions straight back at him. 'Oh, I don't think there are ill feelings.' Savage and uncivilised feelings, certainly.

'Good. Good.' Staverton fell into step beside him. 'You'll understand I was very much upset seeing poor Harbury shot down, of course.'

That sounded perfectly genuine.

'A…a shocking thing! Not at all what I—what one expects.' Staverton fiddled with a fob on his watch chain. 'And I… I blame myself.'

'Yourself?'

'Well, yes.' Staverton fiddled with his cravat. 'It was *my* suggestion that we should drive out to Hampstead, persuade my ungrateful daughter to return to her marriage, her *duty*—and look what happened! Naturally I wish to bring the young wretch to justice, in some way make up for my part in it.'

'Young wretch?'

Staverton leaned closer. 'The boy from the coffee shop. The thing is—'

'Staverton, while I sympathise with your grief over Harbury, Wright cannot have been involved,' Martin said. 'He has a cast-iron alibi. Huntercombe, no less.'

The Viscount shrugged, giving Martin an edgy sideways glance. 'Well, as to that, what if Huntercombe were mistaken in *which* Black boy his servant had with him? After all, why would he pay any attention? No, I think a little further investigation will reveal Huntercombe has been sadly misled. And I'm sure it's not something you would wish—just starting your career at Whitehall—to be embroiled in.'

'Something stinks like a dead rat.'

As Selbourne's words earlier rang clear, Martin jettisoned the notion of leading Staverton along, before punching him in the nose.

'Embroiled?' He slid the merest hint of concern into his voice. 'Do you really think Huntercombe has been duped?'

Staverton pounced. 'Exactly! Lacy, there is something very peculiar about this business. It… it strikes me poor Harbury's death would be most convenient for some. And the thought of a man of Huntercombe's reputation being drawn in—' His shudder was the last word in artistic, his expression pained. 'I have no idea why Whitehall thought to concern itself this morning, but I am very much afraid you have been duped along with Huntercombe, dear boy.'

'Duped.'

Words of advice slid into his mind. *He who says least, hears most.*

Staverton adopted an expression of fatherly concern. 'Indeed. I fear you can have no idea of the danger you court. No doubt…' he smiled sympathetically, patting Martin's arm '…that unfortunate business the Christmas before last when it was rumoured Miss Carshalton had fled to *you* makes you a very useful asset in a situation where someone may be thrown to the wolves.'

Martin slid his hands behind his back to hide his clenched fists. 'Oh.'

'Oh, indeed.' Staverton's fatherly persona beamed. 'And poor Catherine!'

'Poor Catherine?' Martin allowed surprise to surface. Not the fury, or suspicion, just the surprise. After all something had to show, or even Staverton might become suspicious.

'Indeed. A dreadful thing to see her caught up

in this mess. Carshalton will be very much distressed to know she has been led so badly astray.'

'Astray.'

Staverton continued. 'Yes. God knows what radical notions the child has been stuffed with by that scoundrel Selbourne! I dare say he permits her to soil her mind with the rubbish put out by the Wollstonecraft female!'

'Very likely.' Martin assumed suitable disgust at the thought of Kit reading *A Vindication of the Rights of Woman*.

Apparently he succeeded, because Staverton nodded. 'And setting herself up to know the law! Ford was sadly taken in, too, I fear!'

'I appreciate the warning, Staverton.'

Staverton smiled. 'Well, I dare say having been rusticated for much of the past year and more, you are not quite apprised of things yet.'

Rusticated. Martin let that stand. If Staverton didn't know what he'd been doing or where he'd been doing it, so much the better. And better yet if Staverton thought him an easily duped fool.

'No. It's very good of you to take the time, Staverton. I'll bear all this in mind.'

'Oh, think nothing of it, my dear chap! One doesn't like to see a promising young fellow go astray, after all, and I fear poor Catherine will require a firm and experienced hand to control her!'

Martin clenched his fists, remembered that

pounding Staverton to a bloody pulp was not part of his strategy and forcibly unclenched them.

They had reached a hackney stand.

'I'll bid you good day, Staverton.' Martin managed to incline his head politely. 'You've given me a very great deal to think about. You may be sure I'll bear it in mind.'

Staverton clapped him on the shoulder. 'Very wise, Lacy. I'll have a word in the right ears on your behalf, never fear.'

Martin watched for a moment as Staverton strolled off. If Staverton's words reached his immediate superior eyebrows would be raised.

He stepped into a hackney.

'Where to, guv?'

'Whitehall.'

Settling back into the seat as the horse clattered off, Martin thought the rat Selbourne had smelt was even larger and nastier than he'd suspected. He was going to have to do some discreet digging to find out what Staverton didn't want him looking at. And why was the fellow so nervous? He was behaving as though he'd caught a tiger by the tail. As though something had not gone quite as planned and he'd had to improvise.

Chapter Five

It was early afternoon before Selbourne's Books opened.

Ignatius settled behind his desk, reaching for a pen and paper. 'I'll send a note out to Hampstead for Barclay. Best they know about this immediately. And I'll send Morgan to Huntercombe.'

Kit stared. 'Morgan?'

Ignatius glanced up at her briefly, then kept writing. 'Yes. One of the boys at the Lion can take a note to Barclay, but for Huntercombe—' He let out a breath. 'That's a little more sensitive. Morgan can take it and come back in with Huntercombe tomorrow.'

'Won't he come in anyway? Lord Huntercombe. When he receives a note from Sir Richard asking about Caleb, surely—'

'He will.'

'You can speak to him then, can you not?' It was

difficult for Ignatius to manage alone in the mornings. He needed Morgan more than he'd admit.

Ignatius shook his head. 'Best he knows as soon as may be.' Another glance. 'There are others he may wish to alert quickly.'

The cat, Hodge, leapt up on the desk, butted at his shoulder. Ignatius petted the creature.

Puzzled, Kit asked one of the questions that had been jostling in her mind all the way from Bow Street. 'Uncle, why did you request Lord Martin's help? Just our testimony would have been enough to clear Caleb of suspicion. And how did you know where to find him?'

She had deliberately waited until they were alone to raise the subject.

Over the road, since word of his release had spread rapidly and the rest of the staff had appeared, Caleb had opened the Phoenix. Customers flooded in, eager for a soupçon of gossip to flavour their coffee. No doubt several of them would come across to the bookshop after they had squeezed as much news as possible from the Phoenix.

Ignatius drummed his fingers on the desk. 'I wanted a little more weight behind it.'

'Sir Richard would have listened to you. And I think he would have—well, he *did* listen to me.' And why Martin in particular?

The old man shook his head. 'There's something fishy about this, girl. Can't quite put my finger on it, but it stinks to high heaven. It's not as simple as

Staverton leaping on the chance of Harbury's death to strike back at Psyché and Will through Caleb.'

For a moment Kit didn't understand what her brain was telling her. 'You…you think he *planned* it? This is what you need to tell Lord Hunter-combe?'

'Staverton?' Ignatius snorted. 'I wouldn't have thought him clever enough to plan this. He's not entirely stupid, but he's not much on tactics if what I hear from the Lords and elsewhere is anything to go by. He's the sort to fall in with someone else's plans and help carry them out.'

'But Harbury was his son-in-law!' Although she loathed Staverton, she couldn't see him arranging the murder of his son-in-law merely to get revenge on Will and Psyché.

He drummed his fingers again. 'I know. I need to think about that and write these notes.'

Adjusting his eye glasses, Ignatius dipped his pen in the inkwell. The purring cat had settled, paws neatly tucked under him, on the desk in front of him.

She hesitated. Sometimes oblique was better. 'Moth offered Martin her paw.'

He looked up over his glasses, the pen poised. 'Did she now? Well, well, well. Something else to think about.' He directed his gaze at the dog sprawled by the fire. 'I'll wager she didn't offer Staverton her paw.'

Kit grinned. 'No. She growled at him.'

'Sensible. Why don't you run upstairs and let Morgan know I'll need him?'

He started writing and Kit let it go. If Ignatius said he wanted to think about something, you wouldn't get another word out of him on the subject until he'd finished thinking.

Reordering and dusting the biblical commentaries in between serving customers, Kit focused her mind on what she knew already. If Ignatius thought Staverton had been carrying out someone else's plan, who was pulling his strings?

What could she infer about this shadowy someone from what they already knew? It had to be someone utterly ruthless. Carefully she replaced Calmet's *Dictionary of the Holy Bible* on the shelf. While she couldn't rule out a woman, it seemed more likely to be a man. Women, she thought, thinking of Martin's mother the duchess, could be ruthless enough, but *ladies*, for the most part, had so much less freedom to go where they pleased, meet any man they pleased without being encumbered with servants. A gentleman would find it easier to plot and Staverton would be unlikely to take orders from a woman.

So probably a man, which didn't get her very much further forward. What else? A man, one Staverton wouldn't perceive as being beneath him, a man who understood tactics, strategy, and surely one who had something to gain from Harbury's death. Although… She frowned as she dusted the first volume of Coke's *Commentary*. What did Staverton have to gain from Harbury's death? The man had been his son-in-law, after all, and from what she knew the marriage had had his complete approval. He'd been furious when his daughter successfully negotiated a deed of separation from Harbury… Ignatius's words slid back into her mind…

'It's not as simple as Staverton leaping on the chance of Harbury's death to strike back at Psyché and Will through Caleb.'

Ignatius was right. The sooner Lord Huntercombe knew the better. Morgan had left as soon as the letter was written, although he'd plainly not liked leaving Ignatius overnight.

Kit had walked out to the pavement with him.

'I promise I'll look after him, Morgan.'

'You do that, Miss Kit. Make sure he eats his supper. Be firm. It's the only way.'

Smiling a little, she put the first volume back and took out the second…

What if Harbury's death hadn't been the point? Or not the main point. What if accusing Caleb had been the point?

And striking at Psyché and Will through him.

She perched on the ladder, her hands shaking so that she had to grip the book to stop it sliding from her grasp. If Staverton had a motive to cause trouble for Psyché, she didn't have to look very far to find someone else who had been made to look a fool last year.

Her own father.

The man who had given orders for the murder of Martin's ten-year-old nephew, Harry. Huntercombe's stepson. He'd tried a hold up there, too. From what she'd been told, only Lady Huntercombe's courage and quick thinking had saved the boy. Harry Lacy, formally known by the courtesy title Viscount Thirlbeck, was heir apparent to the Duke of Keswick.

Her *sire*—damned if she'd ever call him *father* again—had been so eager to marry her to the heir to a dukedom that he'd ordered the murder of a child. Her stomach lurched. Very likely the death of Martin's elder brother, the erstwhile Viscount Thirlbeck, killed in another supposedly botched hold up two years ago, lay at Carshalton's door as well. Lord Huntercombe believed that, although it had been impossible to prove anything.

Carshalton's views, his hunger for political power to shore up support for the slave trade in Parliament, sickened her. From his point of view her projected marriage to Martin had been all about political influence. Her stomach churned; she wanted to shove away the accusing knowledge of Carshalton's criminality, but she forced herself to look at it head-on. Bitterly she accepted that his blood ran in her veins. Even if she never used his name again or acknowledged him, she couldn't ignore the truth: she was his daughter—tainted.

But it didn't seem quite right. Oh, she could see him doing it for revenge; But to have Harbury murdered just to revenge himself on someone else? She couldn't see how striking at Psyché and Will through Caleb would advance him. And surely no one had needed to die. All they'd needed to make the accusation was a shot fired during the hold up. They hadn't needed Harbury's death to make an accusation stick; merely being convicted of holding up the coach would have been enough.

She frowned. Pistols weren't terribly accurate at any distance. Maybe killing Harbury had been accidental and...

The crash took her unawares.

Mr Daly had knocked the writing slope Ignatius kept for the use of his customers on to the floor. Several regulars used it for casual correspondence. It was kept stocked with paper bearing the shop's letterhead, a quill, a pen cutter and an inkwell. Occasionally the ink well had spilled, or someone had broken the pen.

A new customer, a man she'd seen only a couple of times before, had been using it a few moments earlier, making notes about a couple of books he was apparently interested in. He'd purchased an inexpensive volume of sermons and left. On his previous visit she'd asked if he wished to be entered in their customer catalogue with notes on his interests. She was proud of the catalogue. Ignatius kept it all in his head, but she had spent hours working on the cards over the past twelve months. Most of their customers liked the idea. This fellow had declined roughly so she'd left him alone this afternoon.

Now the slope lay upended on the waxed floor, the inkwell shattered and ink advancing on the Turkish rug by the hearth. Probably because Mr Grumpy—her private name for him—had left it too close to the edge.

Shoving the Reverend Coke back into his place on the shelf, Kit scrambled down the ladder as fast as her abbreviated skirts allowed.

'Don't worry, Mr Daly. Here. Let me.' She had another dusting cloth tucked into her pocket and whipped it out to block the flood of ink he was attempting to control with a pocket handkerchief.

Moth had risen from her snooze in curiosity, but subsided since no walk offered, nor danger threatened. Kit concentrated on blocking the ink from reaching the rug—

'Here.'

Ignatius dropped another dusting cloth into the fray. She slapped it down in the path of a rogue rivulet, unspoken curses jostling in her head.

'Thank you, Uncle.'

'I'm most frightfully sorry, Selbourne. Miss Selbourne.' Daly wrung his hands. 'So very clumsy of me. I lost my balance a little when I stood up and grabbed at the table. Think I caught the slope instead.'

'Never mind, Daly. Accidents happen,' Ignatius soothed the man.

Kit, having staunched the flow of ink, looked at the slope and winced.

The broken inkwell could be replaced along with the broken quill. But the slope itself was damaged. In one corner the dovetail joint had broken and the lid had ripped free of one hinge, splintering the wood. She was clever enough with a screwdriver, but this was more than she could repair.

'I think it requires Talbot's skill, love.'

Wrinkling her nose, Kit nodded. 'I'll bring down my slope first.'

She ran up the stairs to the apartment. The writing slope Ignatius and Aunt Agatha had given her for her eleventh birthday sat on the table in their front parlour. Picking it up, she hurried back down.

Setting it in place of the broken one, she smiled at Ignatius. 'I'll take the other around now.' She glanced around. 'Where is Mr Daly?'

Ignatius had the broken slope on his own desk. 'Bought his books and gone. Thank you, love.' He hesitated, glanced up at her. 'Take Moth. You shouldn't be going about alone at the moment.'

Kit stared. 'Very well.'

'Take your muff.' He held out the plain velvet muff she used to keep her hands warm in cold weather.

'Uncle, it's not that cold and I'm carrying a writing slope.'

His gaze narrowed. 'Only one way. Take it.'

Puzzled, she took it, felt the familiar extra weight and stared at him. 'Why—?' Her breath caught. 'You don't think Staverton—'

'Better safe than sorry.' His mouth settled in a grim line.

Letting out a breath, she took the muff and slipped the chain over her neck. 'Very well. I'll let Moth run in the Square on my way back.'

The cabinetmaker examined the damage.

'Made a right mess of this, didn't he?' His fingers touched the splintered wood tender as a mother with an injured child. 'You'll have to leave it with me a few days. Joint to rebuild and I'll have to match the veneer.'

He set it down gently, then bent closer, frowning. 'What's this, then?'

Scarred, sensitive fingers ran over the leather writing surface where it had come adrift at the lower right corner. The craggy brows snapped close in a scowl as he lifted the triangular flap as tenderly as a doctor might have examined an ailing infant. 'Someone's used a knife on this!' His outraged glare skewered Kit.

She stared. 'What?'

Talbot returned his attention to the damaged lid, poked at the rent in the leather. 'Something under here.' He ran his fingers around the edge of the leather. 'See? Someone sliced an opening and...' He drew out a heavy, folded paper.

He began to open it, but Kit reached across and took it quickly. 'It must be something of my uncle's. I'll give it to him.' She slipped the paper into her muff.

Talbot shook his head. 'Love letters, eh? You take my advice, Miss Kit. Fellow you can't tell Mr Selbourne about isn't the one for you!'

Kit felt her cheeks burn. 'Honestly, Mr Talbot, if I was using it to pass or receive love letters, don't you think I would have checked the hiding place?'

Talbot chuckled. 'No telling what foolish thing a female will do. Off you go now. I'll send a message when it's done.'

Reaching the corner where she would have turned north for Soho Square, she glanced down at Moth who wagged her tail expectantly, tongue lolling.

'Sorry. We can't. You'll have to chase the pigeons another time.'

The tail slowed and Moth nudged her hand.

Kit shook her head. 'Come on.'

She set off along the street, the dog at her side. She had to get the document, whatever it was, back to Ignatius. Part of her wanted to take it out and look, but it wasn't hers. She couldn't think of anyone who would send her clandestine letters, let alone hide one in the slope. Nor could she think of any good reason for anyone to pass Ignatius a letter in it. Nevertheless, she wouldn't breach his trust by reading it without his consent.

She lengthened her stride. The afternoon was closing in with a light mist. Lights were appearing in houses and shops. She doubted there would be many customers left in the bookshop, but she frowned, seeing the heavy window shutters on the bookshop were closed. That was supposed to be her job these days. Hopefully one of the neighbours had helped Ignatius.

Whisking into the shop out of the chill, Kit slammed to a stop under the jangling bell—

Instead of an empty shop, or maybe one or two lingering customers chatting with Ignatius, several men were in the shop, including one at the top of a ladder, pulling out books willy-nilly, shaking them and tossing them down to another man who stacked them roughly.

Moth growled.

'Sit. Wait.' She quelled the dog with a sharp gesture and strode forward. 'What are you *doing*? Some of those books are—'

'Kit.'

Ignatius, seated at his desk, spoke softly.

She stared. 'What are they—?'

'A search, my dear. These officers are from Bow Street. Perhaps you would slip over to the Phoenix and order coffee?'

'Sir, there's no need to send Miss Selbourne. One of the men may go.'

The familiar deep voice struck at her senses. She turned slowly, shaken to the core.

Tawny gaze fixed on her, Martin stood holding aside the curtain that covered the entrance to the back storage and kitchen area. Shock held her speechless as he came forward and another officer came out behind him. To her absolute disgust, Moth trotted forward, tail wagging.

'Here! You up there. Handle those books carefully unless you wish to pay for them!' Scratching the dog's ears, Martin glanced at another man at the desk the customers used. 'Smithers, I don't know what you think to find in such an obvious place.'

One hand still in the muff, Kit's breath caught sharply as the officer he'd spoken to ran his finger along the seam of leather and wood on her own writing slope. Her lungs seized as he tried to get his fingernails under the leather. First one corner, then another.

Frowning, he scratched at the seam. 'Seems the right place for a letter, my lord.' He poked at the corners again.

Kit forced her breathing to steady. 'Of course,' she said, dripping sarcasm, as she slid her hand out of the muff, careful not to rustle the paper inside. 'We keep all our most private correspondence in a writing slope available to the customers.'

He gave her a sharp look. 'Didn't say anything about private, Missy.'

Martin took a step forward. 'Smithers—'

'Smithers, is it? How do you do?' She spoke straight over Martin, determined to speak for herself. 'One does rather assume that when an officer from Bow Street is hunting for a letter it's something one would very much rather keep private and that box is there for the use of any customer who needs it. Which makes it not very private at all.'

So, who *had* used the broken slope to hide something? Her mind went to the man who had used it earlier... And how the hell did Bow Street know about whatever it was? Because judging by the very specific way Smithers had checked and rechecked the writing surface, it looked as though he'd been sure of finding something under there.

'Be that as it may, Missy, there's something—'

'Smithers.' Martin's voice held the snap of command. 'You will speak to Miss Selbourne with all respect. Meanwhile, you may go and order the coffee.'

The man rose slowly. 'As you wish, my lord.' He shot Kit a narrow-eyed glare. 'Beg pardon, miss.'

Martin inclined his head. 'Take this.' He handed over half a crown. 'Ask Wright to please send over coffee for seven.'

Smithers looked somewhat placated as he took the coin and walked out.

Kit steadied her breathing. She'd checked the

shop slope that morning to ensure the inkwell was full and there was enough paper and so forth. If the leather had been cut then, she would have noticed. As far as she had noticed only the newcomer had used it. She could ask Ignatius once they were alone.

Kit glanced at Ignatius. His face was grey—in the half-hour since she had seen him he'd aged. 'Uncle, are you feeling—?'

'I'm perfectly well, love.' A touch of asperity. 'Merely surprised. The magistrate on duty received a tip-off.'

'A tip-off? About what?'

He shrugged. 'That I might have had something to do with the murder of Lord Harbury.'

'*What?*' She rounded on Martin. 'And you lent yourself to this…this charade—'

'Kit, Lacy called on me privately.' Ignatius spoke lightly. 'Most fortuitous. His presence has kept things…civilised.'

She nodded, knots slithering and twisting in her stomach. Ignatius might adopt a light tone, but he didn't know about the damn letter. It was sheer luck it hadn't been found, but what if it had? She should show it to him, but she couldn't take the risk with Bow Street searching the shop and if they found it on her…

'I think I'd rather tea than coffee at this hour. Excuse me.'

She whipped through the curtain into the kitchen.

Trembling, she forced herself to think, weighing the risks as she untied the ribbons of her bonnet, then hung it on the hook by the door. Decision made, she turned to the fire.

If it was the wrong decision, so be it: she had to protect Ignatius. It was the work of a moment to stir up the coals, add more and swing the kettle over the fire to cover her actions. Her hand trembled as she reached into the muff, and her fingers touched the heavy paper—she hesitated. Before simply destroying whatever it was, maybe she should first read it, then—what the devil was the teapot doing there? Distracted, she looked around. The teapot was on the window ledge, not the table, and what was the caddy doing on the chair? Or—

'Kit. I'm sorry. You'll find things a little out of order in here.'

Chapter Six

Kit swung around, her face pale as Martin let the curtain fall behind him. Her frightened, almost guilty expression was a blow to the gut. For a moment it was as though he saw again the cowed, bullied girl she had once been. Then that girl was gone and the fiercely independent young woman with—

'You've cut your hair.'

He hadn't realised this morning, but now with her bonnet discarded he saw the modishly short hair, tousled, gilded brown waves framing her face instead of the elaborate formal arrangements she had once worn.

She glared. 'My hair is irrelevant. They searched in *here*? This area is private.'

'I understand that. Er…the privacy, I mean, not your hair. But—' Lord, he was making a mull of this! He kept his voice pitched low to ensure the Runners did not hear and tried to forget her hair that made his fingers itch to slide through it. 'The magistrate on duty spoke to Ford who took over and delayed the warrant long enough to get word to me, but I couldn't stop the search.' He let out a breath, wondering whether or not to tell her he'd been coming here anyway. 'Believe me, I thought about it, but it would have looked fishy. And frankly I don't have the authority to block a duly sworn warrant.'

'But you took command?'

He couldn't blame her for the anger in her voice, but he needed her to understand.

'Yes. Otherwise the place would be a shambles. Smithers is a good officer and he's convinced this tip-off is important.'

There was something odd about the way Smithers had focused on the writing slope. As if he'd been expecting to find something in it.

Kit hung her muff by its chain on a hook near the back door, along with her cloak, and busied herself with the teapot, her back to him. 'And did this tip-off come from Staverton?'

He didn't think so, but—there was his odd conversation with the very nervous Staverton this morning. 'It's possible.'

She glanced back at him, her brows slightly drawn. 'But not very likely.'

She could read him too well. He shook his head. 'No. The man Smithers described wasn't Staverton.' Assuming Smithers had given them all the information. He suspected the man was holding a couple of cards very close to his chest. Like being told to look somewhere very specific. Such as a writing slope…

'Smithers?'

'Yes. He was approached in a tavern by a man who professed to have important information that Selbourne's Books was being used to pass criminal information.'

'A *tavern*?'

Martin shrugged. 'It's not unusual for the Runners to frequent a tavern, Kit. It's the sort of place they do get useful tips. It's not as though they have the option of frequenting drawing rooms.'

She grimaced, straightening. 'Good point. And I'm sorry.'

'Sorry?'

'For being angry with you. For dragging you into whatever this mess is.'

'That's two apologies too many.' He was involved because he wanted, *needed*, to be. Because he could sense the tangled web of disaster coiling around Kit and Selbourne and he'd be damned before he let it touch them.

She scowled. 'I shouldn't have kissed you this morning either, so—'

'If you're going to be sorry about that I'll be really annoyed. And for the record, irrelevant or not, I like your hair.'

His temper smouldering, Martin stalked back

through the curtain before saying or doing something he'd regret. Like sliding his fingers into those silky, tousled curls.

By the time the officers finished searching upstairs and down it was nearly half past seven. They had, thank God, realised the futility of checking every single book in the shop. Especially after Selbourne had pointed out that any customer might at any moment decide to mount a ladder and investigate a volume for himself.

'Hardly where I'd keep secrets.'

Still, there were enough books off the shelves that someone was going to be very busy reshelving them. Kit, perhaps? Surely Selbourne was too old now to be clambering about on ladders.

Kit had remained in the kitchen and something fragrantly spicy wafted into the shop. Martin watched as the dog scrambled up from her place by the fire and trotted out to the kitchen in response to a sharp whistle from Kit. The cat followed with marginally more dignity.

The Runners were a little disheartened, because they'd found nothing more shocking than a number of volumes of erotica on an upper shelf. Smithers had wanted to impound those, but Martin had told him to take it up with Sir Richard and sent them back to report in at Bow Street.

Ignatius snorted. 'As if I'd be fool enough to hide papers in the shop! The first rule of any shady enterprise is *not* to keep incriminating papers at all.'

Kit came out from the kitchen area as the Runners were pulling on their coats and set a bowl before her uncle. 'Oh, I don't know. It would be safe enough if it was written in Aramaic, say. Even I don't read that.'

Martin's heart squeezed as Selbourne smiled up at her affectionately and patted her hand.

'You'd learn fast enough if you found a mysterious document in Aramaic. What's this?'

'Your supper. Eat it. I'm under orders from Morgan.'

From Kit's firm tone Martin suspected Selbourne wasn't eating enough for her liking. He could believe it—the change in the once robust old man was very clear. Even this morning he'd noticed it and now Ignatius looked haggard. As if he'd aged a decade since Martin had seen him that morning.

Martin waited. He needed to talk to Selbourne. Preferably without Kit present. But the old man needed to finish his supper, and what he'd found out that afternoon, coupled with this search, would spoil anyone's digestion. Kit, however, showed no sign of going upstairs. She moved around, tidying up with a sort of concentrated energy. Putting books back on the lower shelves, reordering books here and there, wielding a dust cloth as if it were a weapon.

She had something on her mind. The faint frown, the slight pursing of her lips as she worked her way through a problem—all so familiar.

Moth strolled back through the curtain and collapsed by the fire with a contented sigh.

Selbourne set down his spoon. 'You've fed the dog?'

'And Hodge.'

Selbourne nodded. 'There's a concert this evening. You'll want to change.'

'Concert? Oh.' She set down the dust cloth, her brow wrinkled. 'I'd forgotten. I'll be ready in twenty minutes. Goodnight, my lord.'

Martin bowed. 'Goodnight, Miss Selbourne.'

Kit changed into her favourite gown for cooler evenings. When she had fled from Carshalton's house she had left all her clothes behind. Hiding in Psyché's apartment, she had realised that for the life she was planning those clothes would be useless. Consequently when she replaced them she had done so with gowns she could manage by herself. Even this gown, her evening best, was possible for her to put on without a maid. She tidied her hair, pinning a lace cap over it. Plain, but that didn't bother her. The company was mostly shop people like herself and Ignatius—everyone was more interested in the music than in what a young woman wore on her head. Not at all like the balls and assemblies to which Martin's mother, the duchess, had once chaperoned her and for which Carshalton had insisted she be dressed as richly as possible.

She liked pretty clothes, but now, dressing herself in a gown of deep blue wool with the tiniest of embroidered flounces at the hem, she knew she was happier than she had ever been when she had a roomful of silks and satins requiring the assistance of a maid to wear. Instead of needing a maid to arrange her hair—and taking an hour to do it—she could tidy it herself in less than five minutes.

The one thing her old life had nearly given her that she wanted was lost to her and she accepted that. If she *had* married Martin, she could never have known this freedom, this independence. It would never have occurred to her even to try for it.

You can't know that. You don't know what marriage to Martin might have been like.

She pushed those thoughts away. Rather than wondering what their marriage might have been like, she needed to think about what she'd learned from Martin. Smithers, the Runner who had been so diligent in searching her writing slope, had been the one the unknown gentleman had approached with information. If Mr Daly hadn't broken the shop slope, Smithers would have found the document.

Her stomach lurched. She hadn't dared read it while there was any chance of Martin or one of the Runners coming into the kitchen. The blasted thing was still tucked into her muff hanging by the back door. But the Runners were gone, and she couldn't see Martin searching her muff. Still. The sooner she got back downstairs and showed it to Ignatius the better. Then they might have some idea of what was going on.

To her surprise, when she opened the door on the lower landing voices floated up. Not distinct enough for words, but she recognised Martin's deep tones.

She stepped lightly down the stairs, avoiding treads that squeaked, until she reached the point where she remained hidden, but could hear the conversation.

'I can't give you an answer, Lacy. Not until I've had a chance to consider what you've told me. After this morning—well, what I suspected then was bad enough. I need to think about this.'

Her breath caught. He sounded so tired, defeated almost.

'Sir—'

'I know. I know. But I have no answer for you. And it's not just myself I have to think of.'

Kit stayed very still.

'Sir, you must know that I would—'

'I *do* know it, Lacy. None better. And if I were in any danger of forgetting, I have that daily reminder over there.'

Kit blinked. What?

Martin's low chuckle brushed her senses. 'You were absolutely right about those paws.'

Paws?

Ignatius snorted. 'Damned thing eats us out of house and home, but she has her uses and she's never chased Hodge.'

Moth was a daily reminder? Of what?

Martin laughed. 'I don't owe you an apology, then?'

Ignatius never did say where he found Moth. Just that she arrived on the Christmas night after I ran from Carshalton and Staverton. But she recognised Martin...

'What did you call her in the end... I mean, what's her name?'

'Not so far, boy. Leave it now. She'll be down soon and I'd rather not answer the inevitable questions quite yet. There are things I've never told her about my past.'

Kit's cheeks burned. She had eavesdropped on Carshalton shamelessly, but Ignatius was another matter. She crept back up half the flight and started down again, deliberately noisy to cover her duplicity.

Stepping into the shop, she affected surprise as Martin rose. 'My lord. I didn't expect to find you still here.'

Thank goodness her voice didn't wobble even if her pulse still danced around like a silly schoolgirl.

'I needed to talk to your uncle.'

Ignatius nodded. 'We'll talk further when you come home, Kit.'

Kit stared. 'When *I* come home? You aren't coming?'

'Not tonight. Convey my regrets to Gifford. Lacy will escort you.'

From Martin's expression this was news to him as well. Damn it! Surely Ignatius wasn't matchmaking? He knew everything was at an end between them, that a marriage between them now would be anything but convenient.

'There's no need for me to go either,' she said. 'We can—'

'No, pet.' As firmly as he spoke the old man's voice was laced with affection. 'You go. Enjoy the music. I'll be poor company this evening.'

Martin spoke. 'Sir, would it be better if—'

'No.' Ignatius cut Martin off far more sharply. 'After the concert will be soon enough. I might have more for you if I sit and think in peace for an hour or so. Escort Kit—it'll be safer.'

'Safer?' Kit couldn't believe it. 'I've never needed an escort, not with Moth. You said so, yourself. And if I did Mr Gifford or one of the others would walk me home.'

'Yes,' Ignatius agreed. 'But tonight I'm saying that you take an escort. And...' he met her eyes '...your muff.'

He'd insisted on that earlier, too. 'Very well.'

He glanced at Martin. 'You will oblige me in this, Lacy?'

Kit turned and glared at Martin, but he was looking at Ignatius. 'Yes, sir.'

Something about his voice, and the steely look that passed between the two men, told her that she had as much chance of persuading them otherwise as she did of holding back the Severn Bore.

'I'll leave Moth with you,' she said. She hated to leave him alone when he looked so worried and frail.

He smiled, shaking his head. 'No. I'll be happier if you take her. I'll go up, but I'll leave the door unbolted for you in case I doze off.' He held Martin's gaze. 'When you come back we'll talk, Lacy. Not before.'

'Sir—'

'Your word, Lacy.'

'*Merda.* Yes, sir.'

He'd been neatly outflanked. Not only could he hardly refuse Selbourne's terms after dropping that bombshell on him, he was damned if he'd let Kit go out alone, even if she *was* accompanied by a dog who'd ended up the size of a young donkey. He couldn't believe Selbourne had been letting her do so. Damn it all! The old man was supposed to be protecting her and he was more worried about her getting cold hands than being assaulted on the street. Take her muff indeed!

He heard Selbourne lock the door behind them and turned to Kit. 'Which way, Miss Selbourne?'

He shifted to put himself between her and other people hurrying by, some with lanterns, others depending on the light cast from windows. Hackneys rumbled by in the street, weaving past delivery carts and barrows, although most of the shops were closed.

She faced him. 'There's really no need for this. With Moth—'

'Kit. Which way?'

'My lord—'

'I swear, Kit, if you *my lord* me one more time—'

'Well, you started it. Calling me *Miss Selbourne* in that stuffy way! And if you didn't want to escort me—'

'Who said I didn't want to escort you?'

'Swearing about it in Latin was a clue.'

'It was Spanish, actually, and—you understood that?' He stopped. The hole he was digging got deeper with every word. 'Right. That wasn't exactly what I was swearing about.' How could he tell her that spending the evening with her was painful because it had to end? 'Kit, I'm not leaving you to wander about Soho at night with only your dog as escort. I gave your uncle my word.'

She glared at him and he blinked. Where had that come from? The girl he had known— He discarded that thought immediately—the girl he had known would not have been capable of fronting a magistrate in his office to stand up for a friend.

'I am perfectly capable of looking after myself.'

He tried a smile. *Be tactful.* 'Of course you are, but—'

She stopped dead in her tracks and spoke through gritted teeth. 'Do *not* patronise me.'

'I am *not*—' He broke off as they stepped out into the road. He'd been about to do precisely that.

He switched tack. 'Can we agree that your uncle wished you to accept my escort? That I gave my word and I am doing it to oblige him?' Easier if he told her what was going on, or as much as he suspected, but giving Selbourne his word had hamstrung him. Nor was it a conversation they could have on a busy pavement.

She was silent as they crossed, frowning. She was thinking about it, he realised. Thinking about it and considering her response. Just as she had always done. Only when he had first known her, she had been guarded to protect herself in a hostile society. Now she was thinking about her *own* wishes and preferences.

'Very well. I'll accept your escort to oblige Ignatius.'

She's been accepting your escort to placate other people since you first met her.

He drew a deep breath and said the last thing he wanted to say. 'If you prefer it, I can simply escort you to the door and wait for you.'

Her eyes flew to his. 'What?'

'I won't force my company on you if you'd rather—'

'It's not that.' She walked on, frowning. 'I don't want you to feel obligated.'

Honesty. She needed honesty. 'I am obligated—Selbourne asked me to escort you, but since I enjoy your company—' he smiled at her startled look '—it's not exactly an imposition for me. It's your decision, Kit.'

Silence was a living thing between them and he waited. Waited for the decision he had not given her, but had accepted was hers.

At last, after a space in time that had stretched to eternity, she said softly, 'I enjoy your company, too. I always did. If you would like to attend the concert with me, I would be pleased.'

Some of the weight lifted from his heart.

'Then—' He held out his arm, elbow crooked. After a moment she set her hand on it lightly. Through her gloves, his own shirt and coat, the feather touch seared him as it had always done.

They walked on in a not uncomfortable silence, the dog trotting unleashed at their heels. Gifford's Music Emporium was not very far away and several other people were entering as they approached.

Kit shot him a sideways glance. 'The music will be good, but the company won't be like the soirées you used to escort me to with your mother.'

He smiled. 'I enjoyed those evenings because there was good music and you were with me.'

Startled eyes met his. 'That was Catherine, Martin. She's gone. There's just Kit now.'

'There was always just you, Kit,' he said quietly.

On one level Martin enjoyed the concert. More than he had expected. Not that he didn't like music, he did. But after what he'd had to tell Selbourne and the consequent worry, he'd expected to be distracted. And he was. But the string quartet flowed around him, unlocking feelings and thoughts better left undisturbed. Because Kit was beside him again, an ache in his heart that assured him that he was still very much alive.

The dog lay quietly beside Kit's chair, her nose on her paws, and snoozed. No one seemed at all bothered by her presence, which suggested it wasn't the first time she'd accompanied Kit to a concert.

Although it wasn't the first time he'd escorted Kit to a musicale, he'd never escorted her to one held in a concert hall above a music shop. Or one where it appeared the company was there to listen to the music rather than be seen.

Glancing sideways, he saw the quiet, concentrated focus of the Kit who had once told him she preferred concerts because she liked music more than talking to people. Only, he'd liked to think she'd enjoyed being with him too.

'I enjoy your company, too. I always did.'

Had she really enjoyed his company when they first met? Enough to marry him?

Not that he'd meant to marry her. Not at first.

But at his mother's insistence he'd escorted her while she chaperoned Kit, or Catherine as he'd known her then. His father had asked him to consider the match seriously.

'You need to marry, boy. The succession hangs by two fragile threads. I have one son left—you.'

'Sir, there's Peter's son.'

'If—and it is an if—the brat is legitimate, a child's life is still fragile. And after you it's some third or fourth cousin in America I've never even met. This Catherine Carshalton—her breeding's not what I'd want for you, but she seems pleasant enough. Quiet, biddable. And there's the money.'

So he'd considered… And slowly he'd seen past the quiet, demure front Catherine Carshalton used to hide her intelligence, and come to like her. Unfortunately he'd been far slower to see what was behind Carshalton and his mother's furthering of the match—Carshalton's hunger for power feeding his mother's obsession with obliterating what she saw as Peter's disgraceful mésalliance.

You were forced on her by your mother and her father. When she was finally free to choose for herself…

Even in her apparently willing acceptance of his marriage offer she had been constrained—she had viewed him as the lesser of two evils—a man who might treat her kindly as opposed to her father who—he forced his fists to unclench, remembering the night at a ball he'd caught her wrist lightly and she'd cried out...

'I'm sorry. I hurt you. Let me see...'

Stripping off her glove in that alcove at a ball, seeing the dark bruising on her wrist, the clear finger marks, and knowing he couldn't possibly be responsible...

'Who did it?'

The splintering, molten rage that someone had hurt her, that some bastard might have tried to force his attentions on her...

She'd hedged, saying it was an accident, nothing at all. But finally she'd broken...

'My father. He discovered that I visited my uncle when I was supposed to be shopping...'

'I think you had better marry me.'

The offer had been out before he'd realised the words were there. Even then, with that protective, possessive fury roiling his gut, he'd told himself it would be a *suitable* marriage—after all, she was an heiress—with some affection on both sides. And naturally a man expected to protect the woman he was going to marry.

He'd taken her to visit Ignatius Selbourne himself after the betrothal, seen the affection between them and promised her that he would never stop her visiting him. He'd liked Selbourne anyway, but even more so when he'd seen the old man's affection for his great-niece.

And with Selbourne he'd finally seen hints of the real Kit, the woman she kept hidden from everyone else, most of all from her father.

Two weeks later, the betrothal broken in a scandal that had rocked London, with whispers that he'd wanted his nephew dead, or worse, that Kit had wanted his nephew dead, he knew he'd lost a great deal more than a convenient, richly dowered bride.

All these months he'd worried about the girl he'd been forced in all honour to abandon. That girl was no more. In her place was a confident young woman, who, according to Selbourne, was well prepared to take over the bookshop and run it.

The bullied, frightened young girl had become an independent businesswoman. One who had fronted the Bow Street Magistrate's court this morning to help someone.

As you once tried to help her?

Now it looked as though she needed his help again. Only this time he doubted the danger threatening her could be resolved with anything as simple as marriage.

During supper after the concert Martin noticed with a grin that, although Moth couldn't be said to beg, she paid close attention to the food and a couple of biscuits disappeared into Kit's muff.

He bent down and murmured, 'What about the cakes? Doesn't she like those?'

A stifled snort escaped Kit. 'They don't travel quite as well as biscuits.'

He choked. 'Ah. Very practical. A glass of wine?' He shot her a grin. '*Not* for your muff.'

She hesitated. 'I should go home, but—'

'Miss Selbourne! How nice to see you. Ignatius did not venture out this evening? I hope he is not unwell. And who is your friend?'

'Mr Gifford.' Kit smiled at the old music seller. 'Ignatius was rather weary. This is—'

'Martin Lacy, at your service, sir.' He discreetly nudged Kit's ankle with his foot. No need to make the old chap a present of *my lord.*

Gifford bowed. 'A pleasure, Lacy.' He turned back to Kit. 'I hope Ignatius is not too knocked up by all the drama this morning? I understand Bow Street arrested young Caleb Wright?' He scowled. 'Ridiculous thing to do! As if that lad would hold up a coach! Told him so myself when I stopped in for a coffee and the newspapers.'

Kit smiled as she laid a gentle hand on the old man's arm. 'A mistake, sir. Caleb is quite safe and Ignatius is a little tired.'

Gifford nodded. 'Well, a shame Ignatius didn't feel up to coming out.' He smiled at Martin. 'I hope you enjoyed the concert, Lacy. Now—a glass of wine?' He beckoned to a servant carrying a tray. 'A nice burgundy for you, of course, Miss Selbourne. And you, Lacy?'

'The same.' Trying not to look surprised, he took a glass and offered it to Kit.

'Burgundy?' he murmured as they strolled away with Moth at their heels. Young ladies were supposed to drink ratafia, or lemonade.

She gave a half-smile. 'Ignatius always assumed I'd like what he likes.'

'And if you didn't?'

She frowned. 'Then I could say so and have something else. I wasn't clear—Ignatius simply treats me as me. As Kit. A person with likes and dislikes. He doesn't worry about what is, or is not, proper for a young lady.'

He glanced down at her. 'Since he taught you Latin well enough to understand my less than polite Spanish, that goes without saying.'

A swift glance up and he glimpsed the old Kit. Uncertain, worried that she had offended by knowing something considered improper for a woman.

'No.' He stopped, turned her gently to face him. And, unable to check the need to touch her again, he raised a hand to brush her cheek with his fingertips.

She stared up at him, cheeks flushed, her soft lips parted, and the memory of that morning's kiss rushed over him. And their only other kiss—

A winter's morning, in his gig, drawn into the side of a hedge, his ring on her finger and her

mouth soft and innocent beneath his. Their be-
trothal kiss...

He swallowed, removed his hand. Safer not to
think of this morning, or that other kiss so long
ago. 'You must know that was *not* a criticism.
Merely an observation.' He tried to lighten the moment. 'And if it *had* been a criticism, I would like
to think you would treat it as it deserves.'

She looked intrigued. 'And how should I have
treated it?'

'With a swift kick to the shin.'

'I'll bear that in mind. Why did Ignatius go to
you this morning?'

He could give her that much. 'He didn't exactly. He went to my immediate superior. For the
rest... Finish your wine and I'll escort you home.
I'm sorry, but—'

She sighed. 'You gave your word about it. Is
that it?'

He nodded shortly. 'There's that. But it's also
absolutely not the sort of thing we can talk about
here.'

Chapter Seven

Kit left the subject alone as they walked back to the shop. Ignatius had taught her years ago that a promise made must be kept. And that if one had the least respect for another, one did not tease them or beg them to break a confidence.

You should have the same care for another's honour as for your own.

She had realised very soon after meeting him that Martin's code of honour was inviolable. His word was his bond. That was partly why she had broken their betrothal so quickly—so *he* didn't have to do it. At first she had thought to protect him from knowing what his mother had done, but she had quickly seen the folly of that. Protecting the duchess for whatever reason endangered Harry. But at least Martin had not been forced to break the betrothal, something he would have considered utterly dishonourable.

Kit took the front door key out of her pocket,

wishing that the evening was not over and that she hadn't enjoyed it so much. She wished that having Martin beside her again, listening to a concert, smiling at her—even with the worry of the morning's events and the worry she had seen in her uncle's eyes—didn't still make her heart sing and her blood dance.

She turned to Martin as they reached the shop. 'This matter you have to discuss with Ignatius, it's bad, isn't it?'

'Yes,' he said simply. 'It's bad. But I have already promised him and I swear to you now that I am here to help you.' He held the lantern up to make it easier for her.

'Help *me*?' She put the key in the lock. 'You mean, to help Ignatius?'

'Both of you.'

The key refused to turn. She frowned. 'That's odd.'

'What's odd?'

'The key—oh.' The door was already unlocked.

As she opened it Moth growled, then uttered a loud bark. At the back of the shop something shifted in the firelit shadows and Kit found herself flat on the floor, a solid weight pressing her down, as a flash and roar exploded and the window beside the door shattered.

'Stay down!' Martin's voice, urgent in her ear, as Moth let loose a fusillade of barks and charged.

His weight left her and she rolled aside, reaching into her muff.

Pistol shot.

Ignoring Martin's injunction and the hammering of her own heart, she scrambled to her knees, the pistol Ignatius had insisted she carry steady in her hand, the metallic taste of fear bitter in her mouth.

Gun smoke hung acrid in the air and pounding footsteps headed for the back of the shop. She didn't dare fire in case she hit Martin or the dog, but she held steady, the pistol cocked in case the intruder got past them and tried for the front door.

The back door banged, and Martin cursed viciously. Footsteps sounded, coming back towards her. 'Good dog. Good girl, Moth.'

She lowered the pistol to point at the floor, but kept it cocked. Martin came into view between the shoulder-height stacks and stopped dead, staring at her, at the pistol.

'Where the hell did you get that?'

She uncocked the pistol. 'My muff.'

'You were carrying—?'

Her name, on a drawn-out moan, came from the back corner near the fireplace.

Kit was on her feet and running before she knew it.

'Kit! Wait!'

She dropped to her knees beside Ignatius who

lay near the fireplace. In the glow she could see the blood soaking his chest and pooling under him.

'*No.*' Frantic, she wadded up her handkerchief, trying to staunch the blood.

'Here.' Martin's much larger handkerchief was pushed into her hand. Even so blood poured out, flooding over her hands.

Cursing under his breath, Martin knelt beside them, his fingers at the old man's waistcoat buttons as with the other hand he stripped off his own cravat. He could have run down the assailant, but he'd dared not leave Kit unguarded and now Selbourne was more important. The old man was losing too much blood.

'Lacy.' The voice was strained, slurred, already fading.

'I'm here, sir.' He wadded up the cravat, thrust it under Kit's bloodied hands, knowing as he did so that there would be no staunching the wound.

'Calling in the rest of that favour, boy.'

'A waste of a favour, sir. Kit, lift your hands a moment.' As she obeyed he unbuttoned the old man's waistcoat and opened the shirt, laying bare the wound. '*Merda.*'

He met Kit's eyes, wanting to reassure her more than he wanted his own next breath. Even without the blood, he could gauge where the knife thrust had gone, barely missing its target, but still doing enough to make death inevitable.

He opened his mouth to lie. And couldn't.

Kit's cheeks gleamed silver in the firelight, as she pressed his handkerchief and cravat directly against the wound that flooded dark over her hands.

'And, Kit...' Even now love threaded the old man's voice.

'I'm here, Ignatius. Don't talk. Let me—'

'No time, girl. Lacy...top drawer...desk upstairs...snuff box.'

'Very well, sir.'

'Dying...'

'Yes, sir.' Kit's strangled sob was a knife-thrust to his own heart.

A twist of the lips that might have been a smile. 'Honest...trusting you, boy.'

'You can, sir. My life on it.'

'Kit. My Kit.'

'I'm here.' Her tears fell unchecked as the old man groped for her bloodied hand.

'All...need...dark.'

His breathing became shallower, as the blood continued to flow between Kit's fingers.

'Lacy! Forgot...wanted the desk.'

Martin leaned over the dying man, held the dimming gaze. 'No, sir. You told me. It's all right.'

'Told you...not...my desk...slope.'

'Don't worry, sir. I'll see to it.'

'Kit...safe...'

'She will be, sir.' Martin made his promise as Ignatius released his last rattling breath.

'No!' Kit pressed harder. 'No, don't go! Please!'

Gently Martin reached for her, pulled her trembling body into his arms. 'Kit, sweetheart. He's gone.'

For a moment she struggled, then with a strangled sob clung to him.

He would have given every drop of his own blood to spare her this grief, but even as he cradled her in his arms a low growl from the dog and pounding footsteps on the pavement, had him thrusting her behind him, his pistol cocked, as a tall form, lantern held high, entered the shop.

'Selbourne? What's—? Kit? What's happened?'

Kit let out a shuddering breath at the familiar voice. 'Will.' She clutched at Martin's left arm. 'It's Will Barclay. Someone… Ignatius… Will, they've killed Ignatius.'

Will came into the shop, Caleb hard on his heels, and set his lantern down on the table. *'What?'* His gaze fell on Martin. 'Who the devil are you?'

Caleb spoke. 'It's Lord Martin, Mr Will.'

Martin rose. 'Martin Lacy, Barclay. I came to see Selbourne about this morning's business. He asked me to escort Kit to a concert. What are you doing here? Selbourne said you'd gone out to Hampstead.'

Will crouched down by Ignatius's body, touched

his fingers lightly to the throat and let out a shaken breath. 'Damn.'

'He's gone, Will.' Kit's voice felt distant, as though someone else were using it.

Will patted her hand, her bloodstained hand, gently. 'I'm sorry, Kit.'

She could only shake her head. It wasn't real. It couldn't be. Surely in a moment she would wake and the nightmare could be sloughed off.

Will glanced up at Martin. 'I'm sorry to make your acquaintance like this. I came back when I got Selbourne's note about this morning. Only arrived a few moments ago. My wife was worried about Caleb and—' he shot a glance at Kit '—she worried.'

'About me?'

Will shrugged. 'She had a bad feeling. So I borrowed a fresh horse.' He rose. 'What do we do now, Lacy?'

As he spoke, Kit's gaze fell on the writing slope. They had left it on the table where the other one usually sat. Now it lay broken in the corner by the shelves that held the seventeenth-century poets, its lid ripped off, the leather writing surface torn loose.

Everything blurred for Kit. Ignatius was gone. She had left him alone and now he was gone. Yes, he had been dying, she'd known that, he hadn't tried to hide it from her.

But this.

Murdered.

Caleb had gone to fetch a magistrate and leave a message for someone called Holford from White-hall.

They wanted her to go upstairs, but she refused. She had left Ignatius earlier. She wouldn't leave him now. She sat on the bottom rung of one of the ladders, holding his hand, dazed, half believing it was a nightmare and soon, soon, she would wake up. But around her were stacks of books that had been taken down from several upper shelves. More than the Runners had taken down.

Not flung around, but stacked. Neatly. And probably quietly.

When they didn't find the document in the writing slope they started searching the books.

Hodge, his tail fluffed, appeared from the stair-well, miaowed piteously and trotted across to her. With her free hand she rubbed his head and he butted against her.

'Poor Hodge. You were down here, weren't you?'

For her own comfort she picked him up, but he squirmed free and leapt down, going to Ignatius.

Martin reached for him, but the cat hissed and he jerked back.

Kit shook her head. 'Leave him. He needs to understand.'

She needed to understand.

Hodge circled, sniffed at the body and nudged at the shoulder hopefully. Finally he walked away, leapt on to the desk and curled up on the desk blotter, precisely where he would have been most in the way.

Did he understand that Ignatius was gone? Would he grieve? Kit sat, numb, wondering if the world could ever right itself.

When the magistrate arrived it was Sir Richard Ford himself and the nightmare tightened its grip.

'What the devil is all this, Lacy?' He strode to the back of the shop, looked down at Ignatius.

'Damn.' It was said very softly.

Ford looked at Martin. 'Do you have the least notion what all this is about?'

Martin didn't answer for a moment, but stared down at Ignatius, his face grim. 'I don't know yet, Ford. We're going to have to find out. Are you prepared to trust the Home Office with the investigation? I've sent a message to Holford already.'

Ford's mouth tightened. 'We can discuss that. There must be an inquest. It would cause too many questions otherwise. I'm assuming Holford won't want too many questions?'

'Not unless we're asking them.'

'Very well. What arrangements have you made for—?' He gestured at Ignatius, puzzling Kit.

Martin responded quietly. 'Barclay went down

to the tavern on the corner. The landlord is sending some fellows up to help us move the body there.'

Kit stirred herself. 'What? Why? His...his bed, upstairs—'

'Kit.' The gentleness in Martin's voice wrapped around her, nearly broke her. 'That's the usual procedure with an inquest. The body is moved to the nearest public house and the inquest is held there. And I'm afraid—' He broke off, grimacing.

Now Sir Richard focused on her. 'Miss Selbourne. Kit. My dear girl, I'm very sorry. He was a good man.'

That jerked her out of the grey nothingness she'd been drifting in. 'I...yes. The very best.'

He spoke carefully. 'You do realise that, as Selbourne's *heiress*...' there was the faintest stress on the word '...you may be considered a suspect in his death. Furthermore you will be required to give evidence at the inquest.'

'For God's sake, Ford!' Martin stepped between them. 'She was—'

'Lord Martin attended a concert with me this evening, Sir Richard.' Jolted from that numbing wasteland, Kit rose from the ladder, stepping around Martin to face the magistrate. 'He escorted me home and we surprised the murderer together. He...he fired at us.'

'Fired at you?'

He frowned over the damaged door jamb. 'Lucky neither of you was hit.'

She forced her brain to function. 'The man we disturbed—it might not have been he who wanted Ignatius dead.'

Because a murder that interested the Home Office wasn't going to be as simple as a burglar who got disturbed at his job.

Martin's face betrayed nothing. Not even surprise.

The shop clock had chimed two when Martin, Caleb, Will and three hostlers from the Red Lion finally slid Ignatius on to a door and took him down the road to the tavern. Ford remained.

Hodge mewed at the front door, rearing up and scratching at the panels for a moment before giving up and disappearing into the stairwell. Martin had been forced to nudge the cat back to stop him following them.

Kit sat at the desk now, her brain refusing to accept that any of this could be true. Ignatius had been dying, yes. But he should not have died like *this*. He should have been allowed to die peacefully in bed. She should have been with him, holding his hand, not uselessly trying to turn back a crimson tide as his life flooded out. She stared at her hands, washed now, and shuddered. Would she always see the blood? Like Lady Macbeth?

To stave off tears, she spoke. 'You are not going with them, Sir Richard?'

'No. Lacy requested that I remain here until he

and Barclay returned.' He snorted. 'Not that he needed to ask.'

She couldn't think why. But then, she couldn't think at all. Not beyond the pounding refrain in her head.

Why did you leave him? Why? Why?

If she had not left he would not have been alone. Moth would have raised the alarm and the murderer might have fled.

The clock ticked inexorably. If only it could be turned back. But even if she could turn it back without breaking it, Time would not care tuppence for one insignificant clock. Time marched on, like King Canute's tides. Relentless, like the blood that had flooded over her hands.

Like Ford's questions earlier as he ascertained precisely what had happened. She glanced at the magistrate. Was she supposed to make polite conversation? With some relief she saw that he had taken a book off the shelves and was reading.

'You should…if it's something that interests you, Sir Richard, take it with you.' She didn't care what the book was, whether it was valuable or not. 'He…he would like you to have it.'

He regarded her for a moment. 'Thank you, my dear. He'll be very much missed.'

'Yes.'

She wished she could be alone.

She was terrified of being alone.

Beside her Moth put a paw in her lap, shoving

her head under her arm. Automatically Kit petted the dog, insensibly soothed.

'I don't like it, Lacy. What about Kit's reputation? There must be another way.'

Walking back to the bookshop along the dark street, Martin appreciated Barclay's concern, but he couldn't afford to indulge it. After examining Selbourne's body he had no doubts. This was not a simple murder.

Ignatius Selbourne had been assassinated.

'I'm sorry, Barclay. There is nothing else that I can think of. Nowhere else that she can go tonight and be safe. If your wife were here you could both take the other bedroom in Selbourne's apartment to satisfy propriety, while I stood guard. As it is—' Martin shrugged. 'If you are concerned about Miss Selbourne's safety with me, then of course you should remain as well. But that won't help her reputation.'

The danger to Kit's reputation was one thing; right now he was more concerned with keeping her alive. He needed to be rational, logical.

Barclay gripped his sleeve. 'You think the killer may come back? For Kit?'

The thought of Selbourne's killer coming back for Kit twisted Martin's entrails into a cold, greasy, slithering knot.

He paused with his hand on the door of the shop. 'Selbourne's killer wanted information. That was clear. If someone thinks that Kit is privy to that information…'

Barclay cursed viciously. Then, 'You say the killer knew exactly what he was doing?'

Martin nodded. 'Yes. The wounds to Ignatius's upper arms would have disabled him immediately. He couldn't fight back after that. Whoever it was knew precisely where to strike to incapacitate, but not kill. Because of that I think the purpose was to get information from him before killing him. Our arrival scuppered that, so the killer finished it. The strike to the chest was mortal—we were lucky Selbourne lasted as long as he did.'

All he had to do was make sense of those confused, dying words.

Ford rose, setting down a book, as Martin walked into the bookshop. The magistrate raised a finger to his lips, nodded to the desk.

Martin's heart tore a little—Kit, her head pillowed on her arms, sound asleep at the desk, her cheeks blotched red with the tears she had shed. The dog lay beside the desk, not stretched out relaxed, but sphinx-like. On guard.

'Exhausted.' Ford spoke softly. 'I'll return to Bow Street now and make arrangements for the inquest. It will have to be tomorrow, or rather today.'

Martin nodded. 'I mentioned the likelihood to the landlord.'

Sir Richard shrugged into his great coat. 'The

sooner we get it over with the better. If Holford wants you to investigate this morning's doings, and I think we can include this, I'll do my best to keep my Runners out of the way.' He held Martin's gaze. 'However, we cannot avoid an inquest. Selbourne's murder will cause quite a stir.'

Martin nodded. 'Yes. I don't think they took that into account. And it's very possible whoever ordered it didn't fully understand what Selbourne was. They knew he had a few connections, but not why.'

Sir Richard grimaced. 'Does Miss Selbourne know?'

Martin shook his head. 'No. He told me this evening that he hadn't told her. He'd never thought there was a need.'

And now he was going to have to do it. The sooner the better.

He let Ford out, locked up after him and checked the windows, shutters, and door in the kitchen area.

Walking back into the shop, he found Moth's lambent gaze on him, her head cocked.

Warily, he approached Kit, but while the dog's tail did not thump there was no warning growl. Slowly he placed his hand on Kit's shoulder. He wished he didn't have to wake her, that he could leave her to sleep, but she'd be in an agony of stiffness in the morning if she spent the night at the desk.

'Kit. Time to go upstairs now, love.'

The endearment was simply there. He shut his eyes, hoped she hadn't heard, as she stirred under his hand, sat up.

'What...? I... I dreamed.' She blinked up at him. 'Martin? What are you—?'

He saw the moment that memory stabbed her, owned her, and his heart ached for the grief he read in her eyes. And when he told her what he suspected it would be worse.

'It wasn't a dream,' she whispered. 'He's really gone. They killed him.'

She got to her feet a little unsteadily and, seemingly automatic, picked up the muff lying on the desk.

'I'm sorry. So sorry.' Hollow, inadequate words. He left his hand on her shoulder. 'Come upstairs. Get some rest.'

Tomorrow would do to tell her the danger she was now in.

At the first landing she turned to him. 'There is a parlour on this floor.' She indicated a door to the left. 'The bedrooms are on the next floor. Mine is at the front. Ignatius uses—I mean, he used the smaller room at the back. You...you can have that one. If you give me a moment I will change the sheets and—'

'Kit, it's all right.' He touched a careful hand to her cheek, felt the silken skin, damp with her grief under his fingertips. 'Leave the bedding. I'll be fine.'

'But—'

'It's fine,' he repeated, and removed his hand. 'Go on up, sweetheart. I'll sit down here for a while.' Again the endearment had slipped out and he cursed himself.

'Oh.' She scrubbed at her curls. 'There is brandy in there. And his desk.'

'His desk?'

A tear slid down her cheek. 'Something in the top drawer, he said. Something he wanted you to have.' Another tear followed the first and all he wanted was to pull her into his arms and hold her, comfort her.

'His…his desk is the messy one.'

He watched as she continued up the stairs with the dog, shadows surrounding the little pool of light from her candle as if they might devour it.

Chapter Eight

Martin stirred up the fire, chose a book from the shelves lining the walls and settled down in one of the leather wingchairs before the fire in the parlour. The cat washed itself by the fire, studiously ignoring him.

He wished to God that Psyché Barclay was here for Kit, but the dog would have to do. A dog, he knew, was a comforting thing. And sometimes you needed to be alone to lick your wounds. He remembered the night he had returned to his lodgings, his betrothal broken, the knowledge of his mother's criminality throbbing like a rotting tooth, until he wanted nothing more than to rip it out. Unlike a tooth, knowledge could not be ripped out. Once known, you couldn't unlearn something.

At least his father, for all his foolish attempts to take his grandchildren from their mother, had been innocent of the greater evil of plotting Harry's death. But Martin had sat in front of the fire and brooded alone. How could his mother have believed he wanted the dukedom at all, let alone at the cost of a child's life? How could she have been so obsessed with the idea of him inheriting?

He was brooding now. The room seemed to close around him, the walls lined with books and the two desks, one tidy and one anything but.

Why didn't you insist on discussing this mess with Selbourne instead of going to a concert? If you had, he might be alive. Kit would not be grieving...

'Something he wanted you to have... His desk is the messy one.'

Much as looking in that desk, even with Kit's permission, went against the grain, he could think of only one thing Ignatius Selbourne might have wanted him to have. And perhaps it was for the best that Kit didn't see it.

He rose, picked up a candle, went to the desk and opened the drawer. It held only one object—an enamelled snuff box.

Lacy...snuff box.

Martin stared at it. In the candle's flicker he could almost believe that the water rippled, that the willow framing the swans, their necks entwined as a heart, danced in a breeze. Of all the damnably romantic images Selbourne could have possibly chosen... Reluctantly he reached in and took it out.

The latch was a little stiff, as if it were not used much, and he eased it open with careful fingers. Inside the lid an inscription caught the light.

To my dearest Ignatius with all my love
    Your Agatha
    1752—forever

He swallowed. Those words, etched in the gold, glimmered in the candle's flicker, echoing across the decades. A gift, then, from Selbourne's wife.

But it was what the box held that Selbourne had really wanted him to have. Martin drew out the tightly folded slip of paper and set the snuff box and its secret on the table. Unfolding the paper, he read.

December 26th, 1803
My very dear Lacy,
    If you are reading this it means fate has intervened and I have not been able to return this little item personally. It also means that my prayers have been answered and I have not had to give it to Kit. I kept my word to you. She knows nothing of this.
    I will continue to hope that you will one day be able to return it to her. Know that you have my blessing and affection always.
    Selbourne

Swallowing the lump in his throat, he refolded the note, slipped it into the pocket of his waistcoat and took out the snuff box's last secret. For a moment he looked at it. Such a small thing, yet it held a promise made and broken, joy and grief. With a sigh he placed it in his pocket with the note and went back to the fire. The book held no appeal now and, leaning his head against the back of the chair, Martin closed his eyes, remembering the first time he'd seen this book-lined room…

Christmas Night 1803

Martin had been followed to Keswick House on the Strand and he knew at least one watcher was still there when he left. He had to assume all entrances were being watched. At four o'clock the light was dying. In the great house his father, the duke, sat alone now with his thoughts and self-recriminations. It had been a miserable Christmas dinner for both of them. His father had merely nodded when he said he was leaving London for the time being. A request to borrow a closed carriage for a couple of days received another nod.

Drawing his cloak around him as he left the ducal stables after giving a set of instructions that had probably startled the staff, Martin set off on foot, trusting to his sword, the pistol in his pocket and the weather to keep himself safe from footpads. Careful not to glance around, he strolled along like a man without a care in the world.

His world was in ruins.

His first stop was a brothel off the Strand. He didn't doubt that his shadow thought nothing of that. After he came out with two cloaked women, handed them both up into a waiting closed carriage and gave loud instructions to the coachman, he thought he had the fellow's attention. Ducking into a gin shop, he waited. For a moment the shadow hesitated, but then he hurried off.

With a grim smile Martin left the shop, his gin untasted, and followed, remaining well back, until he saw his quarry hurry up the steps of the Carshalton mansion in Bloomsbury. Then he slipped into the shadow of the steps leading up the front door of the next house, waiting, waiting. Reminding himself that it took time to get a message to the stables, time to harness the horses... He heard the rumble of the carriage before it trundled around the corner from the mews to pull up at the front door...the front door which opened immediately. A footman scurried down, clutching a pair of valises, closely followed by two gentlemen.

Carshalton and—Martin's hands clenched into fists—Lucius Winthrop. Breathing evenly, he clung to control, watching as they got into the carriage and it set off.

Grimly satisfied, Martin stepped out of the shadows and set off on the last part of his journey.

Even knowing his plan had worked, he'd circled around to approach Soho from the north. Probably a pointless exercise. Someone would be watching here, too, and he didn't doubt any visitor would be noted, but he wasn't going to make it easy for the blighters.

Fear, not for himself, but for Kit, had dogged him ever since her father and Winthrop had descended on his lodgings at three in the morning demanding her return.

She ran from her father and she didn't come to you for help.

That burned.

His own fault. That one shocked moment when he'd nearly believed her part of the plot against Harry. She hadn't tried to defend herself, but returned his ring and walked out of his life.

How could she come to you? Maybe she believed you were involved in plotting Harry's death.

He believed, *hoped*, she was safe, but he had to know before he left the country on this assignment.

He hurried by on the opposite side of the street to his destination and spotted the watcher easily enough, loitering by the gate leading into the inn yard of the Red Lion. He kept going towards Greek Street and crossed there, hidden by the veiling snow.

On the corner of the alley he needed several lads huddled together, laughing.

'Give it to 'im, Ned! 'E's a bloody thief, this 'un!'

The yip of terrified pain brought Martin up short.

Another yelp.

Never draw attention to yourself on the hunt...

'Get the rope on 'un. We'll see how well 'e dances on air!'

The first boy crashed to the icy pavement with a startled yell. The second hit the wall of Murchison's Drapery Emporium and slid to the ground, dazed. The rest took one collective look at Martin's naked sword and fled, sliding and slipping in their haste to abandon their mates.

A small, bedraggled dog—a puppy—with a rope about its neck and a brick tied to its tail, cowered in hopeless terror against the wall.

'Christ!' This was all he needed.

The two boys he'd felled had scrambled to sitting positions and were scuttling backwards.

'Get out of here before I give you a real taste of what you were dishing out,' he growled.

'Just a bloody mongrel dog,' one boy spat. 'Allus hanging around thievin'. You think we won't find 'im again?'

Martin smiled. 'Because this time ended so well for you?'

His sword glinted in the faint light off the snow.

'Let's *go*, Rab,' muttered the second boy. 'No job ain't worth gettin' skewered for.'

Job?

'An excellent point,' Martin said. 'Rab, you really should listen to your marginally more intelli-

gent friend.' He tossed the second boy a shilling.
'A reward for thinking.'

The shilling was snatched out of the air and
the boy was gone in a flash, Rab hot on his heels,
whether in fear or pursuit of the shilling Martin
didn't care.

He stared down at the pup, muttered a curse
and bent to remove the rope, fully expecting the
pup to snap. It whined, gave his wrist a dab with
its tongue, then cowered again.

He untied the brick. 'You'd better find the nearest muck heap and hide under it before they come
looking for you.'

The pup whined again and lifted a front paw.
The size of the paw belied the size of the pup.
It would be a damn big dog. Or it would be if
it lived that long. Another whimper and, damn
it, the bloody thing was shivering. And if his instincts weren't entirely off, in rescuing the creature
he'd accidentally run off a set of watchers without
arousing any suspicion.

'Oh, for God's sake!' He bent down and scooped
it up. 'What the hell am I to do with you?'

He tucked the creature under his coat, where it
snuggled in, and discovered in passing that *it* was
definitely *she*.

A few minutes later, after making his way
through assorted back lanes and traversing two
snowy yards, Martin picked the lock on the back
door of the building he wanted. His companion

in crime, judging by the silence, had fallen asleep under his coat.

The door open and his lantern fully shuttered, Martin slipped inside and shut and relocked the door. No point inviting unwelcome interruptions.

An ominous *click* was his only warning.

'Turn around slowly and keep your hands up.'

Martin didn't move. 'Before you shoot me, sir, may I put the pup down?'

'Lacy?'

'Yes, sir. I apologise for the intrusion, but—'

'You damned young fool! What the devil are you about breaking into my shop? Turn around!'

This time Martin obeyed. The faint glow of embers from the kitchen fire illuminated Ignatius Selbourne standing in the doorway, a pistol trained on him.

He held absolutely still and then breathed a sigh of relief as Selbourne uncocked the pistol.

The old man's voice was cold. 'If you've brought Kit here, you've made a mistake.'

Martin's stomach lurched. All day he'd clung to the belief that Kit would have gone to Selbourne, that she must be safe with him. He'd been so damn sure that she'd be here, he hadn't given any thought to where else she might have gone, or what danger she might have fallen into. If she hadn't come here, if she hadn't made it, where the hell was she?

He stared at Selbourne, his brain struggling to

get past the clawing panic, to *think*... Gradually reason fought clear. Selbourne had no reason to trust him. Quite the opposite. The man had every reason to believe he'd conspired with his mother and Kit's father.

'Sir, I don't ask you to trust me, or tell me anything, but you need to know—Carshalton came to my lodgings looking for Kit.'

'Did he now?' The icy voice held scorn.

'Yes. I encouraged him to think I'd hidden her, so he's had me watched all day.'

There was a moment's silence and Martin thought Selbourne's eyes narrowed slightly.

'And now you've led them straight here? Bright boy, aren't you?'

Irritation pricked him. 'Since I knew I was being followed I did something about it.' He took a breath. 'You're being watched, too. A fellow by the Red Lion and a group of lads at the entrance to your back lane.'

Selbourne seemed to be considering. At last he said, 'I've got eyes, boy. You'd better come upstairs. Douse that lantern and leave it here. No point burning the place down.' He turned and stalked away.

Martin followed him out into the shop and up the narrow stairs in the dark.

'Watch your step,' the old man said. He led Martin into a comfortably furnished sitting room lined with books. The remnants of supper for one sat on a tea table by the fire, along with a bottle of brandy, and a large tabby cat was curled up on the hearth.

'Sit.'

It was more of an order than an invitation and Martin obeyed.

'So. Where'd you hide her?' Selbourne asked as he lowered himself into the other chair.

Martin's churning fear subsided a little. 'You're bluffing, sir. For some reason Carshalton came to me first. Why, I can't say, but—'

'Nor I.'

Martin cocked his head at the tone. 'Can't, or won't? Anyway, if you didn't have her safe, you'd hardly be sitting here with a bottle of brandy.'

Selbourne continued to watch him, not giving a damn thing away. He'd be a damnably good interrogator, but Martin knew a little about waiting himself.

After a moment Selbourne's gaze shifted to the lump under Martin's coat.

'What the devil is that?'

The pup, possibly roused by the voices, but more likely the scent of roast beef, poked her head out.

'Is that a *dog*?'

'I believe so.' Martin unbuttoned his coat and set the pup down on the rug. She looked around, tail tucked tightly between her legs, the brindled coat and size suggesting that somewhere in her ancestry a mastiff had been involved.

The cat rose with an outraged growl, fluffed to tigerish proportions and leapt halfway up one of the ladders servicing the bookshelves. It looked down at the interloper in disgust.

Selbourne snorted. 'More like a bear. Look at the feet.' He took a slice of beef and offered it to the pup. The pup hesitated only for a moment, then lunged for the offering. The meat disappeared in three gulps. Several slices followed, after which the pup, replete, curled up by the fire and let out a contented sigh.

'So.' Selbourne leaned back in his chair. 'He said you were damned good.'

Martin raised his brows. Who was *he* and good at what?

'Good at analysing intelligence. Seeing patterns,' Selbourne elaborated, as though Martin had spoken aloud. 'Holford keeps me informed.'

Martin fought not to react. His superior, the quietly spoken, middle-aged Holford breathed the very essence of discretion. Why the hell—?

Selbourne laughed. 'I trained him, boy. Known him since he was younger than you.'

Martin could only stare. Selbourne—*Selbourne*—had been part of the game?

The old man continued. 'He also said there was absolutely no possibility you would have connived at your nephew's death.' Selbourne scowled as he stretched to take a brandy glass out of the cupboard near his chair. 'I'm not sure I believed him.'

He poured brandy. 'Here.' He handed Martin the glass.

'Thank you, sir.' He wasn't only thanking him for the brandy.

Selbourne sat, still scowling. 'She's not here.'

He went cold all over. 'Then—'

A thin smile flickered. 'Because he went to you first, I had time to get her to a friend. Between us we've got him chasing his tail. I spent most of the day tearing around pretending I was looking for her. She's—'

'No.' Martin flung up a hand. 'You shouldn't tell me. I only need to know she's safe.'

Selbourne nodded slowly. 'I was going to say she's safe enough for now. And if I can keep her hidden until she turns twenty-one in March she'll remain safe.'

'Carshalton had Winthrop with him—they had some idea she was going to marry him this morning.'

Selbourne's eyes were icier than the street outside. 'After a fashion. Marriage the medieval way was what they had in mind.'

'The medieval— *Christ!*' Scalding rage hammered through every vein. 'I'll kill—'

'*No.*'

Selbourne's voice sliced like a winter-hard blade. 'Leave it. For now, at least. The important thing is to keep her hidden. Once she turns twenty-one she's safe. She can stay with me then. Meanwhile I've called in reinforcements.'

'Reinforcements?'

Selbourne's smile was all lethal promise. 'While I was supposedly looking for Kit all over London today, I sent a very discreet message to Huntercombe.'

'Huntercombe?' Martin stared. 'Why—?'

'Because he's always been fond of the child,' Selbourne said. 'And after Carshalton tried to have his stepson murdered?' The smile edged towards vicious. 'Believe me, he'll protect her.'

'She's safe then.' Martin took a swallow of his brandy and felt some of the fear and tension melt away in its scalding warmth.

'Trust me for that.'

He did, but despite knowing that Kit was all the safer if he didn't see her, he had to swallow the bitterness of disappointment. But perhaps it was better for her this way. In the meantime he had to tell Selbourne what he'd done.

'I sent Carshalton off on a wild goose chase northwards,' he said grimly.

'Oh?' Selbourne sipped his brandy.

Martin explained.

Selbourne stared at him and a grin slowly spread over his face. 'You sent Carshalton and Winthrop chasing your father's carriage north out of London? In *this* weather?'

'Keswick wasn't using the carriage and it seemed like a useful occupation for them.'

'A carriage carrying two whores?' Selbourne gave a crack of laughter. 'Lord! I'd give a monkey to see Carshalton's face when he catches up!'

Martin shrugged. 'I told my man to get them as far as Barnet. It's only one stage, but in this weather I'm hoping that by the time they catch up, it will be too late to turn around and return tomorrow.'

Selbourne nodded. 'Very likely. And since it's snowing again, he might even be held up for longer. Well done.' He tossed off the rest of his brandy. 'I'm in your debt, boy. If there's ever anything I can do for you—'

'There is one thing.' From his pocket he drew out the ring Kit had returned to him and held it out. 'Will you keep this for me?'

Selbourne frowned. 'Why?'

Martin shrugged. 'In case—' He broke off. Holford might share what he liked with his old master, but Martin had no such dispensation to tell Selbourne he was leaving England shortly. 'In case. It's hers anyway. If…if you ever think it right, give it to her.'

The shrewd old eyes searched his. 'And what should I tell her if I have to do that?'

'Tell her—tell her that it was always hers, that I wanted her to have it.' He rose, placing the ring on the table between them, before words that must

not be spoken could spill from him. 'I should go.'
He bent down, intending to pick up the sleeping
puppy. God knew what he was to do with the creature.

'You can't take a dog where you're going, boy.'
Selbourne's voice was quiet.

Martin looked up sharply. 'You can't—'

'Channel Fleet. Intelligence and analysis. Code
breaking.'

After a moment's shock, Martin said drily,
'Don't forget the translation.' He shook his head.
'Even my father doesn't know that. All he knows
is that I'm leaving London for a time to let the
scandal die down.'

Selbourne nodded. 'So Holford said. Leave the
pup for Kit. She loves dogs and Carshalton would
never permit her to have one.'

'I know, but—' Bad enough to think she would
forget him, but he didn't want her to waste her
life grieving for what might have been. Hoping
for something that could never be. 'Don't tell her
I was here.'

'Not tell her you came? Why not?'

He wanted her to know. Wanted her to know
he had cared. That he had worried about her. But
he wanted her to be happy, to live her life without regrets.

'She shouldn't be encouraged to think of me.
It's better if she puts all that behind her.'

'As you have?'

There was no answer to that. 'Goodnight, sir. Thank you.'

Selbourne shoved himself out of the chair. 'For what? Keeping the pup?'

Martin smiled bitterly. 'For that, too.' He hesitated. 'Look, don't tell her anything unless you have to give her the ring.'

Selbourne nodded. 'Very well. I'll see you out and lock up.'

'You might use the bolts this time,' Martin suggested. 'You don't want just anyone breaking into your kitchen.'

Selbourne smiled. 'Quite so. You've lost me a wager with Holford coming here, you know.'

'I… *What?*'

'I left the bolts undone for you,' said Selbourne. 'I saw Holford this morning. He agreed to get the letters about Kit to Huntercombe and assured me that you'd reach me faster.' Selbourne's fingers drummed briefly on the wine table. 'In fact, he said you'd refuse to leave the country if I couldn't guarantee to keep Kit safe.'

What?

Holford was damnably acute.

In the end words came from deep within. 'Thank you, sir. I know she'll be safe with you. Otherwise—' He swallowed.

Selbourne held out his hand. 'Thank you, Lacy. Godspeed. I'll pray I never have to give her that ring, that you can give it back to her one day.'

Martin gripped the offered hand. 'That can't be. But if there is ever anything I can do for you, you have only to ask.'

Chapter Nine

March 1805

Kit stared at the closed door of her bedroom. As a little girl she had slept in the smaller back room, but on her return last year Ignatius had shown her to this one.

'I've been using your old room since you left five years ago. You have our old room, pet.'

Had there been too many memories in this room for him? Tears burned as the memories pressed in on her. When she had first lived here with Ignatius and Agatha she had still woken in the night crying for her mother. How many times had Agatha or Ignatius come in to comfort her? Finally one night Kit had simply gone to them. After that the dreams and loneliness had lessened. She still grieved, but she was no longer quite so alone.

Six years later Agatha had died and after less than a month Carshalton dragged her back to

Bloomsbury. At first she couldn't understand why he'd bothered. His vaunted reason, that she could not remain with Ignatius without Agatha's presence and that as her father it was his duty to provide for her, was a lie. He hadn't bothered to visit her or asked her to visit him in six years. Ergo, he gave somewhat less than your average damn about her. He wasn't fulfilling his duty as a loving father, but asserting his property rights to her person.

It took her less than a week to understand that while a ten-year-old girl had been a nuisance in his household, that same girl at sixteen was a very different proposition. On the cusp of womanhood and marriageability, she was a potential asset to be moulded to his expectations. Whether Agatha had died or not, he had intended to take her back. Agatha's death had merely brought it forward.

He had expected her to marry. To marry to *his* requirements. An alliance that would further his influence in Parliament, particularly in the House of Lords. The proposed marriage to Martin had been supposed to achieve that. And she—she still squirmed at the memory—had been prepared to submit simply to escape Carshalton.

In the end she had escaped without Martin. She had fled to Ignatius who, with the help of Psyché, Will and Lord Huntercombe, had hidden her. Between them they had kept her safe until her twenty-first birthday put her beyond Carshalton's power.

She was grateful to all of them. Psyché and Will

especially had become her dearest friends. But Ignatius...the room blurred.

She clenched her jaw, forced back the tears. She wasn't a little girl now requiring someone to comfort her and banish a nightmare. Neither tears nor Martin could bring Ignatius back. Martin, whom she had told to use the room where Ignatius had slept only last night... A tear slipped past her guard.

She brushed it away. Tears were useless, girlish things.

Think of it as your old room. Not his. Not now.

Breathing carefully against the useless, she stared at her muff. All very well for Martin to tell her, *'Go to bed, Kit. Try to sleep. There is nothing to do tonight.'*

Carefully she took the unfired pistol from her muff. Ignatius had been strict about care of her pistol.

'Never leave it loaded too long. For a start the powder gets damp and it will likely not fire at all when you do need it. And if it does fire it's likely to misfire. Unload it and clean it.'

She did it easily, the movements swift and automatic, bringing back the memory of Ignatius, his old hands guiding hers, showing her how to load, unload, how to clean the weapon. And taking her out to Huntercombe's house at Isleworth to teach her to shoot. She was a better than decent shot, thanks to Ignatius and the marquess, but she had never aimed a pistol at a living creature, let alone fired at one.

She had wondered if she could. Now, tonight, she knew.

If she could have taken a shot to protect Martin or her dog she would have fired. And if she had known... Oh, God! Had she known that Ignatius lay dying—

She forced her hands to steady. Might-have-beens were as useless as tears. She had to be rational. Logical.

And that meant no more delay.

She needed to know what was in that document. Reluctantly she reached into the muff again.

Martin stared at the ring he'd last seen in this room. The ring Kit had returned to him and that he'd given to Selbourne to keep for her.

'If you ever think it right, give it back to her.'

Ships sank. He'd known that he might not survive his posting to the Channel Fleet.

Now he held Kit's ring and sat alone in this room with only his memories for company. Well, not quite alone. The cat now sat bolt upright on the hearth and watched him with unblinking green eyes. After the fierce hiss downstairs, Martin eyed it cautiously.

Did animals understand death? He thought dogs did, but a cat...?

'He's gone—' What was its name? 'Hodge. He's gone, Hodge.'

The cat stared back, the black tip of the tail twitching. What the hell did a cat's tail mean? He could read a dog's tail easily, but a cat was a mystery. He'd always thought he didn't like cats. Dogs were the thing, loving, affectionate, always trying to please you. Cats now, they were independent, always holding their own counsel, reserved… But the cat had tried to follow Ignatius from the shop. He'd nudged the creature back gently with his foot and it had mewed, scrabbling at the door as he closed it…

'I'm sorry about that, Hodge. But I think he'd rather you were here safe.' God help him, he was talking to a *cat*. Did he think it might reply? Irritated with himself, he opened the volume of Bewick's *Birds* he'd taken down earlier.

The cat rose and Martin eyed it sideways. It strolled across to his chair on those silent paws and rubbed its head against his boot. Did it somehow know he was reading a book on birds?

'*Mrowp.*'

Perhaps that was an apology for the earlier hiss. Still wary, he reached down, scratching behind the ears. Another rub against his boots and, with a lazy spring, the cat was in his lap.

Martin froze as the creature circled with exquisite precision and curled up into a tight ball, its tail curled around its nose. He couldn't think when he'd last had a cat in his lap. Probably never. He sat very still. If the damned thing took exception to anything now the way it was positioned... Slowly he became aware of the purr, a deep rumble, as the cat relaxed.

Ready to snatch his hand back, Martin stroked, his fingers sinking into soft, thick fur. An answering squirm and the rumble increased in volume. Even he knew that a purring cat was a happy cat.

Oddly comforted, he slid the ring into his pocket and opened the book. Apparently no one was going to be alone tonight.

The clock had chimed four when he heard the rustle of someone out in the hallway. About to dump the sleeping cat on the floor, he heard the click of the dog's toenails and sank back into the chair.

Kit.

A moment later the door opened and she walked in. A warm, dark red dressing robe tied with a sash, he assumed a nightgown beneath it and slippers. No nightcap, her soft curls were rumpled around her pale face.

The startled gasp told him immediately that she hadn't expected to find him there.

'I'm sorry. I thought—couldn't you sleep?'

The dog walked straight to the hearth and sprawled by the fire with a contented sigh.

'Something like that.' If she hadn't yet realised

he was standing guard, four o'clock in the morning was not the time to frighten her. He should send her away—he had not the least right to see her like this, but shadows lived in as well as under her red-rimmed eyes. Something in him ripped a little more—she'd been crying. Damn propriety. 'You?'

'No. I… I thought to sit by the fire.'

Although he gestured to the other chair, she remained by the door, her expression uncertain. 'I didn't mean to disturb you.'

'You aren't.' Damn it. She was apologising for walking into her own parlour. 'You'll forgive me for not rising. I'm, er, somewhat incommoded.' He gestured to his lap.

She came a little further, frowning. 'What—?' Her brow cleared. 'Oh. He's not usually quite so forward. I… I didn't know you liked cats.'

A desperate attempt to make conversation if ever he'd heard one.

'Neither did I. Apparently your cat has decided to convert me.' He tried to keep his voice light to match her gallant effort. It rang weak and tinny.

The shadows in her eyes seemed to deepen. 'He's not really my cat. Ignatius—' She broke off and there was a terrible aching silence. 'It doesn't matter, does it? He's mine now.'

'Kit—'

'Why did you stay?'

He chose his words carefully. 'You can't have thought I'd leave you alone tonight.'

She cocked her head. 'No. Perhaps not. But Will would have stayed. Quite as improper, but he would not be in danger of finding himself with Huntercombe's pistol to his head over it.'

'And his wife?' He'd met Will Barclay's wife. A formidable woman and not one he'd care to annoy. Huntercombe, he hoped, would understand.

The ghost of a smile flickered. 'Psyché? She would be more likely to boot his—tear strips off him if he didn't stay. Why you? And more to the point, why did Will agree?'

He'd just run headlong into the difficult part of protecting a woman who could think for herself.

'Will you sit down?'

She remained standing, clutching the front of her robe, her knuckles white. 'Tell me. They were looking for something, weren't they? In the slope. Whatever it was the Bow Street search didn't find.'

Damn. 'I believe so. I think Ignatius found it first and—'

The bleakness in her eyes stopped him. *Oh, sweet Christ...*

'No. It was me. I... I killed him.'

Shock held him silent, as slowly she reached into the front of her dressing robe, then brought out a folded document. 'They were looking for this. I came down here to think. To decide whether or not to show it to you.' She held it out to him. 'And here you are. Standing guard over me. So I have to trust you, because Ignatius would never have been part of this. He suspected something this morning, didn't he? That's why he went to you for help.'

'Yes.' Martin took the paper, unfolded it and read. It took a second reading before he could comprehend what he was seeing.

Kit's legs no longer felt as though they were hers. She sat in the other chair, felt the leather give under her in its familiar embrace. Moth came and lay before her, resting her chin on her slippers.

'I read it just now. There…there wasn't a chance earlier.'

The letter was seared in her memory.

My dear S.,

After much thought we are resolved that it is necessary to remove a certain Lord H. from any further votes on our Sacred Cause in the Lords. We feel that this will also serve as a Warning to Another closely connected with him.

Both gentlemen are known to be driving out to Hampstead on Monday evening next in order to visit Lord H.'s recalcitrant wife. I do not doubt that we can rely on you to arrange everything to our satisfaction.

One regrets the necessity, but we must and will resolve this matter for once and for all.

Yours affctly,

W. W.

'Where was it?'

She explained about the broken writing slope, taking it to Talbot and coming home to find the Runners searching the shop.

'You didn't think to show it to me then?'

Her stomach knotted. 'No. *I* hadn't read it. It wasn't mine, so I was going to give it to Ignatius, but he sent us out and then…' The knots twisted into an icy lump. 'Then it was too late. I killed him. If he'd known, if he'd seen it—'

She couldn't go on and the fire couldn't reach the chill shaking her. Her gaze fell on the snuff box sitting on the wine table beside Martin. Was that what Ignatius had wanted Martin to have?

It was only an object, but she remembered it from her childhood.

'My misspent youth, pet. But the box is pretty. And your aunt gave it to me.'

And he had kept it and treasured it, especially after Agatha died. She remembered him holding it sometimes in those first weeks after her death, perhaps thinking of the time they had both been young and joyous, all their lives before them.

And further back as a child she had loved to hold it, pretending herself into that serenity of peace and love in the dark days after the death of her mother. Floating with the swans on their dream of blue water framed in the tendrils of a weeping willow, she could forget her grief for a little while.

Now it was Martin's and nothing could ease the pain and guilt that ripped at her.

Martin rose, lifting Hodge and setting him gently by the fire. 'Kit, he still would have sent us out. He wanted to think and this would have added to that.'

He came and crouched down before her, taking her cold hands and holding them in his gentle, warm clasp. 'No one could have predicted his death and no one was responsible except the man who held the knife and the one who sent him.'

'But if I'd stayed—'

'You would be dead, too.'

His voice, harsh and shaking, shocked her. And then his arms came about her and she was held safe, sheltered, as she wept.

Martin was there again, his smile only for her and his arms enfolding her in warmth and safety. His kiss when it came was different now, all heat and fire, a demand that echoed in her own blood. A demand she answered and returned. Here it was at last. Everything she wanted, but thought lost. Here, in this place, this time, she could have everything. But slowly the mists sliding from the books intruded, sliding between them, twisting in cold threads that dragged them apart...

Kit woke again in the bitter grey light of dawn with the heavy, comforting weight of Moth behind her knees. For a moment she lay still, clutching at the remnants of sleep... Something, there was something, and if she slept a little longer she would not have to—the memory of warmth and love faded, replaced by cold, seeping mists.

Knowledge bore down on her, merciless and bright, banishing oblivion.

Ignatius was gone. Dead. Murdered. He lay in the back cellar at the Red Lion awaiting the inquest. She had learned the futility of hiding from the truth when Mama died. Truth always caught up with you. It was better to be facing the right way when it did.

And with the dawn came a hardening of the resolve she had sworn to last night after Martin had left her at the door to her room.

Kit, I'll find them. I swear it to you.

He'd made that promise, and she could do no less. Whatever she could do to find those who had wanted Ignatius dead, she would do it. No matter the cost. First, she needed to know why Ignatius had gone to Martin of all people. He worked somewhere in Whitehall. Surely Whitehall didn't investigate murders? That was Bow Street's job.

Behind her Moth's tail thumped softly on the bed.

Kit reached back to pat her. 'I'm awake.'

More soft thumps and a swift lick on the hand. Easier to face the day if she made a list of things to do. Her bladder told her what the first thing was.

After relieving herself, followed by a quick

wash in cold water and dressing hurriedly, Kit
came out from behind the dressing screen to find
Moth sitting patiently by the slightly open door.
Seeing Kit, she rose, whining.

'Come along, then.'

Reading beside the fire in the parlour, the cat
again curled in his lap, Martin heard the click of
the dog's nails on the floor, Kit's light footfalls and
the creak of a couple of stair treads as they went
down. He'd hoped she would sleep for longer. The
clock on the chimneypiece had barely chimed six.
He'd checked on her several times, leaving her
door ajar, so the dog would have more warning if
an intruder got in and past himself, but also so he
could hear more easily if she dreamed.

The cat had been somewhat unimpressed each
time he'd got up, but each time he returned the
creature had leapt on to his lap again and settled
down. The warm weight was oddly comforting
and the beast purred when he stroked it.

If Kit was up though, perhaps there would be a
cup of tea, or, please God, coffee available… He
ran a hand over his jaw. Lord, he needed a shave,
too. Even as he thought it, he heard the unmistak-
able sound of a bolt being drawn back downstairs.
Dumping the cat by the fire with a great deal less
ceremony than he had used during the night, Martin leapt to his feet and sprinted for the door.

Less than a minute later he burst through the

curtain into the kitchen to find Kit, the back door wide open behind her, staring at him in shock.

'Are you...is something wrong?'

'Wrong?' He could barely get the word out. 'You just open the door? After last night? Without letting me know?'

She stared at him, clearly confused. 'What? I...' Her voice shook a little. 'Moth needed to go out. As she does every morning.'

Martin took a steadying breath. 'And if someone, knowing your morning habit of letting the dog out, had been waiting for you?'

'For me?' Her face paled, but she lifted her chin. 'Moth would have growled if someone was out there.'

Moth's growl wouldn't have mattered a damn to a sniper waiting on a rooftop. He fought his panic down, remembering the disabling wounds on Selbourne's arms. Logic. He had to be logical. Whoever had killed Ignatius had wanted information first. If they thought Kit had that information, they wouldn't send a sniper.

He swallowed down more panic. Now the image of someone coming after Kit with a knife seared him. 'Kit, come away from the door. Please.'

Face still pale, she obeyed.

He stepped past her to the door and looked out. A light mist shrouded the yard. Moth sniffed around the edges, seemingly unconcerned about the possibility of knife-wielding assassins. Remembering the dog's reaction to the murderer, Martin was prepared to accept her reading of the current risk.

Apparently Hodge accepted it as well. He wound through Martin's legs and down the steps, disappearing behind a small outbuilding, presumably to do what a cat had to do.

'Tea? Coffee?'

He glanced back at Kit. 'Coffee, please.'

He was going to need it for this conversation.

Chapter Ten

Kit brought the tea and coffee through to the shop. Somewhat to her surprise Martin had not only relit the fire, he had also found the cups and sugar. He leapt up and took the tray from her.

'Thank you.'

She indicated the reading table. 'Put it over there, please.'

He set the tray down and looked at her over it. 'How are you feeling?'

Numb. Exhausted. Disbelieving. 'I… I don't know.' She took a careful breath. 'You…do you take milk? Sugar?' Her brain refused to work, to remember these things she had once known about him.

For a moment he was silent before coming around the table and pulling out a chair for her. 'Kit, sit down. Let me look after you.'

She stared for a moment, almost confused. But the chair was right there. She sat down. Watched as he poured the merest dash of milk in her tea-cup, then poured the tea. Exactly as she liked it.

'You remembered.'

He sat down and looked at her with a wry smile. 'Yes. Why wouldn't I?'

Her own memory focused. 'Sugar. You take sugar in your coffee.'

A small lump of sugar, no milk or cream.

He dropped in the lump, stirred. 'Yes.'

She was talking for the sake of talking, so she didn't have to hear her own thoughts, the clamour of guilt and grief. She pushed all that down, sipped her tea and let the silence hold her for a few moments.

Martin reached for the coffee pot, pouring himself another cup. 'I've been thinking about that letter.'

Her hands shook and her cup rattled as she set it in the saucer. 'Yes?'

His brows drew together as he sipped the coffee. 'Clumsy.'

'What?'

Martin looked up, still frowning. 'The letter was clumsy. Damnably clumsy. It's pretending to be careful, but it's not. Using initials—exactly like a—'

'Scandal sheet.' Through the mire of grief and the fear her brain started to work. 'That's how they avoid libel suits. Everyone knows who is who, but it's deniable.'

Martin leaned forward. 'I thought you'd see it.'

Despite grief, that warmed her.

He went on. 'In the context, S. has to be Selbourne and W. W. is clearly Wilberforce, although anyone less likely to be part of something like this is hard to imagine.'

Kit nodded. She had realised that already. Mr Wilberforce, the leader of the Abolition movement in the House of Commons, was a customer. He and Ignatius had been on the friendliest of terms. Ignatius had always had a stack of pro-abolition pamphlets available. And Martin was right: no one was less likely to order an assassination. The MP was the kindest, most generous of souls.

'So you think it's too obvious to be real? Why did they do it that way, then? Why point at Mr Wilberforce? Surely anyone who knows him—'

'Because mud will always stick,' he said, draining his second cup of coffee. 'Even to Wilberforce. As for the rest, they weren't really trying to disguise anything. But they had to look as though they were, because this is not the sort of thing that you put in writing if you can avoid it. Verbal commands are far less dangerous.'

Some of the fear drained. 'Then you don't think they were looking for the letter?'

He looked up sharply. 'Oh, yes. Having it found by the Runners is one thing. It causes a scandal at the very least, because Selbourne and possibly

Wilberforce are questioned. It brings the whole Abolition movement into disrepute.'

'But to kill Ignatius over it—' Her voice shook, but she controlled it. 'Why kill him?'

He was silent for a moment. 'Two reasons that I can think of. First, he'd seen the intruder. We have—there are people who can work with a description, make a sketch good enough to identify the subject.'

'Really?' She sketched well, but could she do that? Create a recognisable portrait from a mere description?

Martin nodded. 'Yes. Or Selbourne might have recognised the killer. Second, if he saw the letter, then he would warn Wilberforce and the movement.'

'Then the killer is safe now.' Her mouth was dry.

'No. He's not. Nor is whoever sent him and had this letter planted. Because we have the letter. That's the last thing they wanted.'

'Then you'll show it to Sir Richard and—'

'No.' Martin poured more coffee. 'That's the last resort. Once Ford sees something like this he'd have to act and it would cause precisely the scandal Selbourne's killer, the man who ordered it, wants.'

'Why you?'

'Why me what?'

'You work for Whitehall, don't you?'

'Yes.'

She could hear the reluctance in his voice, but

pressed on. 'How many murders does Whitehall investigate?'

He let out a breath. 'Not many. My superior, Holford, heads a very small office that looks into anything that might threaten the stability of the government or the country itself.'

'And *Ignatius* knew that?' Even as she asked, she knew what he was going to say.

'He was one of Holford's informants for years.' A faint smile curved his mouth. 'In fact, he trained Holford. Originally your uncle worked on the Continent. Eventually he came home and opened this shop. By then Holford was in the Home Office and he asked Selbourne to keep working quietly in the background.'

Kit struggled to comprehend. 'I always wondered how he knew so many people, but he never said anything.'

Martin nodded. 'He wouldn't when you were a child and he had stepped back in recent years. He told me last night that he'd never seen the need to tell you, but he was going to now.'

If she distanced herself from it, pretended all this was happening to someone else, better, someone in a story, surely she could think about it logically?

The Runners hadn't found anything and whoever had killed Ignatius had searched her slope last night, so they knew the paper was not there…

'Kit, when you found the letter, you said the cabinetmaker saw it.'

'Talbot thought it was a love letter, that…that I was—am—conducting a clandestine affair—'

Martin raised his brows. 'As you said yesterday—a stupid place to leave something you wanted to keep secret. Is he likely to gossip?'

Her stomach rolled over. 'He might. He wouldn't think anything of it.'

And if he talked in the tavern then it wouldn't take long to get around, and anyone who was looking for the letter and listening—

Fear iced her and she couldn't repress the shiver. Moth whined, nudging her nose into Kit's hand. Automatically she petted the dog.

His mouth tightened. 'You're cold, damn it.'

He got up, put more coals on the fire, then came back and refilled her teacup. He glanced around and picked up the shawl she had left in the shop the previous afternoon.

'Here.'

Gentle hands tucked it around her, his care enfolding her, as warmly as the shawl. She could have put more coals on the fire for herself, she could have filled her own cup. But that he'd done it, had wanted to do it, warmed her from the inside out, did something to dispel the dreadful cold inside her. Ignatius had been some sort of spy, working for the government, and she'd never realised.

'Thank you.' Poor words, not remotely close to expressing her feelings.

Those gentle hands remained for an instant on her shoulders, tightened. Then he stepped back.

If only...

She dismissed useless wishes. Once before she had listened to her heart, and fate and her own honour had kicked her in the teeth. Better to hold herself inviolate, no matter what her dreams served up. She couldn't permit herself to depend on Martin Lacy. If she couldn't stand by herself, then she didn't deserve the freedom she had won.

'It's nothing.' He sat down opposite her again. 'Kit, what I said last night—it holds. You are not responsible for his death. Put that away. We have to think about how it happened. How they got in. Selbourne didn't bolt the front door, did he?'

She nodded, forcing her brain to work. 'No. He said he'd leave it unbolted for us.' She swallowed. 'He...he hadn't been well. His heart and he sleeps—slept—very heavily. With me out he wouldn't bolt it.'

She saw the frown.

'Would you often go out? Alone?'

The even tones didn't fool her. 'No. Psyché and I might have gone together to that concert, or Will might have escorted us. Usually we'd both—Ignatius and I—be home of an evening.'

'But last night you were both supposed to be

out. And you did go out. Who could have known that?'

She blinked. 'Well, anyone on Mr Gifford's subscription list, or anyone who came into the music shop, I suppose. He keeps a list on the counter to which we add our names so he knows how much wine to order and so on. It's not a secret.'

'Then it's possible someone expected you both to be out and intended to search the shop undisturbed,' he said, absently refilling his cup again. 'But even so, they must have watched the shop, seen us leave and then seen the light upstairs. The lock wouldn't take much to pick.'

'And Ignatius heard them and came down, thinking it was us.'

'Yes.' He reached out for her hand, gripped it. 'But don't imagine that puts the responsibility back on you. When they didn't find what they were after they would have gone upstairs to question him. And if you had been there—'

She shook her head. 'Moth would have heard an intruder downstairs. She would have warned us and neither of us would have gone down unarmed. The killer might have fled.'

He nodded. 'That would work only once. After last night we should check the yard each morning for baits before she is let out.'

Her stomach rolled over as she looked at Moth stretched out by the fire. 'You think they'd—' A stupid question. If killing Ignatius hadn't bothered them, poisoning a dog wouldn't as much as touch their conscience.

'Point taken.'

His grip firmed. 'I'm sorry. You have to be careful.'

Her hand in his trembled. She longed, how she longed, to turn her hand under his, return the clasp. Instead she made herself tug very slightly.

He released her instantly. 'My apologies.'

Stiff, formal. And safer, so much safer for her heart if she kept things a little more formal. She had to remember what was important—finding Ignatius's killer and keeping his business—hers now—afloat. To do that she had to make sure no whisper of scandal was attached to his name. And more than her concern for the business and her future, she would not allow the memory of the man who had taken her in, and given her a home and that future, to be destroyed.

She wouldn't permit that to happen, no matter the danger. Ignatius had taken in a grieving ten-year-old when Carshalton found his only child—a mere daughter—an inconvenience. He had protected her again when she ran away, given her a home, a purpose in life.

She had known for months that one day soon she would be running the shop without Ignatius, but the manner of his death changed everything. It was like being in a boat on the river and losing an oar—she was being swept along, struggling to steer or control her course. Obviously she wouldn't be opening the shop today, but—

'We have to think about where you can live while I see to this mess. Somewhere safe, preferably out of London and—'

The knock on the front door had Moth lifting her head.

Kit rose quickly, grateful for the distraction before she could tell Martin exactly what she thought of his plan to tuck her safely away *'somewhere out of London'*.

'I'd better see who that is.'

Martin shook his head. 'No. I'll do it.'

As he started to rise, she took a deep breath.

Always best to ease into a major difference of opinion...

'I do use the peep, Martin. If it's someone I don't know, I'm not fool enough to open the door today.' She made herself speak calmly, as if it weren't a matter for discussion.

He froze, opened his mouth, shut it again and sat down.

Martin sat, mulling over that quiet rebellion as she went to the door, the dog following her, and slid the peep cover aside.

She closed it and turned back. 'It's the Runner, Smithers. With some papers.'

Martin let out a breath. Ford hadn't wasted any time at all. 'The summonses, most likely.'

He thought she paled, but she nodded and turned back to the door, unlocking it. He cursed as he saw her set her hands to the heavy bar.

'Wait.' A few swift strides had him beside her. 'I'll lift that for you.'

For a moment her hands remained on the bar. Then she nodded. 'Thank you. I can do it, but it is heavy.'

He breathed a sigh of relief as she threw the bolts and stepped back as he opened the door.

Smithers stood there. 'Morning, my lord. Sir Richard said as you'd be here.' His glance slid past to Kit. 'Very sorry for your loss, miss.'

'Thank you, Mr Smithers.'

To Martin's surprise she gestured the man in. 'It's a cold morning, Smithers. Would you like a cup of tea? Coffee?'

The man looked as surprised as Martin felt.

'Well,' he said slowly, 'a cuppa tea would be a nice thing, thanking you kindly, miss. Since I've delivered the other summonses I dare say it's all right.'

Martin stepped back and gestured him in. 'There can't have been many.'

'No, my lord. Just Mr Barclay and his servant at the Phoenix over the way.'

The only witnesses. No. Arranging an inquest wouldn't take long under the circumstances. Martin broke the seal on the summons addressed to himself, passed the other one to Kit.

'Ten o'clock?' Ford was really moving things along. That was barely three hours away.

Smithers shrugged, accepting a cup of tea from Kit. 'Thank you, miss.' He blew on it, then, as she moved away and gestured him to a chair, stared. 'That the writing slope I was looking at yesterday?'

Martin saw the faint, satisfied curve of Kit's mouth as her gaze flashed to him and he realised exactly what she'd intended by offering Smithers a cup of tea. Clever. Sneaky even. He had to admire it.

He picked up the ball she'd tossed to him. 'Yes. It seems that Mr Selbourne heard someone down here in the shop last night. The slope must have been broken in the struggle.'

Smithers frowned. 'Dare say that might be the way of it.' He drank some tea, still staring at the wreckage.

'Something bothering you, Smithers?' Martin could only applaud the way Kit had manoeuvred this and he kept the question casual.

Smithers turned to him. 'It's this, my lord. That chap who spoke to me yesterday, the one that gave me the tip-off, well, he said, straight up, that Mr Selbourne used a travelling writing desk to pass secret messages.'

'That's why you were so interested in it?'

Martin held his breath at Kit's question, but she sounded utterly calm.

'Aye.' Smithers nodded. 'Made me think, though, when you pointed out that it was right there for anyone to use, miss. Like you said, not such a good place if anyone was allowed to use it.' He scowled. 'Didn't get much of a look at the chap, though. Place was dark and he wore a hat and muffler.'

The bell jangled, and Martin whipped around. 'Caleb. Good morning.'

Caleb returned the nod. 'My lord. Miss Kit. Lord Huntercombe has arrived. He wants to see both of you.'

Kit's mouth trembled. 'Is…is Morgan with him?'

Caleb swallowed visibly. 'Aye. We had to tell him about Mr Selbourne. He's not in a good way, Miss Kit. Blaming himself, saying he should never have left Mr Selbourne alone.'

Kit's eyes closed briefly. 'He didn't. I did.' For a moment she seemed to sag, then she straightened. 'We'll be over shortly.'

Caleb nodded. 'I'll get back then.'

Martin locked the back door while Smithers gulped down his tea. Thanks to Kit's quick thinking he had the information he needed and the man didn't even realise he'd been questioned.

Smithers finished his tea and set the mug down. 'I'll be off back to the Lion, my lord.'

Martin nodded. 'Thank you.

He let the man out, then turned to Kit. 'Ready?'

'Yes.' She turned to the dog. 'You stay here, Moth. Guard.'

She looked at Martin. 'If anyone attempts to break in, she'll raise the roof barking.'

'Good thinking. And…' he opened the door for her '…absolutely brilliant thinking offering Smithers that cup of tea.'

The Phoenix was closed for another hour, so Caleb opened the door to them. 'Mr Will said we'd stay down here. More room and I'm making coffee. Miss Kit, I'm sorry about Mr Selbourne. We'll get the bug—ah, the blighter, don't you worry.'

She gave him a wobbly smile. 'I know. Thank you.'

She looked past him, saw Lord Huntercombe rising from his seat. And beside him, Morgan.

The old servant looked dazed, lost. 'Miss Kit. I shouldn't have left him. I should have—'

'Morgan, he couldn't trust that letter to anyone else. And if you had been there—'

'I'd have stopped it.' The old man stuck out his jaw. 'Might have thought twice if there'd been two of—'

'If you'd been there we'd have two bodies in the Red Lion's cellar.' Martin spoke bluntly. 'Whoever it was knew exactly what he was about. You couldn't have stopped it.'

Morgan glared at him. 'And who might you be to—?'

Kit laid a shaking hand on Morgan's arm. 'Morgan, this is Lord Martin Lacy. He…he was with me when I came back and found Ignatius. I'm sorry. He's right. You'd be dead, too.'

He patted her hand. 'I should have come back and that's all there is about it. Now here's his lordship, miss.'

Kit turned to face the man who had been her uncle's friend.

'Kit, my dear. I'm so sorry. Are you—? No. Of course you're not all right. Nor am I.'

Huntercombe's frank admission of his own grief stabbed to the core. Kit went to him, hugged him, felt the tears well up again as he held her, as they gave each other comfort as they had when she first came to live with Ignatius as a child.

She had been grieving her mother's death. He had been grieving the loss of his first wife and their children. Their shared pain had forged an odd friendship, one she had depended on. She had looked forward to his visits to the shop, not because he seemed always to have a twist of sweets in his pocket, but because he asked after her studies, accepted her very unfeminine liking for Greek, Latin and mathematics, and always had time to chat.

When she had run away from Carshalton, Huntercombe, along with Will and Psyché, had risked disgrace to help her stay hidden until she came of age. His own solicitor had drawn up the trust that would keep the business and the rest of her inheritance from Ignatius in her hands come what may.

After a moment, they stepped back and she faced him, her eyes damp. 'I'm going to find out why, sir. Whatever it takes.'

Chapter Eleven

Martin walked further into the shop and saw the dark-haired boy sitting quietly in the corner, Huntercombe's spaniel at his feet.

Barclay strolled over. 'You know Harry, of course, Lacy.'

'Yes. I know Harry.'

His breath caught at the boy's hesitant smile.

'Good morning, sir.'

Sir?

'Good morning, Harry.' He walked over, sat down at the table and accepted the spaniel's offered paw. Absently he rubbed the dog's head. 'I thought we agreed last time we met that you would call me Uncle Martin.'

His nephew Harry flushed. 'Sorry, sir. I mean, Uncle Martin. I suppose I forgot. Are you cross with us?'

Martin blinked. 'Am I cross—probably not, but who is *us*? You and the spaniel?'

From the corner of his eye he noted Caleb, with Selbourne's manservant, disappearing into the rear of the shop.

'Georgie and me.' Harry's dark blue eyes, so like his mother's, narrowed accusingly. 'You never come to see us. We wanted to thank you for the portrait of Papa. Uncle Hunt had a copy made so we didn't fight over it.'

Despite himself, Martin grinned. 'Wise man. And, no, I am not cross with you two.' He wanted to know his nephew and niece, but the last thing he could do was explain that he had avoided them because—

'Is it because of what your mama did? And Kit's father?' Harry made a face. 'She doesn't much like him being her father so I should call him Carshalton, I suppose.'

Martin took a moment with that, made sure he'd heard the boy correctly. 'You know what happened?'

The very welcome scent of bacon and eggs, and coffee, wafted from the back of the shop.

Harry stared. 'Well, of course we know.'

The girl, too? What was she? Seven?

Harry went on. 'After the coach was held up Mama and Uncle Hunt explained. Georgie had nightmares, you see.' He flushed. 'I did, too. It helped a bit, knowing *why* someone tried to kill me. And Fergus...' he rubbed the dog's ears

'…slept in our room for a while.' A grin. 'He slept on our beds and Mama pretended not to know.'

Shaken at the thought of the children having nightmares, Martin hauled in a breath. 'Harry, for all your mama and Uncle Hunt knew, I might have been part of it. I stayed away to protect you. And I'm very sorry about the nightmares.'

Harry didn't look convinced. 'They weren't your fault. Kit wasn't part of it and she said you weren't either. That it was your mama and Kit's… Carshalton, that is. She said you didn't want to be a duke.'

He had to smile. 'No. I can't say that I do.'

'Me neither.' Harry pulled a face. 'I wanted to go to sea. But Uncle Hunt says people depend on me and I have to do my best regardless.'

Martin reached out and ruffled his hair. 'No, you don't have a choice. Bad luck.' With that attitude there was every likelihood Harry was going to be a very excellent duke.

Kit wasn't part of it and she said you weren't either.

'Do you see Miss Selbourne often?'

Harry nodded. 'Uncle Hunt brings us sometimes when he visits the bookshop. And she came to stay for a while last summer. Will she keep running the shop?'

'I…don't know.' He didn't doubt that she was capable of it, but would she want to after this? And if she didn't, what would she do? Time to change the subject. 'How does your mother go on?'

Harry smiled. 'She's very well, thank you. She had a baby, you know.'

'I did hear that. Congratulations.'

'We got a puppy instead. And now she's having puppies as well.'

'Oh.' He wondered what to say about that. Tried to recall when he'd worked out how puppies, and babies for that matter, came into the world.

'Uncle Hunt says Fergus is the papa and that we can only keep one puppy. We have to find good homes for the others.' A considering look came into his eyes. 'Would *you* like one, Uncle Martin? As a proper thank you for the portrait?'

'I…yes, actually.' His manservant would probably cope in the unlikely event that he ended up with one of the pups. 'But only if Huntercombe approves. And Georgie, of course.'

Harry rolled his eyes. 'Georgie? She's plotting for all the puppies to go to people we know well so that she can see them sometimes.'

'Right.' He suspected Huntercombe might be somewhat less than pleased about one of his prized spaniels going to himself at all, let alone with the expectation that Harry and Georgie saw more of him.

Caleb reappeared carrying a large platter heaped with bacon and eggs. Morgan carried a stack of plates. Harry scrambled up to help Barclay push several tables together.

Martin helped set out chairs as Caleb disappeared again. He returned with two pots of coffee while Barclay fetched cups.

A few moments later they were all seated, including Caleb. Morgan retreated to the kitchen area, saying he'd already broken his fast and would clean up.

Harry had managed to seat himself next to Martin and was asking him where he lived now. 'Mama says you were away for a while and that you have moved.'

'*No!*'

Harry jumped in his seat and Martin swung around sharply.

On the other side of the makeshift breakfast table Kit had set down her knife and fork and was looking in disbelief at Huntercombe. 'How can you even suggest it, sir?'

Barclay laid a hand lightly on her shoulder. 'Kit—'

'I'm not going to be frightened out of my home! Ignatius always expected me to take over the shop and run the business after his death.'

'Kit, this is not the situation we expected.' Huntercombe's voice was steady, but Martin heard the underlying tension. 'Ignatius has been murdered. From what Will has told me it, appears that the killer was after information—they may think you have that information. We don't even know what it is. Until we—'

'But, sir, we—'

'Kit.' Martin cut off whatever she'd been about to say. He trusted the marquess and was starting to wonder about the man's connection to Holford and Selbourne. And he knew Huntercombe trusted Will Barclay unreservedly, as Selbourne had. But with two servants—he supposed Caleb was a servant—and the boy there, it was best to keep that letter private for now. He needed to speak to Holford.

Kit looked across at him, eyebrows raised. He gave a slight shake of his head. Her brows rose even higher, but then she relaxed, nodded.

Seeing the marquess's thoughtful frown and hoping to cover the reason for his intervention, Martin said quietly, 'At least listen to what Huntercombe has to say.'

The look Huntercombe shot him could have sliced granite, but his voice when he spoke to Kit was affection itself. 'My dear, you *can't* stay there alone. That you were there last night is bad enough.'

'But I wasn't alone. And—'

'I'm all too aware of that, Kit. And while—' another chilling glance sliced through Martin, this time accompanied with a polite nod '—I accept that last night Lacy's presence was the only solution, it cannot continue.'

'You wish me to remove to Grosvenor Square?'

Martin held his breath. If she could be persuaded to do that…only a plan was revolving in his head. It wasn't a plan he much liked and he would wager that Huntercombe was going to hate it. But it might be their only chance.

Huntercombe nodded. 'Or to my Isleworth house. Or even to Cornwall.'

Martin let out the breath. 'With respect, sir, are you planning to be in Cornwall yourself?'

He braced himself as Huntercombe turned to him slowly.

'I am very grateful that you remained in Selbourne's apartment last night, Lacy.' The marquess's voice bit. 'I suggest you don't test my gratitude too far.'

Martin inclined his head. 'So noted.' His own voice was equally cool. 'My question stands.'

'Then, no. I was not planning to return to Cornwall. I will be travelling between Grosvenor Square and Isleworth while Parliament is in session.'

'Then Kit will not be safe in Cornwall.'

Huntercombe's grim gaze held his for a moment. 'That bad, then.'

'And I'm not going anywhere, anyway.'

'Kit—' Huntercombe's voice remained steady '—your reputation—'

'With respect, my lord, it is not your decision.' Kit was pale, one small hand balled into a fist betraying her tension. 'I am of age and I do not believe the terms of my trust allow you to dictate my personal life. Quite the opposite.'

'Kit, be reasonable.' Huntercombe poured himself a cup of coffee. 'I cannot dictate to you, but you won't be opening the shop immediately. I take Lacy's point about protecting you directly, but I can't do that if you remain here in Soho. At least until the murderer is caught—'

'And what if he isn't caught?' Kit demanded. 'I can't hide at Moresby House or Isleworth indefinitely.'

Huntercombe smiled. 'You know very well that you would be more than welcome. But it won't come to—'

'No. I won't put your family at risk.' She turned to Martin. 'It would be a risk, wouldn't it?'

Martin looked down the table, caught Huntercombe's arrested gaze and drew a deep breath. 'Yes.'

Kit's mouth firmed. 'That settles it.'

Huntercombe frowned. 'I can send the children home with Lady Huntercombe, but—'

'That will cause an even bigger scandal than if it gets out I remained in the apartment last night.' Martin swallowed the last of his coffee. 'Not even your reputation would survive it, sir.'

Huntercombe's fist clenched. 'Then how the deuce do we protect her?'

Martin braced for the explosion. 'I'll guard her.'

'What?' Huntercombe's jaw dropped.

Martin hurried on while the Marquess was still stunned. 'Look, while I might personally prefer to lock Kit up safely in the Tower of London—' he ignored Kit's snort '—until this is over, her being at the shop, supposedly vulnerable, might be our best shot at smoking out Selbourne's killer.'

'Supposedly vulnerable?' Huntercombe glared at him. 'Where do you find the *supposedly*? She'll be a sitting duck unless you watch over her night and day! And if you do, which leaves her reputation in shreds, then they may not come at her anyway, not until we lower our guard.'

Always sensitive to movement behind him, Martin was aware that Harry had made himself as small as possible, probably hoping not to be ejected from what must be a thoroughly fascinating scene.

'They won't know.'

'How so?'

Wary, Martin turned to answer Kit's question. 'With your agreement, what I propose is this: I have lodgings, I'll leave my manservant there to make it look as if I am coming and going as usual. I ostensibly go about my business as usual.'

Kit stared. 'Ostensibly? What are you really doing?'

'You're here,' he said. 'Over the road, that is. Either in the shop or the apartment, but visible in the shop as much as possible, even if it's not open.

Shutters open, the doors locked and barred. Are there tasks you can believably carry out?'

She nodded. 'Yes. I need to put all those books away. I could conduct a full check of the stock. Go over the accounts. That sort of thing.'

'Good. You are in full view. You open again when you feel it is right.'

'I'm not seeing where my agreement would be in question, Martin.' Her eyes narrowed. 'Where is the *ostensibly* part of this?'

He'd just arrived at the sticky *ostensibly* part…

'In the evening you come over here where you'll have people about you. I'll go to my job each day and arrive here after dark. Barclay escorts you back to your shop and you admit me through the kitchen door.'

She stared at him, her eyes wide and startled, lips slightly parted.

Martin went on. 'No one knows I'm staying there, save the Barclays, Huntercombe, Morgan, Caleb, and—' he grimaced '—Harry, and I suppose Lady Huntercombe.' He looked around. 'Best not mention any of this to your sister, Harry.'

Harry shook his head. 'Not jolly likely, sir.'

Under the circumstances Martin let the *sir* stand.

Huntercombe had the look of a man backed into a corner. 'For God's—'

'Sir.' Kit's voice was pleading. 'Ignatius was your friend. You *must* understand how I feel. To let his murderer go free because I ran away? I cannot do it, sir. I simply *cannot*.'

Huntercombe let out a breath that sounded as though it hid a curse. 'The conflict of two opposing rights.'

He ran a hand through his hair and glanced at Barclay. 'Will, what do you think?'

Barclay nodded. 'I had the same reservations as yourself, sir. But I've had a night to think it through, and—' He shrugged. 'Apart from the Tower? There's no alternative. If Lacy is discreet, it should be safe as far as Kit's reputation is concerned.' His mouth flattened. 'I'm damned if anyone involved in murdering Ignatius is going to get away with it; that and keeping Kit alive trumps the proprieties.'

Martin breathed a sigh of relief as Huntercombe nodded, his expression wry.

'Always the calm voice of reason, Will. Thank you.'

Barclay smiled. 'I learned from the master. Except—' he frowned '—given what's happened, I'll need to ride out to Hampstead and escort Psyché home. So, Kit, for a couple of nights could you stay in Grosvenor Square?'

Kit sighed and nodded. 'Yes. That makes sense.'

'Let's begin as we mean to go on.' Huntercombe frowned. 'I need to speak to Lady Harbury anyway. Harbury's death alters the terms of the trust governing her ownership of Highwood House. I can escort Psyché back to London, Will.'

Martin eyed the marquess thoughtfully. Rather than leaping at an unassailable reason to get Kit safely under his roof, the man had surrendered the advantage voluntarily. What the devil was going on here?

He couldn't think about that now. 'We still have this inquest to get through intact. Let me be very clear; we do not, under any circumstances, give the impression that we believe Selbourne's death is anything other than a burglary in which the thief was disturbed by the householder.'

At this point Huntercombe glanced ruefully at his stepson. 'Harry, you will say nothing about any of this to your sister nor to anyone else. And you will kindly permit *me* to inform your mother about this—you may be there, but *I* will do the talking.'

'Yes, sir.'

'And you will *not* be attending the inquest.'

Harry's face fell. 'Oh, but, *sir*—'

'No. You will remain in one of the Lion's private parlours with Morgan.'

Martin hid a grin. There was no gainsaying that tone and Harry didn't try. He didn't even look terribly sulky about it.

Chapter Twelve

To Martin's relief the inquest, conducted by Ford, proceeded without a hitch, returning a verdict of murder against a person or persons unknown.

Huntercombe left for Hampstead from the Red Lion on horseback, leaving his stepson in Will Barclay's care to return to Grosvenor Square.

He drew Martin aside briefly under cover of Harry asking Kit if there was anything in the shop he might purchase for his mother.

'I'm trusting you to keep her safe, Lacy.'

Martin couldn't blame the man for his grim expression. 'In all ways, sir.' He bit his lip. 'Harry mentioned that business with Carshalton—he said that you don't believe—'

'That you had anything to do with it?' Huntercombe asked. 'I don't. Nor does Emma. Is that why you've held back from the children?'

Martin shrugged. 'There were plenty of whispers. And the last thing I wanted to do was give

Carshalton a scapegoat if he tried again. Beyond that—' He met the Marquess's gaze squarely. 'My father and I behaved very badly to Lady Huntercombe. My presence can only distress her.'

Huntercombe raised his brows. 'Really? I suggest that you permit her to decide what will and won't distress her. You can practise that very thing while you're dealing with Kit.'

'Sir—you have my word. You must know that I will do nothing to take advantage of this situation. I fully understand that marriage between Kit and myself is impossible.'

Huntercombe was silent for a moment, his expression unreadable. Then he held out his hand. 'Keep her safe for now, Lacy. We'll discuss the rest later.'

Martin stared after him. What *rest* could there be?

Kit had no idea what Martin and Huntercombe had said to each other, but from the thoughtful expression on Martin's face as they walked back to the shop, she suspected it had surprised him. Will and Harry strolled with them. Caleb had gone on ahead with Morgan to open the Phoenix.

'I say, here's Caleb coming back.'

Harry pointed, and sure enough, Caleb was hurrying along the pavement towards them, weaving through the pedestrians.

He came up slightly out of breath.

'Miss Kit. Stop. They're waiting for you at the shop. Lord Staverton and—' his face hardened '—Carshalton.'

Kit's stomach lurched.

She had not seen Carshalton since the night Will and Psyché had risked their lives to smuggle her out of the Phoenix...

Snow lay heavy on the pavement as she was hurried along to the waiting carriage and she heard the familiar, furious voice.

'By God, it is her! You stupid little bitch, Catherine! Stop or I'll shoot you myself!'

She turned... Will and Psyché, running, as they'd planned. And Carshalton, pistol raised, the flash as he fired and Will fell. Her own choked scream as she fought the strong hands forcing her on.

'You can't help them. Come!'

Ignoring the sticky churning knots in her belly, she forced herself to think logically. What did they want? And how could she use it against them?

'Will, you, Caleb and Harry should go straight back to the Phoenix. Before they see us all together.'

'What?' Will's jaw went to granite. 'Damn it, Kit. Do you think—?'

'Your first loyalty is to Huntercombe and keeping Harry safe,' she said bluntly. Oh, Carshalton wasn't a fool. Harry was safe enough, but she wouldn't have him faced with the man who had ordered his murder. 'I have a plan. Trust me.'

Will muttered a curse. 'Very well. Thanks, Caleb.'

Caleb laid a light hand on the boy's shoulder. 'Come along, Master Harry, his lordship will have all our hides if we let you within a stone's throw of *that* precious pair.'

Harry snorted. 'I can easily throw a stone that far and I'll wager you can. In fact—'

Will cuffed Harry's head lightly as he flanked his other side. 'Come on, Caleb. Let's get him home before he tries it. Lacy, you're hereabouts for the afternoon?'

Martin nodded. 'Count on it.'

'Will?' Kit touched his sleeve lightly.

He glanced back at her, questioning.

'There's no time to explain. Watch the front for me.' She could do this. She had to. For Ignatius. And for Psyché and Will.

Will gave her a quick nod and followed Harry and Caleb. As they crossed, Harry's clear voice floated back. 'I'm not scared of him! I haven't had bad dreams for *ages*.'

Georgie had nightmares... I did, too...
Martin realised he'd clenched his fists as Harry's slightly embarrassed admission echoed, along

with the memory of what Selbourne had confided all those months before…

Marriage the medieval way was what they had in mind.

And the look on Kit's face when Caleb had told her who was waiting…

'Martin, listen. You need to—'

Kit's voice died away as very deliberately Martin drew her hand through his elbow, settling it on his arm. He'd wanted to kill Staverton then. That hadn't changed.

'Martin.' Her voice dropped to a whisper. 'The last thing we want him to think is that we—'

'Kit, I know why you had to run from Carshalton's house that particular night.' That he hadn't been there to protect her had eaten at him since Selbourne told him.

She stared up at him, her eyes stricken. 'What? You can't know—'

'Yes, I can.' He kept his voice quiet, but he couldn't help the edge. 'And your hand stays precisely where it is.' It was little enough, but by God he'd protect her now.

'Martin, listen. If he thinks I'm alone he'll say more.'

'Say more?' Her words jolted him. 'About what? And what do you mean, *thinks* you're alone?'

'Exactly that. The *more* is something I thought about yesterday, before the slope got broken.'

Under his hand her fingers clenched convulsively on his arm. 'Will you trust me?'

'Trust *you*?' He stared. 'It's those bastards I don't trust!'

Her fingers tightened on his arm. 'We have to look like I'm begging you to come with me.'

'I *am* coming with you, Kit.'

She let out a frustrated sound. 'You need to pretend to see them and decide *not* to come with me. As though the sight of them has put you off.'

'Leave you? Like hell!'

'Listen!' She gripped his arm tightly, her expression urgent as she glanced along the pavement to where Staverton had now seen them, was nudging Carshalton. 'If you leave me here and go around to—oh.' The flare of urgency died. 'You don't know how to find the back door from—'

'Yes, I do.' Understanding crashed over him. 'Pretend you need to let the dog out and leave the back door open.' He shot a glance down the pavement towards the door of the shop and feigned a start, meeting Staverton's smug gaze. Removing Kit's hand from his arm, he bowed over it even as she clutched at him.

'Let me handle it.'

Grimly he looked at her. 'Very well, but don't imagine for one moment that I like this.'

Martin walked away from her, every instinct screaming in revolt, and lengthened his stride like a man who wanted to be anywhere else...

He broke into a run the instant he was out of sight around the corner. Easier in daylight without snow on the ground and an icy pavement beneath. Nor, as he gained the lane that led into the twisting warren behind the shops, did he have to deal with a gang of street boys amusing themselves torturing a puppy as they lay in wait. He wound his way through the maze, hand on his sword, until he reached the yard behind Selbourne's.

Moth looked up from her sniffing around, gave a low bark and trotted across to him.

'Good girl.' He scratched her ears. 'Time you went in.'

The dog beside him, he crossed to the open door. No sign of Kit, but at the sound of voices in the shop some of his tension eased. So far, so good. Kit's light tones and the heavy bass he knew as Carshalton's.

He moved into the kitchen and over to stand against the wall beside the curtain. The dog's nails clicked on the flagstones as she pushed back through the curtain.

'I thought you put that creature out!' Martin smiled in savage satisfaction at the nervousness in Staverton's voice.

'I did. Now she's come back. Moth.' A click of fingers. 'Sit.'

'Now, my dear Miss Carshalton—'

'Selbourne,' she corrected. 'I changed my name

legally as my uncle's heiress. Not an uncommon procedure.'

'Without my consent such a change is invalid.' Carshalton dismissed that instantly.

A chair creaked as someone sat down.

Kit's voice remained steady. 'Not once I was of age. Convention might suggest that a daughter seek her father's blessing or consent. The law doesn't care. You were saying something, Staverton?'

Martin could have cheered as she addressed him by his title, equal to equal, refusing to offer any hint of subservience.

Staverton adopted a patronising tone. 'I am here not to quarrel, but to plead with you—' There followed a scrape and rattle of coals… 'My dear Catherine, you cannot think how it pains me to see you carrying out such a menial task. Have you not a servant?'

'He is occupied. What brings you here, Staverton?'

'Naturally the news of Selbourne's demise distressed us. We wished to reassure ourselves that you were safe after such a dreadful experience, but to see you brought so low!'

Staverton's oily tones were enough to make Martin want to punch him—he wondered at Kit's restraint.

'Staverton, if it distresses you to see the fire stirred up, I suggest you leave.'

'You'll speak with respect, girl! And shut that dog up!'

Carshalton again, his deep tones threatening. And he'd stirred Moth to a warning growl.

His fists balled, Martin reminded himself that Barclay and Caleb were watching from the Phoenix, it was broad daylight and that if Carshalton *were* fool enough to try anything, he was close enough to foil it himself. If the dog didn't beat him to it—the ominous rumble continued.

'Perhaps Staverton might try the same. Instead of assuming I'm too feeble a creature to manage the fire.'

The icy whip of Kit's voice slashed.

'Listen to me, girl! You'll—'

'Dear Catherine, it is not that I think you feeble, as you so amusingly put it—' Staverton rushed into speech, cutting off whatever threat Carshalton might have uttered '—but that I hate to see you lower yourself to such a demeaning task. And, of course, so does your father. Which brings me to the point—'

'That was quick.' Back to the faintly veiled sarcasm. 'Moth. That's enough.'

The growling subsided. Mostly.

'Quick?'

'It usually takes you a great deal longer to get to the point.' No veil at all.

Tension thrumming in every vein, Martin settled to listen.

* * *

Kit viewed the shock on Staverton's face with satisfaction. He'd never heard her answer back before, of course. She had never done so in Carshalton's house. At best she would have been confined to her room and more likely given a beating.

She controlled a shudder. Even now Carshalton's favoured sandalwood cologne turned her stomach. She breathed carefully.

'Catherine, such impertinence is most unbecoming and not at all like you. This and your visit to Bow Street yesterday—and look how *that* turned out—tells me that Selbourne was a most pernicious influence on you.'

Fury blistered beneath her assumed calm.

'Dreadful, I assure you.' She started to pick up books, sorting them into piles on the desk. Better to keep her hands busy. How *dare* he criticise Ignatius?

Movement from Carshalton caught her eye. He was looking at the stained rug near the fire where Ignatius had died. He met her gaze and a satisfied smile curled his mouth.

Cold slid through her.

Staverton seated himself at the reading table and frowned. 'Catherine, at your father's request I am acting as intermediary here. And indeed for myself, with your father's permission.'

She looked up from the book she was holding, met Carshalton's hard gaze again. Her insides shook. If not for Moth... She steeled herself. 'How fascinating, Staverton. Continue then.'

'I must say that I was sorry to see you with Lacy, just now. I hope that cur is not pestering you with his dubious attentions now that what protection you had is gone.'

'Sir Richard asked him to escort me home from the inquest.' She hoped her voice was indifferent enough.

Carshalton snorted. 'Played least in sight when he saw us.'

Kit scowled. 'He remembered an engagement.'

Staverton smirked. 'I'll wager he did! Catherine, you must see that had you accepted my offer all those months ago you would not have been subjected to such public embarrassment as an inquest. A mistake on your part, you must own.'

The hell she must! She set another book on its pile. 'I'm sure you would see it so.'

'Then I hope you will look more favourably now that I renew it. With...' he gave an ingratiating smile that showed most of his front teeth, but missed his eyes entirely '...your dear papa's blessing, of course.'

Renew it? Good God!

'No.' Unnecessary even to think.

Staverton widened his smile. 'Now, my dear, I've no doubt that you think your behaviour in the last fifteen months renders you unfit for such a high position, more, that my own self-regard must preclude such an alliance, but—'

'Staverton, I'm afraid I haven't given my "unfitness" or your self-regard any thought whatsoever.' She dusted off the book she was holding, willing her hands not to shake as she placed it on a pile. 'I simply don't wish to marry you. Or anyone else for that matter. I'm perfectly happy as I am.'

'I am sure you *believe* yourself to be happy, but a female can scarcely be so unless she fulfils her highest purpose in becoming a dutiful wife and mother.'

'Logically,' she said, 'I think I am happy, therefore I *am* happy. Rather like Monsieur Descartes: *Cogito, ergo sum.*'

Staverton stared. 'What?'

Kit sighed. 'Never mind. You were saying? Something about renewing an offer of marriage? One you neglected to mention to me in the first place.' She deliberately said nothing about how they had intended to force her into marriage.

'Never reveal everything you know, pet.'

Ignatius had given her so much good advice. And Staverton had revealed that they didn't know that her knowledge had spurred her flight.

'You would have been told on Christmas morning. It was very foolish of you to flee to Lacy, hoping he would reverse his decision not to marry you, but I can forgive a naive young woman's misguided attachment.'

'How very generous of you.' She'd be lucky if his sanctimonious tones didn't induce her to throw up. Instead she focused on what he'd revealed—they still thought Martin had ended the betrothal. When she'd confronted Carshalton over the plot to murder Harry Lacy she'd been too cowardly to tell him she had broken it.

'Naturally your dear papa and I felt for your sensibilities and believed that a quietly arranged marriage to a man of standing and title was the best way to salvage your reputation.' He smiled again. An even more unconvincing arrangement of his features. 'I fear I must take the responsibility for not speaking to you earlier—I, ah, thought a Christmas morning proposal would be a romantic gesture.'

'A romantic gesture.' Kit spoke thoughtfully. That was something else she had learned from Ignatius.

'Repeating what they've said encourages them to keep going. Sooner or later they slip up and reveal something.'

Staverton hurried on. 'Yes, that gives you to think. You may imagine our concern when you were found to be missing at breakfast time.'

'At breakfast time.'

Carshalton had been pounding on the front door of Selbourne's Books at four o'clock on Christmas morning. The commotion had reached her hiding place above the Phoenix.

Fear hammering through her with every heartbeat, not just for herself but for Ignatius. The almost overwhelming conviction that running away was folly, that he'd find her in the end, that she should go back and endure...because without the hope of marriage to Martin nothing much mattered any longer.

She clenched her fists on her desk. Catherine, that terrified young girl, was gone. Dead. She had died somewhere between here and Bloomsbury on a snowy Christmas Eve over a year ago. Moth rose from her sprawl by the fire, came and shoved her nose under Kit's elbow.

She glanced down, laid her hand on the dog's head and steadied.

You can do this. They can't touch you.

'Yes.' Staverton's smile oozed a little more. 'It was most unfortunate that Selbourne, for his own selfish reasons, chose to interfere when you finally arrived on his doorstep rather than bringing you home. But now that he is gone, you must realise your position—without male protection you cannot possibly hope to lead any sort of respectable life.'

'You think I can't run a business?' She stroked the dog's head, scratching her ears gently.

'Run—' Staverton stared. 'You imagine you can run a business? Run a *bookshop*?'

He couldn't have sounded any more shocked had she said she was planning to run the brothel around the corner.

'No. I don't imagine it.' She kept her hand on Moth, drawing strength and confidence from the warmth of the rough coat. 'I know it. I've spent the last year learning how to do so.'

'My dear, this is most unfeminine. The proper course is to reconcile with your father and marry respectably.'

'I doubt it.'

'You'll think again, girl. Unless you want to be caught in Selbourne's mess.'

Carshalton's voice held a flat threat.

'Now, Carshalton. We shouldn't frighten poor Catherine. The scoundrel clearly used her to create a veil of respectability for his doings.' Staverton attempted a sympathetic smile. 'Catherine, I am sure you would not like to be embroiled in whatever Selbourne was engaged in. Your father is rightly concerned about your safety as I am sure—'

'Stubble it, Staverton. We'll have plain speaking now.'

Carshalton rested his elbows on her desk, intertwined fingers showing white. 'Selbourne got himself into a mess, didn't he? He was murdered for a reason—meddled in things that were none of his business. If you don't want that to come crashing down around your ears, you'll come back with us now and I'll keep you out of it.'

'Keep me out of what?' Kit allowed a hint of fear to creep in.

Carshalton sat back, his smile smug. 'That's got

your attention. What do you think will happen to your precious business when it's known Selbourne arranged Harbury's death?'

Kit's breath jerked in. She wasn't faking anything this time.

Carshalton smiled in satisfaction. 'That's right. Think about that. Maybe he hoped Harbury's widow would be grateful. Wouldn't be the first time a man married late in life.'

'A man with a history of manipulating vulnerable young women,' Staverton put in.

Kit steadied herself. She wanted nothing more than to tell the pair of them to go to hell, but she needed them to think she was cowed. 'He…he wouldn't have done that!'

Carshalton's smile widened. 'You don't want to see Selbourne's name ruined, do you, girl? Because that's what's going to happen if you're stubborn. But if you see sense and do as I say, then I'll do what I can to stop it.'

She swallowed her fury, allowed her voice to tremble. 'You're…you're going to ruin Ignatius if I don't do as you say? But he's already dead.'

'That's right. He is.' Carshalton spoke with icy precision. 'Selbourne died.'

'But if…if I come with you now, his name won't be ruined? You can stop it?'

He smiled. 'I can.'

She drew a very careful breath. Fury scorched

the fear, but she put a wobble in her voice. 'I... I need to think. Please... I need time.'

Carshalton rose, took one step towards her and stopped dead as Moth lifted her lips in a rumbling snarl and her hackles bristled.

'Shut that dog up before I do!'

Kit's blood congealed as Carshalton's hand crept towards his pocket, his glance darting from her to the dog.

'Now, Carshalton.' Staverton sounded nervous. 'No...no need for that. If Catherine needs time to consider my offer, I can wait.'

Kit held her breath, watched, ready to fling herself across the dog if Carshalton brought out the pistol she didn't doubt he carried.

'I...thank you, my lord.' And that nearly choked her. 'I need time. To think.'

Staverton's smile this time was absolutely genuine—smugly triumphant.

Carshalton stalked to the door, turning to glare. 'Consider this while you're thinking, girl. If you won't see reason and do as you're bid, then there's Bedlam for unnatural, unbiddable females.' He gripped the door handle. 'And don't think you can turn to Lacy. He doesn't want to be caught in another scandal and he didn't seem so very keen to face us, now, did he?'

She forced herself to remain silent, unmoving, her eyes level on his, while her stomach rolled in slow, sickening swoops and the scent of sandal-wood threatened to overpower her.

With a final glare Carshalton stalked out, followed by Staverton, and the door slammed.

Kit breathed a sigh of relief. There. It was over. And she hadn't—

Her stomach heaved and she bolted for the kitchen.

Chapter Thirteen

Hearing flying footsteps, Martin stepped aside as Kit shoved through the curtain. Moth followed at her heels as she raced for the back door and vomited into the yard.

'Kit!'

He went to her, stood helplessly as she bent over retching. Damn it, he should never have permitted— No. He forced himself to step back from that. Much as he needed to protect, he couldn't stand in front of her. He'd realised that when he understood her plan. Silently he gripped her shoulder, as the dog whined and nosed at her hand.

When the racking paroxysms were over and she straightened, he went to the kettle and poured a cup of water. 'Here.'

For a moment she stared at it as if she'd never seen water before, then rinsed her mouth and spat into the yard.

She set the cup down. 'Th-thank you. I'm…perfectly all right now.'

That, her gallant pretence at unconcern, was more than he could take.

'The hell you are.' He dragged in an unsteady breath. 'And even if you were, I'm not.' He caught her shoulders and pulled her into his arms, holding her close, feeling that instant of startled resistance before all the barriers fell and she clung to him, shaking.

Those few short minutes listening to Kit confront her father and Staverton had been an eternity. And when he'd realised Carshalton had a pistol… His arms tightened involuntarily, then he felt her arms slide around him and knew completion. She shuddered, arms tightening, and he cradled her closer, mentally cursing Carshalton to the darkest circle of hell.

Broken, incoherent words, shaken loose from the depths of his heart, he murmured helplessly into the soft, tousled curls. Comfort, reassurance, whatever she needed.

She drew back a little and those smoky grey eyes, shadowed with grief, edged with tears, gazed up. Her mouth trembled.

'I'm sorry. I thought he was going to shoot Moth for a moment. I'm… I'm being a watering pot.'

The wild urge to kiss those words from her lips rose up. The moment stretched, time suspended between them, as every reason he couldn't kiss her reared up to mock him. He consigned every last one to perdition… Her eyes widened, the soft lips parted, as they had once so long ago. She had wanted his kiss then, too, had responded in the sweetest…

In the shop the doorbell jangled, their lips a heartbeat apart.

'Kit? Where are you? Are you all right?'

Will's urgent voice ripped her free of the spell, the certainty that Martin was about to kiss her, the absolute knowledge that she wanted the kiss with every fibre of her being.

Was that her sigh, or his?

It didn't matter. His face rigid, Martin put her from him very gently and strode over to the curtain, pushing it aside. 'She's safe, Barclay.'

Will appeared, his face white. 'Lacy. Thank God.' The tension in his face eased. 'I assumed you had gone around the back, but—' He looked at Kit. 'When you didn't come to the door and wave—'

She pulled herself together. 'I'm sorry. I'm—' *Fine. Perfectly fine.* But this was Will who'd been shot because of her. No lies. 'It shook me a little. That's all.' No point hiding it; lord, she could smell it for herself. 'I was sick. Are you going to escort Harry back to Grosvenor Square?'

'Shortly, yes.' Will subjected her to a penetrating stare. 'Morgan is very uncomfortable about the propriety of him living here without Ignatius.'

'What?' Kit shut her eyes. 'He won't stay?'

Will grimaced. 'He's gone to see about lodgings. He says he'll come in daily, but, Kit, he's an old man and this has been a shock to him.'

She bit her lip. 'Yes. Ignatius was more a friend than his master. He'll want to retire. Ignatius left him enough for that—an annuity.'

Martin touched her hand lightly. 'This may work better for our purposes anyway.'

Will nodded. 'Exactly. I should be on my way. Ah, Caleb will be over in a few minutes. He offered to take that rug around to Sayid for you, Kit. Chap's a rug dealer,' he added for Martin's benefit. 'He'll get the stains out if anyone can.'

Kit shuddered. 'I don't want it back. Mr Sayid can keep it.' She'd buy another, but she couldn't look at that rug again, no matter how clean, and not see Ignatius's blood on it. At least the waxed floor had meant the blood had not stained the wood. She wasn't sure she could have lived with that.

As it was, she'd lost Ignatius, and now Morgan was leaving. Once they had settled this business she was going to be on her own. She stiffened her spine. She could do this.

She had to.

Caleb appeared shortly after Barclay's departure and removed the rolled-up rug. He reappeared twenty minutes later with a large pot of coffee.

'Mr Sayid said he was happy to give you another in exchange. He can get the stains out easily enough because you weren't silly enough to try it yourself and use hot water. He'll bring one around tomorrow.' Caleb smiled a little. 'I think he's picking out a good one.'

For a moment Martin thought Kit might burst into tears, but she steadied.

'Thank you, Caleb.'

'No problem. Enjoy the coffee.'

As the door closed behind him, she looked at the clock above the fireplace and said with an assumption of brightness, 'You must be ravenous. I forgot all about food. Pour the coffee while I fetch something.'

She set down the book she had picked up and disappeared out to the kitchen.

A few minutes later she returned with a platter of sliced bread, cheese, dried apples and cold sausage.

Setting it on the desk near him, she grimaced. 'It's not exactly what you're used to, but this is what we usually have in the middle of the day. There's no time for much cooking.'

He grinned, layering sausage and cheese on bread. 'Better than what I got at sea very often.'

'At sea?'

'While I was out of London.' He could tell her some of the truth. 'When I first knew you, I did some work for the Home Office translating, reading code—'

'You never said anything.' She frowned at him. 'I thought you were just a normal sort of duke's younger son.'

'Expensive and lazy?'

She flushed. 'I never thought that. I *liked* you. I just didn't know you had a position like that.'

He laughed. 'My parents were horrified. Especially Father when he realised it involved reading other people's letters. My mother thought it would give you a disgust of me that I was *jobbing for the government.*'

She was silent for a moment. 'Given how my father made his fortune I've very little room to criticise. Is that why you said nothing?'

He could have kicked himself. 'No. I wasn't really supposed to talk about it much at all. Not what I actually did. I intended to tell you after we were betrothed, but—'

'There was no chance.' Her voice was very soft.

'No.' No chance for anything. To say goodbye, to try to find a way *not* to lose her. And once the scandal broke, the whispers about the attacks on Harry and his own supposed guilt, Holford had been under pressure to dismiss him.

'Is that why you were posted to the Channel Fleet?' she asked. 'Because of the scandal?'

He shrugged. 'Partly. Holford called in a favour at the Admiralty. My Spanish is fluent, as well as my French. I'm also good at deciphering codes. He persuaded them I'd earn my keep, so they sent me out on a supply ship.'

'I wish I'd known.'

It was barely a whisper.

'Why?'

She stared, her mouth a flat line. 'I *worried* about you, that's why! No one could tell me where you were. I even wrote to your father!'

His turn to stare. 'What?' The duke hadn't mentioned that.

'He wrote back.'

'He did?'

'Quite nicely. He wrote that *he* had no idea where you might be and if I happened to find out would I be so good as to tell him? Why do you limp?'

It was very slight now. It surprised him that she'd noticed. 'An accident while I was ashore near Cadiz. I slipped running. Ripped something in my leg.'

'Not a bullet?'

'No.' Bullets were the reason he'd been running, but they'd missed, and his companion had kept him upright and got him to the waiting boat.

'And you don't mind eating down here? It's rather informal, but usually the shop is open and I'd have to bring it all back down again to be washed.'

That tentative question brought the practicalities of the situation home to him. Damn it, he was treating her like a servant. Sitting on his backside while she prepared the meal and was no doubt thinking she'd have to clear up after him.

And she worried if eating in the shop was too informal for his aristocratic self.

Wondering if he'd lost his mind, he said, 'I'll help you with the dishes.'

He knew the dishes got washed somehow. Not that he'd ever thought about it before and he couldn't blame Kit for the stunned look she bestowed upon him.

She helped herself to cheese and dried apple. 'Maybe I should check to see if the sky is still in its appointed place.' She smiled at him. 'Don't worry about the dishes. I—'

The knock on the front door had her turning. An odd expression flickered over her face. 'Well, speaking of dishes.'

She rose and started for the door. 'You're about to meet my housekeeper.'

He froze. 'You have a housekeeper?'

She looked back. 'Of course.'

'Kit, if she gossips, then—'

Again that odd expression. 'She won't. But I should have warned her.'

Kit opened the door. 'Jenny, I forgot you'd be coming.'

'Kit, my dear. I wasn't even sure if I should come. I'm so very sorry.' She enfolded Kit in a hug.

Not at all like your average housekeeper. More like a friend. A woman in her middle thirties, he judged, affectionate, sympathetic. Attractive, taller than Kit, with an air of controlled dignity, she wore her plain gown and apron with quiet elegance and her bonnet was modest, but trimmed with bright blue ribbons. Everything about her said *lady*, not housekeeper.

In the act of untying her bonnet strings the woman froze and Martin felt the force of her blistering gaze. Hostility, suspicion.

'Kit. What are you—?'

'Ma'am.' He rose, bowed.

Kit rushed into speech. 'Mrs Archer, may I present Lord Martin Lacy? He was with me when… when I came home last night.'

Martin bowed. 'How do you do, Mrs Archer?'

He felt the icy gaze and accompanying silence as an accusation.

'How do you do, Lord Martin.' Polite, uninflected. He doubted she was reserving judgement though. Merely comment and he suspected he had Kit's presence to thank for that.

'Kit, I'll go on upstairs and get started.'

'I'll come up, Jenny.' Kit sent Martin an apologetic look. 'There is something I must discuss with you.'

Mrs Archer sent another suspicious glance at Martin and the two women disappeared upstairs.

* * *

Kit reappeared fifteen minutes later.

'I'm sorry. Jenny had questions.'

'About my presence.'

She bit her lip. 'She doesn't like it, but she agreed it was probably best when I explained why you were here.'

'You told her *that*?'

'Yes. A little bit. Not about the letter. And not about your job.'

He couldn't blame her, but— 'Most people don't explain things to the housekeeper.'

Her mouth flattened. 'Jenny—Mrs Archer—is rather more than just a housekeeper, Martin. And she won't gossip.'

'Very well.' He had to accept that and not question how she could be so sure. He was depending on his own manservant not to gossip.

Feeling Kit's gaze on him, he looked up to see her watching him, head tipped to one side.

'You aren't going to ask how I know that, are you?'

'No.'

She let out a frustrated breath. 'I have to trust you.'

He tamped down the faint hurt that she even had to think about it. 'If you can't, then I shouldn't be here.'

'I don't mean for myself. I mean, about Jenny.'

Ah. She hesitated to share another's story without permission. 'There's no reason that I can think of that you have to tell me anything about her.'

'That's because you don't know the story,' she said drily.

'True. But, Kit, if she would not like me to know her story, then *I* have to trust you.'

'*Touché.* However, Jenny did give me permission to tell you. She thinks otherwise you will worry about her gossiping.'

'Kit, if you tell me that she—'

'Mrs Archer, as she is called nowadays, used to be my governess.' She took a slice of cheese. Ate it. 'She abducted me.'

Martin reached for the very cold coffee pot. Cold or not, he definitely needed coffee. 'Maybe you had better tell me about that.'

Chapter Fourteen

April 1793

At first Uncle Ignatius was delighted when she and Miss Andrews arrived soaking wet shortly before opening time. Kit, not wishing to drip all over the books, stood still before the fire, clutching her valise, gazing around in delight at the shelves and shelves of books. World upon world, all enclosed in leather bindings, releasing their magic when you opened them. She breathed in the leather bindings, even the dust, and wished she could spend more time here. Sometimes now that Mama was gone she allowed herself to daydream about living in the cosy apartment upstairs and helping Ignatius sell books.

She turned to ask if she might help him sell a book while they were there, but he was asking Miss Andrews what had happened to her face and Kit saw that her governess had pushed back the veil she had worn on the hurried walk from Bloomsbury.

She couldn't hear what Miss Andrews said in answer—like the lady in Shakespeare, Miss Andrews's voice was *'ever gentle, sweet and low'*—but she heard what Ignatius said quite clearly.

Dear God!

After which he locked the front door and hurried them upstairs, calling for Aunt Agatha. Kit cast a longing glance back. Even cold and wet, she was reluctant to leave those worlds of leather, ink and paper, the glorious bookishness. But she had been trained to obedience and Uncle Ignatius would not want her dripping all over the books. And perhaps they had some arnica upstairs that poor Miss Andrews could put on her bruised face.

Aunt Agatha met them at the top of the stairs. 'My dears, how nice! But you're soaked. Come by the fire and…oh!'

She had seen the bruised face.

'Agatha—take Kit up to the second bedroom. Miss Andrews says there is a change of clothes in her valise.'

'Very well.' Aunt Agatha nodded and took Kit's hand, drawing her on up the next flight, but Kit saw how she touched the other woman's arm in passing. Gently, as if in comfort.

Kit sought to explain. 'She banged her face again, Aunt.'

Agatha's hand tightened on hers. 'Again? It's happened before then? In here, pet.'

Agatha whisked her into the second bedroom, a smaller room than the one where she and Uncle Ignatius slept, but cosy and friendly with a bright counterpane on the bed, an overflowing bookcase and watercolours of flowers and misty hills on the walls.

'Let's remove these wet clothes before you catch your death of cold.'

The sodden garments were stripped from her with brisk efficiency and she was rubbed down hard enough to leave her skin tingling.

'There.' Agatha smiled, but it didn't quite reach her eyes. 'Hop into your dry clothes and wait here while I fetch some hot soup and you'll be as right as a trivet.'

'Not right as rain, Aunt?'

Warm and dry now, Kit essayed the silly joke and the smile briefly reached Agatha's eyes.

She rose from her knees. 'That too, pet. I'll be back soon.'

Kit waited, but soon seemed to be taking rather a while and, wondering if she really ought, Kit crept down to the parlour, heard her aunt's voice.

'My dear girl, you mustn't do that. We can help you. Can't we, Ignatius?'

'We certainly can.' Kit had never heard him speak like that. Fierce and comforting all at once.

Like…like a sword raised to protect. 'Whether or not we can keep Kit here—and we'll try—'

Keep her? She might be able to stay?

'I promise, we can help you.'

'I couldn't leave her there alone and I couldn't stay! I couldn't! Even though he'd marry me if he knew that—'

But Miss Andrews's voice broke and dissolved in a terrible weeping. Kit heard the murmur of comforting voices and crept back up to the bedroom, suddenly feeling cold again. She found a volume of Shakespeare's sonnets in the bookcase—Mama had loved the sonnets—tucked herself up in the counterpane on the bed and started to read.

After another long time, she heard Agatha calling up to her and went back down to the parlour. Ignatius and Miss Andrews were gone.

Agatha set her down at the little round dining table with the soup and sat down herself with some knitting.

'Is Uncle Ignatius selling books?' Perhaps she could help after the soup?

Agatha shook her head. 'He has closed the shop for today. He has an errand or two to run.'

'With Miss Andrews?' Agatha and Ignatius never objected to questions. They said that was how you learned.

Agatha hesitated, then said, 'Yes. Some of

them. My dear, if anyone asks you about Miss Andrews—anyone at all, pet—you are to say she brought you here and left at once.'

That was almost true, but— 'I shouldn't say she went somewhere with Uncle Ignatius then, just that she left.'

Agatha set her knitting aside. 'Yes. Sometimes a lie, to protect someone else, is the right thing. Miss Andrews tried to protect you by bringing you here, but some might say she abducted you, so we have to protect her from that.'

Kit thought about that. She knew she would never need to tell either Agatha or Ignatius a lie to protect someone from them… You could always tell them the truth no matter how frightful it sounded.

'I'd rather live here with you than with Papa. Now…now that Mama is gone.' Saying it brought the tears Papa had forbidden welling up. She blinked them back.

'Stop that caterwauling, girl!'

Agatha said nothing to that and Kit spooned up more soup, considering another question.

'Aunt, can things be haunted?'

'Things? Houses, you mean?'

'What about doors? I think the doors in Papa's house might be haunted and they don't like ladies.'

Agatha stared. 'Why do you think that?'

'Well, Mama used to hit her face on them a lot and now Miss Andrews and some of the maids.'

Kit addressed herself to the soup again, feeling remarkably silly.

'I see.'

The grim tone had Kit looking up sharply, but Agatha found a smile and Kit relaxed a little.

'I promise you the doors here aren't haunted. No one hits their face on our doors.'

'When will Uncle be home?'

Agatha let out an audible breath. 'When he has seen your father.'

All Kit's airy castles collapsed into ruin. 'I have to go back, don't I?'

Agatha reached out and patted her hand. 'Not tonight, pet. You can stay tonight.'

She was in bed, supposed to be asleep when Ignatius finally came home, but sleep, until she was quite sure she wasn't to be dragged home that night, was impossible. She heard voices, Aunt Agatha and Uncle Ignatius, and crept down to the landing to listen.

'Tell me, Ignatius.'

'Well, I've seen that poor girl settled. She's barely quickened and, as she thought, Carshalton doesn't know.'

'You saw that bastard?'

She'd *never* heard Aunt Agatha speak like that. As though she wanted to spit at someone.

'Oh, yes. I saw him.'

Now his voice was like ice dipped in fire. She'd never heard that either.

'And?'

'I told him she'd left the child on the doorstep. That she barely spoke before hurrying off.'

'Will he look for her?'

'I doubt it, love. He'll assume exactly what the poor child intended.'

His voice was gentler now and Kit imagined him patting Aunt Agatha's hand to reassure her. She thought the child must be Miss Andrews, because she herself hadn't intended anything. She hadn't even known where they were going until they were practically on the doorstep.

'Kit?'

She froze, thinking they'd realised she was there…

'He said he'd send a servant to collect her—' Kit's heart turned to lead '—but I said she could stay a day or two if it was more convenient.'

The back of her throat ached and her eyes burned. A day or two was better than nothing, but—

'You didn't ask to keep her?'

'Not directly. You know what he is.'

'Oh, yes.' Loathing rimed Aunt Agatha's voice. 'Any time he knew Kate wanted something particularly he'd make sure she didn't get it.'

Kate. That was Mama.

'Exactly. I said she could stay if it made it easier

for him. No need to worry about another "flighty" governess.'

Aunt Agatha snorted.

'Quite. He said he'd no use for a girl, it would be different if she were a boy, and he was thinking of sending her to school anyway.'

'He could still do that.'

'He could.' Smugness edged Uncle Ignatius's voice now. 'But for all his wealth he's such a nipcheese over spending money on his daughter that the idea of leaving her here, for *you* to raise and school, appealed to him.'

'She's staying then?'

Kit's heart leaped and danced right along with the hope flaring in her aunt's voice.

'Please God, yes.'

Kit slipped back to bed. Her eyes still stung, but almost all of her was relieved that Papa *didn't* want her. Instead she could stay here where they did want her and wouldn't mind that she still cried for Mama.

Soho, March 1805

'He—' Martin stopped himself right on the cusp of saying *seduced*. 'He raped her. Miss Andrews, Mrs Archer.'

There had clearly been nothing of seduction about it. Why try to make it sound respectable?

Kit nodded, her expression blank. 'Repeatedly.

He…he wanted to get her with child. Excuse me. I'm going to start reshelving the books.'

She tucked several under one arm and started up a ladder, climbing with an ease that told him she did it often.

'He—?' Enlightenment flashed 'He wanted a son.'

'Yes.' She shoved in a book. 'She was pregnant. That's why she ran. But she didn't want to leave me there.'

Sick disgust churned in Martin's gut.

Thank God for Ignatius and Agatha Selbourne.

'And you stayed here.'

She glanced down at him, her eyes wintry. Another book slid into place. 'Yes. He didn't need me. He ignored me. Until Aunt Agatha died—' She broke off, looked hesitant.

'Yes?'

'I'm not sure, I'm guessing, but I think he must have planned to take me back at some point. Once I was—' She broke off.

'Marriageable?' Old enough to be sold off to someone Carshalton adjudged useful to his own ambitions. Like himself.

She nodded. 'Yes. But Agatha died when I was only sixteen. I suppose he thought it was better to take me back then rather than wait.'

Martin let out a breath. 'What happened to the child?'

'The—?' She looked down from her perch,

frowning. 'Oh, Jenny's baby. She miscarried a few weeks after bringing me here. I knew nothing of that at the time of course. She only told me about it last year when I came back to live with Ignatius.'

She placed the last book and started back down the ladder.

'Kit, why don't I pass books up to you?'

She stopped. 'Well, thank you. It's that pile.' She pointed. 'It's very kind of you.'

He shook his head in amusement. 'You can't possibly think I'd sit around and watch you do all the work. I may not have the knowledge to shelve books correctly, but I can pass them up to you.'

Her smile bloomed. 'As long as you know your alphabet it's not very hard.'

He handed her the pile. 'Once you had sorted them into their correct subjects. That takes an element of knowledge. Scholarship, even.' He smiled at her surprise. 'You'd like the library at Keswick House. I don't think you ever saw it.'

'No.' Rather stiffly.

'We'll call on my father one day and you can have a look over it.'

If the duke had answered Kit's letter, quite a few things had changed at Keswick House.

They worked steadily and the piles of books spread about dwindled. By tacit consent they kept the conversation general, avoiding the private. Including talk about that nearly-a-kiss. Although talking about it was not at all what Kit wanted.

She acknowledged that to herself as she perched at the top of a ladder, putting books in order. What she wanted was to make it really-a-kiss. She told herself it was a very good thing that that Will had interrupted them.

A kiss was one thing. A kiss was fine. But kisses led to other things. And those other things might not be quite so fine. At least, she thought in and of themselves those things might be lovely. Judging by both times they had kissed and what Psyché had told her, those other things would probably be more than fine.

It was all impossible.

Wasn't it?

Her father had disowned her as completely as she had rejected him. She had received a letter from his solicitor informing her that she had been disinherited. Would he care now whom she married? And she needed to put that aside and focus on what she was doing—perching at the top of a ladder reshelving books…the top of the ladder, the upper shelves…

Why? Why had the killer started with the upper shelves?

The Runners had started with the slope and the lower shelves. But the killer had started up here. The obvious answer to her mind was that only she ever climbed the ladders now. Customers were strongly discouraged, and Ignatius had no longer been strong enough, plus his heart had sometimes made him breathless and dizzy. Anyone who had been in the shop regularly could have worked that out.

And if she had wanted to hide something in a book, then the top shelves were where she would put it. Because no one else was likely to unearth it. Which meant they had assumed she knew about the letter when it hadn't been found in the slope.

Which was why, she reminded herself, Martin was here, not because he wanted to kiss her. He probably hadn't really wanted to kiss her earlier. He was full of common sense and as rational as she was, and kissing each other made no sense at all.

She shoved a book into place with unwonted violence. There were times when common sense and rationality held no appeal whatsoever. Sometimes she wanted to do something foolish.

Like kissing Martin Lacy out of his senses and herself along with it.

The door opened with a jangle and the Rector of St Anne's walked in.

Slamming a mental door on her unruly thoughts, Kit scrambled down the ladder. 'Sir, Archdeacon. Good afternoon.'

The old man smiled at her. 'Miss Selbourne, Kit, my dear. Please accept my sympathy. I shall miss Ignatius dreadfully. And for you—well.' He took her hand and patted it as he glanced about the shop. 'You're keeping busy, I see.'

'Yes, sir. May I present Lord Martin Lacy? Lord Martin, this is Archdeacon Eaton, the Rector of St Anne's.'

They shook hands.

'Keswick's youngest, aren't you?' The archdeacon nodded. 'Very kind of you to help.'

He looked sorrowfully at Kit. 'My dear, I thought you might wish to discuss arrangements. For Ignatius, you know.'

Kit dragged in a breath, steadying herself. 'Yes, of course.'

Martin listened with an aching heart as Kit made the arrangements with the archdeacon. The man had very kindly already spoken to the undertaker about a coffin. 'Ignatius left instructions with me, you know. He knew how very distressing this would be for you.'

It didn't take long. Kit suggested three days hence for the burial. That gave her time to let people know. She said something about letters. He could help her with that. Whatever she needed.

With the sun sinking and shadows filling the shop, Jenny Archer came down from the apartment as Martin lit the lamps. Kit had disappeared into the kitchen to prepare supper.

Mrs Archer looked around. 'Is Miss Selbourne cooking supper?'

'Yes, ma'am.'

Her expression was grim. 'I did as she asked. The bed in the second bedroom is made up.'

'Thank you.'

'My job.' Her voice lowered further. 'Believe me, if any harm comes to Kit through this, you'll answer for it.'

He nodded. 'Mrs Archer, should any harm come to her I will likely already be dead.'

Her jaw dropped. After a moment she recovered. 'That wasn't what I meant, Lord Martin. This could ruin her. I may accept her assurance that you have no interest in…seduction.' Her mouth hardened. 'There are many who will not.'

Martin let out a breath. 'I know that. But we have to keep her alive. You risked a great deal for Kit twelve years ago.'

The woman shrugged. 'I did what I thought right.'

Martin nodded. 'Yes, but it was a risk. He could have had you taken up for kidnapping. I owe you for what you did. Just as I owed Ignatius Selbourne and his wife. I'm in your debt.'

It couldn't be said that she smiled, but a glimmer of light came into her eyes. 'Believe me, Lord Martin, I have been repaid for that a thousandfold.'

He bowed. 'Not by me. Ah, the funeral will be in three days. Ten o'clock at St Anne's.'

She nodded. 'I'll be there. Good day to you, my lord.'

Chapter Fifteen

In the quiet glow of the parlour Martin enjoyed the simple supper with Kit. The room wrapped around him, at once quiet and full of life. The people who had lived here had been happy. He'd never met Agatha Selbourne, only knew her through the few things Kit had said about her and the story this afternoon, but if something of her remained here he hoped that she didn't object to his presence.

Ignatius, he thought, would understand. Might even be pleased. His fingers closed over the ring in his pocket. Why else would the wily old man have left it in that particular receptacle?

The bowl of hearty soup mopped up with a slice of bread, the dog snoozing by the fire, even the cat, ensconced again on his lap—it all breathed contentment. And now he sat reading, stroking the cat every so often, by the fire, while Kit sat at the desk writing letters to Selbourne's friends. She had wanted to do that herself although her eyes had welled up at his offer to help.

It should be me. But, thank you. Thank you for offering.

Each time he looked at her longing flooded him. Not just mere physical longing, but a longing that this quiet companionship might not be finite. Her slight frown as she concentrated, the way the fire-light gleamed on the short, pretty curls. She hadn't bothered with a cap, or mittens as most women did. Although judging by the ink stains on her fingers, there was likely an element of practicality in not wearing mittens.

Practical. Full of common sense. That was his Kit. *His* Kit. And there was the problem. He still wanted her to be his. In the same sense that he wanted to be hers.

An equal exchange of hearts and melding of lives that he simply couldn't ask for. Not now. It wasn't fair on her. He had to remember why he was there—to protect her. Not to love her. He shouldn't even be thinking about it. And that moment down-stairs when he'd been within a breath of kissing her. When *they* had been within a heartbeat of kissing each other. One more breath, one more heartbeat.

He banished the memory. Until Selbourne's murderer was exposed—not just the man who had wielded the knife, but the one who had sent him, the one who had planned for that letter to be found—he needed to remain Kit's protector in the truest sense of the word.

What did Kit know? Or think she knew?

He'd intended to raise the subject after supper, but he was reluctant to break into her task with talk of the letter, of Carshalton's visit. Even with Eaton's visit and the arrangements for the funeral, he thought working with the books, the rhythm of restoring order, had settled her. Oh, there were still the shadows of grief. They would remain for a long time yet. But she had found some peace. He could allow her one evening.

She looked up and their eyes met, memory an enchantment stretching out to bespell them both. Her lips parted and he had to steel himself against the need to go to her, to take the next breath, feel the heartbeat they had denied that afternoon.

'Hodge likes you.' She sprinkled sand on the letter she had been writing.

The spell broke and he let it go regretfully. 'It seems so. That or I have a particularly comfortable lap.'

'You and Ignatius. And Aunt Agatha. They had him before I came to live with them.' She folded the letter, affixed the seal and set it with the others. 'And he's never sat on anyone else's lap. Not in all the years I've known him.'

A smile trembled on her lips. 'It's nice that he's

found a new lap. For now, at least.' Then, after a deep breath. 'We have to talk about it, don't we?'

She didn't mean the cat and his preference in laps.

She hadn't wanted to speak. The simple comfort of having him there as she wrote to Ignatius's friends had ensnared her so that she was weaving dreams again. Dreams that were foolish enough in sleep and sheer madness when waking. Best to nip folly in the bud early rather than let it flower. Nothing could come of this longing.

He put his book down. 'We should. You said there was something you'd been thinking about yesterday. That made you want to confront Carshalton alone to see what you could get out of him.'

'What he said today, it fits. You see, yesterday, before I found that letter, it occurred to me that he might have been behind Harbury's death.'

'Why?'

He didn't sound sceptical or dismissive. Oddly, he reminded her of Ignatius, who would always make her explain an idea as clearly as possible, helping her find the weak points of an argument and clarify her thoughts.

'Because of the hold up. It's what he tried with Harry. And...and—' She struggled to say it, to remind him of what her sire had likely done... Another reason they could never reach that dream.

She might have rejected Carshalton, but he had still sired her.

'My brother, Thirlbeck. Another hold up.'

She didn't trust her voice, so simply nodded. After a moment she said, 'Until I read the letter I couldn't see a connection, a *reason* to kill Harbury. After all, he was very much pro-slavery. Why would Carshalton want to remove him?'

'And the letter changes all that?'

'I think so. Maybe they didn't even intend to kill Harbury. After all, pistols aren't that reliable, it was dark—'

'The intent was definitely to kill my brother,' he pointed out. 'And Harry for that matter. Otherwise, I didn't inherit. Each time the highwayman made sure he would have them at point-blank range. Just as he did with Harbury. I read the reports, remember.'

'Oh.' She wasn't sure if that supported her idea or not, but it still needed to be taken into account.

'Even so, I think you're right. The letter does change things. Once that came out—and if the Runners had found it, it would have—the scandal would have destroyed the Abolition movement for a generation at least. Even if Selbourne was never convicted and Wilberforce exonerated—it would crush them. Especially if they could tie a Black man to the actual murder.'

'They used Caleb deliberately.' Rage scalded her.

'Yes. A deliberate and cynical attempt to implicate one person in particular.' He shook his head. 'Not a vague description of "a Black man" but a specific person. One who could be tied to several prominent Abolitionists. Selbourne, the Barclays, even Huntercombe.'

'But would Staverton collude at the murder of his own son-in-law?'

Martin frowned. 'You know, that's a very good point. I might have to ask Barclay's wife what she thinks about it. She knew them both better than either of us. But what I can see is that your idea Harbury's death was unintentional might be how it was proposed to Staverton. An attack that was supposed to fail. He told me it was his suggestion that they should drive out in an effort to reconcile Harbury to his wife.'

Kit's stomach lurched. 'That's how Carshalton planned to control you if we'd married—implicate you in Harry and...and Thirlbeck's deaths.'

He nodded, seemingly unbothered. 'It's a pattern and the connection you were looking for. And he has another way to control Staverton.'

'What?'

'You. He's holding out marriage to you, an heiress, as an inducement.' His mouth flattened. 'And you told them you needed time to think.'

Despite the fire a chill shook her. 'You know why I said that. I'll never consent to marry Staverton.'

'It's not what I know that matters.' Martin got

up and paced. 'It's what they believe. They believe that if once your father gets you back under his control, they can force your compliance.'

He stopped in front of her. 'You know how they'd do it.'

She gripped her shaking hands together in her lap. 'Yes. The way they planned it before. But—'

'Kit, they don't understand it wouldn't work.' His face was grim. 'They'll never understand it. And...' he reached down and pulled her to her feet '... I won't risk it happening to you.' He clasped her hands. 'Whatever it takes, even marrying you myself—'

Shock slammed through her. She could have everything, everything she'd once wanted... But not everything she wanted *now*.

'No.' She pushed temptation away. 'You can't do that. Even if I believed my father would no longer go after Harry, I'm not going to marry anyone. I... I don't need to anymore. I have my own business. My own *life*.'

Once before she had been prepared to marry him to save herself. She'd been *grateful* for his offer. She was better than that now. Stronger than that. She didn't need to marry at all and she certainly wasn't going to marry to be rescued and have to be grateful for the rest of her life. She wanted more now.

'No,' she repeated, tugging her hands free.

He made no attempt to recapture them, but stood silent, his mouth a hard line.

'Kit, you can't think I'd be a bad husband. That I'd—'

'You could be the most wonderful husband in the history of husbands.' He would be. She knew that. 'I still have no intention of marrying you or anyone else. Goodnight.'

Kit saw Martin off early the following morning. He said very little, seeming preoccupied, and declined breakfast, although he had accepted a cup of tea and her offer that he use one of Ignatius's shirts.

'You'll go over to the Phoenix after they shut? I'll come after dark.' His hand was already on the door handle.

'Yes. Psyché should be back this morning.' She said nothing about their argument the previous night. What was there to say?

'And you'll keep the doors locked.'

She bit back an annoyed rejoinder. He was worried about her, not treating her like an idiot.

'Yes.'

'Right. We talked about that. Sorry.'

Despite herself, she laughed. 'It's all right. I understand.'

He looked back with the faintest of smiles. 'Do you? Then please understand as well that I never meant to insult you last night.'

'Insult me? You didn't insult me.'

'Oh, yes, I did. By saying I'd marry you to save you. Again. What did you say to me once? For all the wrong reasons?'

Everything in her, all her certainty, shook at the look in his eyes.

'I might have spoken too early because of Carshalton, but believe me, Kit, that's not why I *want* to marry you.'

'You *want* to marry me?'

He stared at her for a moment, then said something she'd once heard when one of Carshalton's horses stepped on a groom's foot. His expression grim, he walked back to her and gripped her shoulders.

'If you don't want this, say so now, or, better yet, slap me.'

After a moment that seemed to last an eternity, he groaned and lowered his mouth to hers. Or he started to. Kit, her wits scrambled, stood on tiptoe and met him halfway.

Mouths met, stars, entire galaxies colliding as his mouth possessed hers, as she answered, opening to him and possessing in return. His taste exploded through her, dark, dangerous, and utterly safe. His arms a sure haven where she could still *be* and not be lost.

Breaking the kiss, he released her, stood looking as dazed as she felt. She wasn't entirely sure her legs were going to hold her.

'There. You tell me the answer.'

Five minutes after he closed the door behind him Kit finally remembered her question.

'You want to marry me?'

But through the leap of joy, another question stabbed: if Carshalton had been prepared to murder a child, how much danger would Martin be in if they married?

Up and down the street shutters were already opening and over the road the Phoenix was being readied for business. She saw Caleb washing down the windows, as Will strolled over to her with a pot of coffee.

'A quick walk when you've had this? I'm sure Moth needs one and you shouldn't go alone, even with her.'

Kit smiled, pushing the memory of the kiss from her mind. 'Yes, but I'm finishing the coffee first.' Maybe coffee would jolt her out of this foolish dream.

He grinned and occupied himself browsing the shelves as Kit gulped down the coffee.

Moth stood by the door, whining.

'Poor Moth.' Kit tied her bonnet strings while Will locked the door for her. 'She hasn't had a proper walk for days.' A walk would do her good as well. It might burn off some of her restlessness and confusion over that damned kiss.

'Take her out again later with Psyché,' Will said. 'She'll need one after the carriage ride in from Hampstead.'

The carriage drew up outside the Phoenix late in the morning. Mr Sayid had just arrived with the new rug, waving away Kit's admittedly feeble protest that she ought to pay for it.

'No, no. Selbourne was my friend. My good friend. You honour him by keeping his business going, making it your business. I honour you both with the rug. The other rug, it will clean, but you would always see it. So. We exchange.' He grinned. 'Buy another rug later. I'll charge you double to make up for it.'

And he patted her hands.

The bell jangled and Moth charged the door, uttering pleased barks.

'Good dog. Good morning, Mr Sayid.' Psyché smiled at the old rug dealer. 'I hear you're giving rugs away now.'

Sayid smiled. 'For this one, yes. Good morning to you both.'

As the door closed behind him, Psyché held out her arms, her own eyes full of tears. 'Kit, I'm so sorry.'

For a moment Kit held out, but she was not proof against Psyché's grief which matched her own.

When they'd mopped up the mutual tears, Psyché let out a breath.

'We knew it was coming, that he was dying. But this.' Her voice was desolate. 'When my great-uncle died it was a gentle thing, we…we could sit with him, *be* there for him.'

Kit swallowed. 'I…we were there. He knew we were there. He said my name. Held my hand for a moment.' Fresh tears threatened.

Psyché nodded. 'Will said you wanted to take Moth for a decent walk. Now?'

'Now.' The quiet morning dusting books and working on the accounts had given Kit time to think. To wonder. 'I need to talk to you. Or rather I need you to talk to me. I need your advice.'

They strolled around to Soho Square, Moth at their heels, while Psyché pondered Kit's question.

'Does making love *have* to lead to marriage?' She blew out a breath as Moth scattered a flock of pigeons. 'That depends on a number of things.'

'Go on.'

'Well, how you feel about the man for a start. And how he feels about you.'

Kit thought about that. 'So, if one of you wants to marry, but the other doesn't—'

'It's not going to end well, no.' She gave Kit a thoughtful look. 'We're talking about Lord Martin Lacy, aren't we?'

'Yes.'

'You two agreed that you couldn't marry.'

'Because of the danger Carshalton posed to

Harry, yes. I'm not sure that still applies, but—I still can't marry Martin.' She didn't think Psyché would be shocked. 'And we…we want each other.'

'If you think Harry is safe, why not talk to Huntercombe, and—?'

'My father probably had his brother murdered. How could I marry him? And there's something else, Carshalton wants me to marry Staverton. If I married Martin, would he be safe?'

'Have you discussed this with him? Are you thinking about having an affair with him? Has he offered that as an alternative?' Psyché's voice was very even.

'No. *He* said he wanted to marry me.' Kit scowled. 'I asked why and he kissed me.'

'Oh. I see. You're wondering about offering *him* an affair instead.' Psyché nodded. 'That's different.'

'Why?'

'Because, unfair though it is, you'd be the one taking all the risks.' Psyché shrugged. 'Such as pregnancy or simply having your reputation ruined if you aren't discreet enough. People might frown at him, issue a few *tut tuts*, but his life won't go down the drain. Women won't treat *him* as fair game because he succumbed to another woman's wiles.'

'I really don't think I've got many wiles, Psyché.'

Her friend laughed. 'Oh, yes, you do. Even if

you don't notice them. Anyway, my advice? Be honest with him. And remember that men have a very peculiar code of honour when it comes to virgins. Especially virgins they have feelings for.' She shot Kit a glance. 'I'm assuming you're still a virgin because I honestly can't think when you've had an opportunity to rectify that.'

Kit burst out laughing. 'Rectify?'

Psyché's bright dark eyes laughed back. 'Perhaps not the most romantic choice of words. Anyway, if you *are* going to make this outrageous offer, be open about it. Don't spring it on him when he's actually got his hands on you.'

Kit grimaced. 'I did think about just getting into bed with him, but it seemed a little unfair.'

Psyché let out a snort. 'That's definitely cheating.'

'And if he says no?'

Psyché smiled. 'What would he say or do if the positions were reversed? If *he* offered you an affair and *you* said no? If you think he wouldn't accept a refusal, then I can't imagine why you would even want to have an affair with him. You have to respect each other.'

'If you don't want this, say so now—or, better yet, slap me.'

She already knew the answer to that.

Practically speaking, then… 'I have to avoid pregnancy.' She knew it was possible.

Psyché nodded. 'Yes. And that may be a sticking point for him. He won't want to risk getting you with child.'

Kit let out a frustrated breath. 'There's the business, too. The trust means I continue to own it, but what if he were to forbid me to run it? It's all so complicated.'

Psyché gave her a friendly shoulder bump. 'No, it's not. You need to think about what, in your heart, you really want. Then make it happen. Always assuming he wants it, too.' Then she looked carefully at Kit. 'There's something else bothering you, isn't there?'

Kit nodded slowly. 'Yes. It feels wrong, but I can't talk about it. At least not yet.'

She needed to discuss it with Martin. Surely he would see that they should warn Will and Psyché about the danger that was closing in.

'All right.'

'All right?'

Psyché smiled. 'If it's not yours to tell, then you don't tell. You'll tell me when you can. In the meantime, practicalities. I have a jar of Queen Anne's lace seeds that I won't be needing for quite a while. I'll give them to you this evening. Just in case. Better to have them and not need them than the other way around.'

'Queen Anne's lace?' She knew the plant of course, with its delicate spiky leaves and graceful umbels of white flowers. 'Whatever for? In the herbals—' and they always had any number of them in the shop '—it says they're good for regulating or bringing down the menses.' As a young girl when her courses started, they had been painful. She and Agatha had looked through the herbals for something to help and the apothecary nearby had concurred with their choice. She hadn't needed them for years though.

'Correct.' Leaning close, Psyché said, 'And bringing down the menses is precisely what you want. Chewing the seeds is one of the simplest, most effective ways to avoid pregnancy.' She let out a breath. 'Something else you should consider, Kit—Martin Lacy from all accounts is no fool. If he wants to marry you, then he has already decided he doesn't give a rat's tail about your father or any danger a marriage to you might bring.'

Chapter Sixteen

Leaving his Whitehall office very late that after-noon, Martin stopped briefly at home to speak to his manservant and collect what he needed, then took a cab to Soho, his mind in turmoil.

Work had delivered a few surprises. He'd re-quested a meeting with his superior and Holford had listened to his outline of the situation, and his suspicions, in silence.

'So to all intents and purposes you're living with Ignatius Selbourne's great-niece to protect her from her own father.' He shook his head. 'Fine times we've come to. Very well. I want Selbourne's murderer brought to justice one way or another, and—'

'One way or another, sir?'

'Lacy, Carshalton has the sort of fortune that makes things go away. He got away with shoot-ing Huntercombe's secretary in the street fifteen months ago. Before that he attempted to murder a child—your own nephew. It didn't work so we couldn't charge him. At this point I'm not going to be too delicate about how we stop him. If indeed you and the girl are right. Talk to Barclay.'

'Barclay?'

'And his wife.'

Martin sat, stunned into silence and Holford raised his brows. 'Huntercombe has used Barclay for years to carry sensitive information. In fact, his current position as property manager and rent steward for Hunt is very useful. No one thinks anything of him riding out of London for a few days. You can trust the pair of them.'

He frowned. 'If you couldn't this entire situation would be impossible to contain. They have to know the danger that's brewing around them and you may believe I'll be speaking with Hunt.'

'Huntercombe works for you as well.'

Holford smiled. 'Not precisely. He was very useful to the Foreign Office years ago when I started out. Then he worked in the Home Office for a while. Let's just say he's still very helpful. As Ignatius was.'

'Understood, sir.'

Holford rose from Martin's visitor's chair. 'I wish I'd known the other morning that I wouldn't see Ignatius again. I'm going to miss him. Now...' His voice became clipped. 'This Beechworth case you think may be connected. You can't leave London, but I can send someone else to escort his widow and the coachman who drove him that night up to London discreetly. It's possible that there may be a little more information there if we ask the right questions.'

Martin was mulling over this conversation when he arrived in Soho. He wasn't entirely surprised to hear laughter coming from behind the shutters of the Phoenix. Tentatively he knocked on the door.

The peep opened, then swiftly shut and the door was opened.

'My lord.' Caleb stood there. 'Come in.'

'Thank you.' He removed his hat and stepped in.

Several tables had been pushed together and the remains of supper lay there.

Psyché Barclay rose. 'Lord Martin. My thanks for the help you gave Caleb the other day.'

He grimaced. 'I'd like to say it was nothing and Kit certainly had it under control. But...'

Looking at Kit, he said, 'You've said nothing of what we discussed last night.' He knew she wouldn't have. Despite her friendship with these people she would not have told something that was not hers to tell.

She shook her head. 'Of course not. I mean, I wanted to because—you're going to tell them?'

He nodded. 'I was going to anyway, but I have permission.'

Barclay raised his brows. 'Holford? You'd better sit down. Wine? Have you eaten?'

Martin sighed gratefully. 'To take your questions in order… Yes. Yes, please. And, no, I haven't. Thank you.'

Kit sipped tea as Martin devoured his supper and outlined his suspicions. Will and Psyché were utterly silent as he spoke. It was Caleb who broke the silence afterwards.

'Did this Lord Holford give permission for you to tell *me* all this?'

Martin frowned. 'To tell you the truth, Wright, it didn't occur to me to ask him about it. There was never any question that I was going to tell you.' He scrubbed his hands through his hair. 'You were the one who might have ended up dancing in mid-air over this. You have every right to know how they tried to use you. They must have had you watched for a while, seen when your day off was. Noticed that you often visited friends. That sort of thing. It was sheer bloody luck that Barclay took you with him that day and that you had absolutely unassailable witnesses to your whereabouts.'

'It's diabolical.' Psyché shivered and Will closed his hand tightly over hers. It made Kit's heart ache, the tangible intimacy between them.

'Yes. A good word for it.' Martin picked up his wine glass, took a swallow. 'Wright, I'm sorry, but I have to ask you to stay close to home unless you're with Barclay. Don't leave the immediate area and don't take any risks. Even visiting your friends may not be safe. If they were to snatch you to get you out of the way, then stage something they could accuse you of—you see where I'm going with that?'

The boy scowled. 'Yeah. I'm a prisoner then.'

Martin nodded. 'I'm afraid so. As Kit is.'

Caleb stared across at her. 'What? They think *you* look like an assassin?'

'No.' She swallowed. 'They think I look like a convenient heiress so Carshalton can continue to control Staverton that way.'

Caleb clenched his fists. 'It's wrong. It's all wrong.'

She couldn't agree more.

'That's the one thing I'm struggling to understand,' Psyché admitted. 'Lucius is a wart. But I honestly can't see him setting Harbury up to be murdered.'

'Kit wondered if it wasn't meant to end in murder, but only a failed attempt.' Martin nodded at Will's hiss. 'That would have been enough on its own to put Wright in prison and ruin anyone who could be connected to it. Would he have agreed to that? Would he have fallen for it?'

Psyché shut her eyes briefly. 'Oh, yes. I can see that. Then he's trapped. He can't talk without implicating himself.'

Trapped.

The word nagged at Kit. How badly had Staverton incriminated himself? The conversation ebbed and flowed around her, but she deliberately blanked it out, put it outside her thinking.

The letter implicating Harbury—how many people could have written it? She knew Carshalton's hand; it wasn't his. Unless he had deliberately disguised his hand, but it had looked too, well, fluent, for that.

'Psyché?'

'Oh, you are alive.' Psyché grinned at her.

Martin rubbed a hand over his mouth to hide his smile. He was fairly sure you could have let off a fire cracker behind Kit a moment ago and she wouldn't have noticed.

'What?' Kit flushed. 'I'm sorry. That was rude of me. I was thinking. There can't be very many people Carshalton would have trusted to write that letter, I shouldn't think.'

Martin stared, arrested. 'No. Not many at all. Where is this leading you?'

Kit frowned. 'It was an educated hand. A gentleman's hand, would you say?'

'Yes. I would.'

She bit her lip. 'I didn't ask what you did with it, but have you got it with you.'

He nodded. 'Yes. You want to look at it?'

'I think Psyché should look at it.'

'My God!' Will set his wine glass down hard. 'You think—'

'You think Lucius might have written it?' Psyché clenched her fist on the table. 'He *couldn't* be such a criminal idiot!'

Holford had told him, point blank, that he could trust the Barclays. Martin brought a small leather folder out of his pocket and opened it to reveal the letter. He spread it out on the table and Kit pored over it. What was she seeing? He'd read the letter for clues and found nothing beyond that the author was educated.

'The W. W. for the signature—you see? It does look very like how Mr Wilberforce writes a W, but the rest of the writing is not his.'

Martin looked over at her. The penmanship, not the words. 'You know his writing?'

'Oh, yes. He is one of our customers. He comes into the shop sometimes, but he often simply writes asking us if we have, or to find, a particular volume.'

'A man may disguise his writing, Kit.' Psyché rose from her seat and came closer. She leaned over Kit's shoulder. 'But then he'd disguise the Ws as well, wouldn't he?'

She was silent for a moment, but Martin saw her eyes widen, grief come into them. 'Will. Oh, Will. What has the fool done?'

Barclay came around the table and put his arm around her. 'It's his writing, love?'

'I think so. Wait. Hetty gave me a pile of my Great-Uncle Theo's correspondence to go through.

There are some letters in there from Lucius. And…
and something more. I'll fetch them.'

She hurried back through the shop and disappeared.

Barclay spoke quietly. 'It's not Lucius Staverton
she cares about. It's her cousin, his daughter Hetty.
And their great-uncle, Theo Staverton, who raised
them. She'll hate that his name is sullied by this.'

Psyché came back with a sheaf of papers. She
sat down and rifled through them. 'Here. This is
one from Lucius. It's only a couple of years old.'
A tear slid down her cheek. 'Except for the Ws,
the writing—' Her voice broke.

'It's identical.' Martin scanned the two letters.
'I'm sorry.'

Kit went to her friend and put one hand on her
shoulder. Psyché reached up and gripped it. With
her free hand she drew out another letter.

'This one. Look at it.'

'It's a different hand,' Kit started.

'Yes. It's from Hetty to Uncle Theo when she
was staying at Highwood shortly before her marriage and he had come into London. Hold it up to
the light. Look at the watermark.'

Kit did so and Martin could see what Psyché
had seen. 'It's identical.'

'It's the paper Uncle Theo always kept in the
library at Highwood. Hetty still orders it. Here.'
She pulled out another letter. 'This is the note

Hetty sent me the other day, asking me to come to her. It's the same paper.'

They left soon after, Psyché slipping the jar of Queen Anne's lace seeds to Kit under cover of a hug. 'Dosage and instructions inside the lid.'

Kit tucked them away into the pocket inside her cloak. 'Thank you. Psyché, I'm so—'

'Don't apologise, Kit. It's not your fault. Lucius has brought this on himself.'

'I can still be sorry for your grief for your cousin, for your great-uncle's memory.'

Psyché hugged her again. 'I know. Thank you.'

Farewells said, they walked across the road.

Martin unlocked the door saying, 'I'll need to write this up for Holford.'

She swung her cloak from her shoulders. 'Of course.'

Upstairs, she hung the cloak behind the door. 'You can use my desk.'

After opening the window, Kit settled into the chair that had been hers ever since she had returned to live with Ignatius. So many nights she'd sat here as a child reading while Ignatius worked at the desk with his ledgers and Agatha sewed.

This past year she and Ignatius had worked together as he tutored her in running the business. She had always thought that when Ignatius died she would have to become accustomed to his chair remaining empty. Ignatius had said something about that when Agatha died…

Chairs aren't really empty. There's always the memory of someone. And chairs are patient things; they're happy to wait for the next person.

She had not expected, nor even wanted, there to be a next person for Ignatius's chair.

Across the road Psyché and Will had their window open, too. Music drifted over. Not modern music, but something older. Psyché had a fondness for older music and this sounded like Bach. Kit had never heard of him before, but Huntercombe had given Psyché two volumes of his keyboard music as a wedding gift last year along with the harpsichord.

This particular piece was unfamiliar and there was that slight carefulness in the playing, as well as stops and starts, repeats, that told her that Psyché was playing at sight and learning. Perhaps trying to forget her pain in the music. Kit's ability at the keyboard was negligible, but she knew enough to recognise a fugue, to hear the strands of the melody twining in and out.

A slight pause and the music began again, a single strand of melody at first, then slipping into a lower register while a new melody wove about it. Thread after thread, weaving a pattern that depended on each independent part, different equalities combining so that one part ripped out would destroy the whole. Just as Lucius Staverton's actions threatened to ruin his family.

How often in the last year had she and Ignatius sat in this room surrounded by books and listened to Psyché's music? She glanced at the clock, her book unheeded in her lap. Soon, too soon, Psyché would finish for the night. She would hear the window sash squeak as it closed and she would know that Psyché and Will were going to bed.

She hoped Will could comfort Psyché. Their marriage was full of comfort—she thought for them it was like this music: equal, interdependent parts creating something strong and lovely that could stand fast against anything. Would marriage to Martin have been like that?

If not for Will and Psyché, she reminded herself, she would have found out what it would have been like being married to Staverton. No autonomy, no independence. She would have been utterly subordinate to his control—a meek accompaniment at best, perhaps not even that. The panic struck and she fought for breath, her fingers trembling as the music wove its eternal logic about her.

'Kit?'

She looked at him.

'Are you all right?'

'All right?' she parried, breathing in the reassuring patterns of the music, gripping the book to hide her trembling.

'You haven't turned a page for at least ten minutes and your hands shook. You're worried for Psyché?'

And she'd thought him engrossed in his work.

'I was listening to the music. Thinking about her.'

The moment stretched between them. He'd been supporting his head, hand to his temple, the way he did when he was utterly focused on something. Now his hand shifted to his chin as he smiled at her and her heart shook.

'I won't ask you to read aloud then.'

Her gaze fell to the page—

Why out of all Shakespeare's poetry did she have to be reading this sonnet on the endurance of love? Even as the question coalesced in her mind, over the road the fugue was gathering all the threads together, bringing them to their inevitable solution and close. Life wasn't like a fugue; it was often messy and incomplete. It was untidy with threads left hanging loose.

The fugue ended and his smile, the one that undid her, deepened. 'My luck's in. Will you read?'

She had God knew how many poems in the vault of her mind. She could recite any one of them. He didn't have to know.

But she had sworn to herself once that she would never lie to him again. Neither directly, by omission, nor by what she always thought of as weasel words. If they could have nothing else between them they could have honesty and that would have to be enough. And after all she knew why she was reading this particular sonnet. Why, despite it being lodged so deep in memory and heart, the volume now fell open at this page. And perhaps it was the best way to lead in to what she wished to ask him.

'"Let me not to the marriage of true minds admit impediments—"'

The familiar words pierced Martin's heart as she continued, words he had heard so often and only fully understood one winter's day when his world had shattered in loss. His hand slipped into his pocket, closed on the snuffbox Selbourne had left for him...

'"It is the star to every wand'ring barque—"'

Her voice broke and she fell silent.

The line he'd had inscribed on her betrothal ring.

Shaken, he stared at her. A tear slid down her cheek. Across the road someone closed a window with a creak and faint thump. And Kit, the self-possessed and independent, wept. Not for Ignatius Selbourne this time.

She wept for him.

'Kit—'

'I'm sorry. I should not have—'

'No.' He hardly knew he was on his feet until he was crouched beside her chair, her hands gripped in his and the sonnets tumbled to the floor. 'Don't you dare apologise. Not for that. Never for that.'

For the past year he'd drifted bereft on a lonely sea because the pole star, his truth north, had been hidden from him. But perhaps not utterly lost.

He took out the snuff box. 'This wasn't what Ignatius wanted me to have.'

'What? Yes, he—'

'It was this.' He opened the box and took out the ring. 'I left it with him. For you. If…if something happened to me, I wanted you to have it.'

Kit stared at the ring he held. The ring he'd given her on that winter's day before their worlds had shattered.

'You kept it.'

'I kept it for you. It was yours. A pledge.'

She reached out, touched the ring. 'A pledge of our betrothal, yes. But—'

'Not only that, sweet.' He was going to say it. Finally he was going to risk it. 'Why do you think I chose that line?'

Her breath jerked in. 'You can't. Martin, it was only ever supposed to be—'

'A marriage of convenience. I know.' He took her left hand, slid the ring back where it belonged. 'I was never very good at doing only what I was supposed to do. It became more.'

He turned her hand over, pressed a gentle kiss into the palm. 'I love you, Kit. I loved you when I first gave you that ring, although I didn't say it. I'm saying it now when I give it back to you.'

'Martin, I can't marry you.'

He took a deep breath. Everything in him braced against the pain. 'Harry?'

'No. I think Harry would be safe, but I still won't marry you.'

He'd misread her. He could ask why, but he wasn't sure he could bear the answer. 'Very well. But I want you to wear that ring for as long as you wish. I'm yours. I don't think that will ever change.'

He should release her hand and step back. Hell, he should never have stepped forward, let alone spoken.

'I'm sorry, Kit.'

She smiled, her eyes on his. 'I'm not.'

For a moment he simply didn't understand. And then it was too late. She leaned forward, cupping his cheek with her free hand, and kissed him. A gentle kiss, the sweetest, lightest feathering of soft lips that a man could imagine. Innocent.

His response was anything but. His arms closed around, his body alight as he drew her close, and deepened the kiss as he had done that morning. And again she answered, her mouth softening, moving under his, opening to the press of his tongue. For long moments there was nothing else. Just Kit, in his arms, her arms about him, their mouths united in a tender dance there in the warm firelight.

Desire rose, hammering in every vein, an urgent ache in his body, a longing that burned through every layer of fabric.

Something bumped between them. Slowly sanity reasserted a semblance of control and he broke the kiss to glance down.

Moth stood there, her bright curious gaze on them, tail waving.

'Moth. Go…go and…sit.'

Kit's dazed voice brought him fully to his senses.

We can't. I *can't.*

She was an innocent. How could she possibly know where they would end if this continued? He was supposed to be protecting her. Not seducing her. Even if he hadn't given his word to Hunter-combe, to Selbourne, Kit deserved better of him than that.

Tell the girl you love her one minute, and ruin her the next? Leave her with no choice?

Thank God for the dog. Eventually, a long way in the future, he might actually mean that.

'I'm sorry, Kit. I shouldn't have touched you. Not…not like that.'

Those smoky eyes cleared a little, considered. 'Not like what?'

Like a lover. Like I have every right to kiss you until the world burns around us.

* * *

The ring on her finger shimmered in the candlelight and she remembered the first time he'd given it to her on a chilly winter's day, drawn into the hedgerow in his gig on the way to Isleworth. He'd let her read the inscription before putting it on her finger and her heart had turned over. She'd thought she'd loved him then and she had.

But after all the grief of losing him, and now the bittersweetness of having him back in her life, she thought that old love had been a pale, weak sort of thing. Yes, she'd loved him, but she'd had no real choice about accepting him even if she hadn't. And she'd thought the inscription a mere romantic gesture, made because he knew she loved reading and poetry and wanted to please her.

It had been more. It had always been more.

Now she had a choice, and she knew better. Knew he loved her and that what she felt for him now went far beyond what she'd felt then. She couldn't let marriage to her endanger him.

They didn't need marriage, did they? Couldn't love be enough?

'No. We can't marry.' She saw the pain her words caused him, saw it in his eyes, in the bitter twist of his mouth, and felt it in her own heart. 'But we can still be together.'

He gripped her hands again, his fingers strong yet oh, so gentle. What would they be like, those strong, gentle hands, on her body? She wanted to know. Wanted to know what his body might feel like under her hands. Wanted the wild beat of her heart, the leap in her blood, the fizzing dance of nerves under her skin to continue. She wanted to give him the same things, give herself, give him everything.

His voice was hoarse. 'No, Kit. I can't. Once this mess is over, once you're safe, it would be easier…less painful, for us not to meet very often.'

She'd thought that once, too. Or she'd tried to think it.

The lie, as well as the pain, was there in his eyes. She had told herself the same lie for over a year. It wasn't that she hadn't been happy, for she had been. Happy and contented in her life with Ignatius. Fulfilled, even, in her work so that happiness had been there for her every day. But under it all had lingered the pain of loss. It had always been there, tempering everything she did, everything she learned and achieved.

He spoke again, his voice not quite steady. 'Seeing each other constantly and not…not—'

'Being lovers?' she suggested.

'Yes. That.' Clipped, harsh. As though he couldn't bear to think about it.

She took a deep breath. She truly understood now how foolish simply walking into his room and getting into his bed would have been. This had to be open and honest between them.

'We can be.'

'What?'

'We can be lovers. I'm offering to—no, I'm *asking* you to be my lover.'

Not his mistress, never that. But his lover, his equal? She could do that.

'Kit. Damn it. If you don't wish to marry me, one day the man you *do* marry—'

'I'm not going to marry, Martin.'

'Sweetheart, you can't know that.'

'Oh, yes, I can.' She had never wanted to marry, per se. She had wanted to marry *him*. And since she couldn't, then it wasn't going to happen. But that didn't mean she couldn't love him. And those were words she mustn't say to him. 'And even if I did, what happens here between us—'

'*Nothing* is going to happen.'

He sounded very sure of that and if he held to it then she must respect it. But she could at least explain why she would never marry anyone else.

'Very well.' She took a careful breath. 'But if it did, then it would be none of his business. Any more than your former lovers are my business. A man to whom it mattered would not be one I could trust. My body would not be the only thing he wanted to own.'

'Kit, if you mean the business and Selbourne's fortune... I understand Huntercombe is your trustee, or one of them.'

She tilted her head—he seemed to be choosing

his words very carefully. 'Yes. The other is his friend, Lord Cambourne, if it matters.'

Martin grimaced. 'Cambourne, too? Bloody hell, I'd be a dead man walking if either of them discovered I'd seduced you. And that's after Barclay finished with me.'

'Well, you aren't.' Now she saw at least part of the problem. 'You stopped well short of that. *I* asked *you*. And I'm not seducing you either.'

Laughter leapt in his eyes. 'Aren't you?'

Uncertainty churned in her belly.

'I don't think so.' Honesty, she reminded herself. 'I thought about it, but I didn't know how to go about it, except getting into bed with you and—'

'That would have worked.' He shut his eyes. 'And why I'm telling you that I have not the least notion.'

'Oh. Well, I decided that was cheating and Psyché agreed.'

A choked laugh escaped him. 'God help me.'

'Anyway, I'm not seducing you, I'm asking. You can refuse.'

He let out a breath and tried again. 'Kit, society has rules about this sort of thing—*gentlemen* have rules. About…about innocents.'

'Would it help if I went out and lost my virginity with someone else?'

'What? *No!*'

'I'm not part of that world any longer,' she said

quietly. 'I'm no longer Catherine Carshalton, heiress for sale. I'm Kit Selbourne, independent businesswoman, and I intend to stay that way. I'm not going to marry. I won't risk it.'

'Kit, any trust Selbourne and Huntercombe had drawn up to protect your property if you married—'

'It's not merely about owning Selbourne's, or about the money being mine.' Could she make him understand how she felt? That it was more than owning the business. 'I belong here. Working here, running it now. Making decisions. I couldn't do that with a husband who at any moment might pull out his legal right to order me not to. Even to force me to live somewhere else. This is my home. My freedom. I won't risk it. Ever.'

She had said enough. She had offered and she couldn't press him. What had Psyché said?

You have to respect each other.

She took a deep breath and picked up her candle. 'Goodnight, Martin. I'll see you in the morning.'

Clicking her fingers for Moth, Kit started for the door. She had to respect herself, too. Asking was one thing, begging was quite another.

Chapter Seventeen

She was nearly to the door before he understood what the problem was. Or he thought he did.

'Kit, wait.'

She looked back, her hand on the door handle, head tilted.

What to say? Because what she was offering— her trust, her heart—was more than he deserved and he wanted it more than his next heartbeat. Yet she didn't want to marry because she was afraid of losing her independence. Somehow he had to show her that she could trust him.

'What if there were a child?'

And why wasn't he saying *no* and going to bed by himself? He didn't want to look too closely at his reasons for not refusing her outright.

'Has that never bothered you before?'

He'd always been careful. He'd used a cundum, finished outside the woman, or they'd employed less risky ways to pleasure each other.

'Yes, it has,' he admitted. Honesty, he owed her honesty. 'I've been careful.'

She flushed a little. 'I can…there are things I can use. Queen Anne's lace seeds, if you chew them—I mean if *I* chew them.'

'Some of those sorts of remedies are no more than old wives' tales,' he said. 'I'm not risking your safety on—'

'This one works. I asked.'

She walked out of the room, the dog at her heels, and a moment later he heard the creak of the stairs.

Damn it. This was madness.

The cat twisting in and out of his ankles, Martin finally walked up the stairs and past Kit's closed door to his own room. He stared at his door. Why the hell couldn't she have just come and got into bed with him?

He let out a breath. He knew why. Because she had been determined not to manipulate him. She insisted on thinking for herself and accorded him the same respect.

Because she was Kit.

The cat miaowed and he opened the door.

Decision made.

Knocking on Kit's door ten minutes later, minus his boots and coat, he wondered if he had lost his mind. She'd had time to think. If she had changed her mind—

'Come…come in.'

The room was lit only by the single candle and the fire she had kindled. And she stood there, eyes wide, staring at him, clutching at the unlaced gown she was clearly about to take off.

The dog sprawled by the fire fixed him with her lambent gaze.

'I… I thought you were going to bed.'

He smiled. 'I am. I hope. If you still want me?' He shot a glance at the dog. 'Is she going to object?'

'What? Oh. No, no. Moth, stay.'

He waited. 'Then, it's yes—you want this? Me?'

Her lips parted. Lord, she was lovely, standing there, wondering what the hell she was meant to do next.

'I—yes. Yes, I do.' She sounded as though she were having trouble catching her breath.

He let out an unsteady breath of his own. 'Then will you permit me to help you with that?'

'Help me?'

'Your gown, sweetheart.' He had never wanted anything more in his life.

Oh.

Once every gown she owned had required a maid to get her in and out of them. Even her stays had laced at the back and needed help. It had been stifling, like being in a silken cage. Nowadays she could manage all her gowns and undergarments for herself and she loved that independence.

She'd never considered being undressed by a man. Her breath shortened and she moistened her lips. Being undressed by Martin…it would be like the prelude to one of those fugues Psyché loved.

He came to her and even as she wondered if he'd simply rip the gown off, somehow she was in his arms and he was kissing her again. And this time it was different.

This time they weren't going to stop.

His mouth, hot and hungry on hers, his tongue licking into her lips, teasing them open, their mouths a mutual possession of heat. Wicked hands that caressed and teased as he loosened her gown so that it slid down, catching at her hips for a moment until she wriggled so that it fell to the ground, leaving her in her shift and stays.

Her breath shuddered in. What—? Her fingers found the buttons of his waistcoat. Frowning, she began on them and discovered that her fingers were trembling. One large, warm hand covered them. Her cheeks burned—was she doing something wrong?

'Sweetheart, if I'm going too fast…?'

At the faint concern in his voice, she found the courage to look up.

'Fast?'

His fingers tightened. 'You're shaking.'

The worry in his gilded brown eyes banished her own.

'No. It's just… I want this too much.'

He bent to brush a kiss to her temple. 'There is no "too much", love,' he murmured. 'Not between us.'

And still she hesitated. Theory was all very well, but all those shibboleths about how a woman should behave—'I'm not being shameless?'—were the very devil to cast off.

His eyes danced. 'God, I hope so!'

He flicked one of the waistcoat buttons open. 'Have at it.'

Laughing now, she undid the rest between kisses until he shrugged it off to join her gown. And somehow his shirt had come out of his breeches and she could slide her hands under it to explore the warm, muscled glory of his back.

She realised with a shock that he had been equally busy with her laces as her stays loosened.

'Lift your arms, love.'

Her breath caught as she did so and he eased the stays off over her head, leaving her in only her shift.

She murmured a protest as he eased back. But it was only to lift her into his arms. She clutched at him as her head whirled.

'Martin!'

He smiled down at her. 'We're going to do this properly. Starting now.'

She was reasonably sure what they were about to do qualified as extremely improper under the circumstances.

He laid her on the bed and looked down at her for a moment before joining her.

Slow. He—*they*—would take this first time slowly. For both of them. He lowered his mouth to hers—

'I thought we would both be naked.'

Laughter shook him, eased some of the tension in his body, as he raised his head again. 'Do you ever stop thinking?'

She frowned, taking it quite seriously. Fascinated, he played with the silky tendrils of hair drifting about her face.

'No,' she said at last. 'Never. At least, not if I'm awake.'

It was true. Selbourne had raised her to think for herself, to analyse and judge; she lived a life of the mind as much as any scholar. And beyond that? He thought it had been her protection, her defence against her father. It was part of herself that she had been able to hold hidden and inviolate.

'I'm going to change that,' he murmured, trailing kisses beneath her ear, absorbing the faint traces of lavender and soap, and the scent that was Kit and Kit alone. A sweetness that called to him more surely than any perfume. Tremors shook her, little quakes of shock that melted through her to him.

'You...don't like me thinking?'

Ah. He nipped her earlobe, licked the spot and nuzzled as she gasped again.

'I love you thinking.' He smiled down at her. 'Your mind is a complete fascination to me.' He slid his hand down over the soft linen of her shift, learning the slight weight of her breast, the curve of her waist. Another tremor shook her and he brushed a kiss to her temple. 'But now?' He fought the selfish urge to have more, to have everything. 'Right now, tonight? This is for feeling.' *For love.*

'But—' she moved restlessly against him, burning holes in his control '—are we going to be naked?'

'Eventually. There's no rush.' Or there damned well shouldn't be, never mind what his body wanted. There *wouldn't* be. Not this time. And if he unbuttoned his breeches, let alone had her naked now, he'd be inside her before *he* could think.

The thought of being inside her, feeling her sweet and wet around him... His arms tightened and she gave a little startled huff, and pressed closer.

'How are you going to change that?'

What? Change—? Ah...

'Like this.' He lowered his mouth to hers, brushing gentle kisses back and forth, teasing, luring her response, until those soft lips parted and she was open to him. He licked into the honeyed taste of her, taking her mouth deeply, completely. And she answered, her tongue dancing with his in the sweet advance and retreat.

Gently he cupped one breast, encompassing that tender, female weight. Her gasp burned through him and he smiled through the kiss, stroking the bare upper curve of her breast. He eased the linen down, found the sensitive peak. His cock hardened even more, aching as her nipple contracted to his touch.

He caught it between thumb and forefinger, squeezed. She moaned, her slight body bowing up in a wild plea for more. And God help him, *he* needed more. Skin, he needed bare skin, the naked softness of her breast in his hand. Now. Five minutes ago.

He released her breast, devouring the soft murmur of protest, and slipped his hand beneath the hem of her chemise, finding the silkiness of her bare thigh.

'Lift your bottom for me.'

She obeyed and he slowly slid the shift up until it bunched around her waist. Each heartbeat hammered through him as her eyes opened and she sat up, her wide gaze on his face. Slowly she set her hands to the linen, lifted it slowly, wriggling a little as it came off, leaving her naked before him. His mouth dried. Slight, pale curves, small breasts that he ached to touch.

He reached for her—

'Your turn,' she whispered, reaching for his shirt. Slender fingers unlaced his cuffs, every featherlight touch a burning delight. He held utterly still as she tugged the shirt from the waistband of his breeches.

A moment later it was gone and her eyes widened as she sat up, staring.

'That's—you've got a dragon on your arm?'

He'd forgotten that. 'A wager with an officer on the ship I sailed with.'

'So you lost the wager?' Curious fingers stroked the dragon, tracing the sinuous curve back up his right arm.

He grinned. 'Certainly not. He wagered a hundred that I wouldn't dare and another hundred that, even if I did, I couldn't remain silent while it was being done.'

'But why a dragon particularly?'

'Because...' he took her back into his arms, felt her tremble '...the ship was HMS *Dragon*. And right now, the dragon is hungry.'

Skin to heated skin, he lowered to the bed with her and took her mouth again.

He slid down the softness of her body, trailing hungry kisses. He found the sweetness of her breasts with his mouth and licked one peak. Blew on it.

'Martin.'

Shocked wonder in her voice.

'Trust me.' He took the peak into his mouth and sucked gently.

Kit was lost and cried out, as pleasure speared her from breast to her aching centre. His hand slid between her thighs and at that gentle urging she parted them, wanting everything she had thought impossible. His mouth came back to hers, taking her helpless murmurs as he found all the secrets, tender kisses and the searing intimacy of his touch there where everything burned and cried out for more. He gave her more and shock slammed through her as she felt her own slickness.

'Martin?'

'Sweetheart?'

She fought to clear her mind as he stroked, circled, and her body ached for more. 'I'm wet. Is that—'

'Yes. It's beautiful. You're beautiful.'

The low masculine growl stroked her, too. Wicked velvet over every trembling nerve. She forgot worry and if her name had been more than three letters… His mouth closed over her breast again, and her name was gone too as he pressed gently between her legs, parting them.

And at last he was there, cradled between her thighs. Heat burned, urgency was a living flame and through it all one thing sang—this would be for her. He eased his cock against that softest flesh, felt the dizzying give and yielding of her body, the wet heat that beckoned him on.

'Kit.' He barely knew his own voice. Harsh and rough with the effort of control. 'Look at me. Are you still sure? You want *this*?'

Her eyes opened and he nudged into her, ready to stop if she asked for that.

She stared up at him, the hard planes of his face, fierce restraint carved in every line. His weight, hard and male, held her. And she knew in that fragile moment poised between *now* and *then*, that if she said *no* he would stop. Already she could feel him, his shaft pressed into her entrance. And it felt as if this couldn't possibly work, that there couldn't be room because it already hurt.

She reached up, traced the tense line of his jaw with shaking fingertips, as he held utterly still.

'I want you. All of you.' Everything. Even the pain.

It did hurt as he came into her so slowly, so gently, and her body trembled at the promise of this possession that couldn't possibly work.

'*Damn.*' A strangled curse. Then, 'I'm sorry.'

His mouth came down on hers and hurt flared, bright and sharp, as he came fully into her, his mouth taking her shocked gasp. For a moment he stayed very still, his mouth a whisper on hers, tender and comforting. Pain faded, lost in the delight of finally being his. The joy of him being hers.

Experimentally, she moved a little, a lift of her hips against him that drew an answering shift of his body within her. Pleasure rekindled even as he groaned and stilled again. She wriggled, wanting more.

'Kit.' His hands cradling her cheeks trembled. 'Stay still. I hurt you.'

Love flooded her. 'That was then. Not now.'

He raised his head a little, smiling down at her. 'Not now?' He eased back and the careful movement splintered pleasure inside her. He pressed back in and she nearly died.

Yes, oh, yes!

Had she said it aloud? She wasn't sure, but he moved, deep and sure. Her body answered, the world contracted to him, her, them, the rhythm of their loving, their frantic breaths and murmurs, and the rising beat of pleasure. Possession, absolute and devastating. Not just being possessed, but possessing in turn, her body leaping to flame with his, dancing ever closer to an unimaginable edge. And then she was there, everything in her that she was or could be wanting this. She took it, took that final leap as the world stormed burning through her.

Even then she understood as Martin pulled from her and collapsed, shuddering, to spend beside her.

He lay quietly, aware as never before of the woman cradled in his arms, relaxed against him, her cheek pillowed on his shoulder, as he rested his cheek against the soft tousled curls. Slowly their bodies cooled and he reached to drag the tangled bedding up over them. With an odd little purr in her throat, she snuggled even closer, her silken skin the sweetest caress he'd ever known. Overwhelmed with emotion, he turned his head slightly to press a kiss to her temple.

Kit. His Kit. If he couldn't show her that she could trust him… Her decision. It had to be her decision. He could neither manipulate nor coerce. He could only accept.

He was nearly asleep when she spoke.

'How did Moth know you? And how did Ignatius have the ring?'

His arms tightened around her as he confessed.

She was silent for a moment. Then, 'You came after me? You came here that Christmas night?'

He kissed her temple again. 'I had to know you were safe. That you'd reached Selbourne. It wasn't much.'

'You sent Carshalton and Staverton on a wild goose chase.' She sat up, the bedclothes sliding off her, a pale sylph in the firelit shadows. 'Ignatius said they followed a lead out of London and couldn't get back for three days because of the snow. That was what bought enough time for Will and Psyché to get me out. Otherwise…' She bent to kiss him. 'Martin, without that time Carshalton would have called in the Runners much sooner. And they'd have caught me.' She kissed him again. 'Thank you.'

He drew her back down to him and she nestled close, skin to skin.

He'd never be able to let her go, so he had to trust that she would come to understand he would never try to curb her. And then there was Carshalton. Carshalton, who still wanted his only child in a marriage *he* controlled. In this world wealth was always power. To keep Kit safe he had to bring down one of the wealthiest men in Britain.

Chapter Eighteen

Martin gave Holford his report and the letters Psyché had provided without explanation.

Frowning, the older man read them, his face becoming grimmer.

Finally, he handed the papers back to Martin. 'This is a disaster. You have evidence here that a member of the House of Lords has involved himself in the assassination of another member of the House—his son-in-law, no less! And that he wrote a letter falsely implicating a member of the House of Commons.'

'Yes, sir.'

Holford shut his eyes. 'A disaster,' he repeated.

Martin agreed, but— 'Psyché Barclay believes Staverton may have been duped by Carshalton. That he was not expecting Harbury's actual death.'

Holford's eyes snapped open. 'I hardly see that arguing his stupidity as a mitigating factor—ah!' He drummed his fingers on his desk. 'You think that this might be used to put a little pressure on him. Good thinking. Leave it with me. We're going to need a little delicacy here. A hint dropped, let him stew in it for a while, then offer him a chance to save himself. Is that what you're thinking?'

Martin grimaced. 'Something like that. I'd prefer to see him hang, but—'

'Be realistic, boy. A trial, literally before his peers, in the Lords? I'm ashamed to say the odds are we'd acquit him.' Holford smiled thinly, 'Social, and possible financial, ruin is a more effective hammer with which to break him. Now, if we could only identify the man who was used to murder Ignatius but Staverton may be able to furnish us with a name.'

Kit stood in the rain the following morning, alone among the mourners as Ignatius was laid to rest. High and low, his friends had turned out to farewell him. Will and Psyché stood with her. They had agreed it was better if Martin stayed away, rather than drawing attention to his interest. Impossible to know what might or might not get back to Carshalton.

Some of the mourners Kit had never seen before. Others she knew only slightly. Yet others were very familiar. Lord Huntercombe attended with a thin man he presented simply as Holford.

Holford bowed over her hand. 'He spoke of you often, Miss Selbourne. I'll miss him.' And very softly, 'Believe me, we're going to get to the bottom of this.'

Huntercombe took her hands. 'When all this is over, come out to Isleworth again.'

She smiled. 'In the summer. Thank you.'

As the two men walked away, a woman all in heavy black and veiled, came close and spoke. *'Mes condoléances.'*

The unconvincing French accent was familiar. Kit found a smile. *'Merci, Madame Mireille. Vous êtes très gentille.'*

The madam of a local brothel, Mireille had been a customer of Selbourne's for years while always remaining discreet about it. Kit was never quite sure how much French Mireille actually spoke, but thought telling her she was very kind would be safe enough.

Mireille inclined her head. *'Merci, petite.'* She strolled on, not speaking to anyone else, as others came to speak to Kit.

Will and Psyché were last, waiting back until the graveyard of St Anne's had cleared.

'Was that Mireille earlier?' Psyché murmured as they walked with Kit towards the gate.

'Mmm.'

Psyché slipped her arm around Kit. 'He would have loved that. I hope the archdeacon didn't realise, though.'

Kit leaned her head on Psyché's shoulder. 'She was fond of Ignatius. That's all that matters.'

* * *

A week later, Martin sat bemused, listening to the flow of conversation around him. He had enjoyed convivial evenings with friends before, of course. Laughter, ribaldry, friendly chaffing. But not much since the scandal. Some of his one-time friends, those who didn't cut him out, were rather awkward around him now.

He was an embarrassment. Oh, his close friends might have dismissed the whispers and outright accusations, but their wider acquaintance still murmured. It had been easier to withdraw, to decline the increasingly sporadic invitations and spare his friends the difficulty of knowing who else to invite.

But here in Psyché Barclay's shop, with several tables pushed together to accommodate them, he was welcome. The fare was simple—whatever hearty soup or stew she had put together over the course of the day. Perhaps a sweet pie to finish with and a decent cheese. Here he had unexpectedly found friends and contentment from the first.

For the past week since he'd gone to Kit's bed that contentment had deepened, despite the worry hanging over them. He belonged again. To Kit. With Kit. He enjoyed sitting with her in the parlour above the shop if she had work to go over. He often had other work of his own for that matter. One of his jobs was translating, occasionally deciphering if a coded letter was intercepted by the post office.

He shared her bed each night and continued to

finish outside her. While he hoped her use of the seeds would work, he would damn well do what he could to keep her safe. He asked her about her work, showed her as clearly as he could that he not only didn't mind, but approved. The last thing he wanted was their hand forced by a pregnancy.

That Kit might feel forced to marry him because of that was unbearable.

As usual when he arrived at the Phoenix, he had found the little group already at supper. Caleb had opened the door to him, gestured him in.

Will Barclay rose smiling from the table.

'Come, sit down.'

Psyché simply filled the extra bowl and passed it down the table to him along with a friendly smile. Kit cut him a generous slice of bread and Caleb asked if he preferred wine or ale.

He had been welcomed to their table and into their group without hesitation from the first. Even the boy, Caleb, he realised fast enough, was not viewed as a servant, but more as a younger brother. Although he insisted on using *Miss Psyché* and *Mr Will*, *Miss Kit*, it was very clear that they all viewed him as an equal.

At first Caleb had been silent and wary with him, but over the past week the boy's stiffness and diffidence around him had eased. Or perhaps that had been his own discomfort—the brutal knowledge that many of his own countrymen, his society and culture deemed Caleb's family and culture as *less*. That they looked on him as something not quite human, a creature to be trained.

And there was Kit. Tonight she sat across from him, her face bright and eager, despite the black gown that leached colour from her. Such a difference from the shy, frightened girl he'd met all those months ago. Relaxed with friends, not playing a part, hiding what she was, afraid of what might happen if she let the compliant mask slip. Here if she disagreed, she argued, said outrageous things without having to fear that anything might get back to her father and earn her a beating. He'd loved her before—now seeing what she could be, he loved her even more.

To Will's comment a moment ago that Mary Wollstonecraft's ideas on the rights of women were radical, she had said simply, 'Justice should always be radical. None of us will live to see it, but one day even women will be allowed to vote.' And she was arguing her corner with passion and logic, pointing out all the changes in government and rule since Magna Carta.

'All this change—unimaginable to John and his nobles, even as they signed the Great Charter,' she concluded.

'Still, women voting,' Will said. 'No—' He caught the challenging glare from his wife. 'I don't say *you* couldn't vote intelligently, but most women—they simply aren't equipped for it.'

'Education,' Martin found himself saying. 'That

was the whole point of Wollstonecraft's book, was it not?'

Kit beamed. 'You've read it?'

Temptation lured, but he wasn't that foolish. 'No. But that was what I took from your comments.'

'I have a copy,' she said. 'You can borrow it.'

He caught the grin on Will's face. 'Thank you.' *I think*.

Beside him Caleb choked back a laugh and nudged the wine jug towards him. 'More wine, sir?' Another change—for the first time he'd used the more relaxed *sir* rather than the stultifying *my lord*.

'Thank you.' Martin poured another half-glass. He had some work to look at tonight.

Caleb spoke again. 'Heard something odd today.'

The tone of the boy's voice had Martin looking sharply at him and he noted that the other three were also paying attention. 'Oh?'

'Yeah. I delivered some coffee beans at the Lion and since it was my meal break I stopped in the yard to chat with a mate.'

Martin nodded. Inn yards were positive sinks of information on all sorts of things, including comings and goings.

'Go on.'

Caleb took a mouthful of ale, swallowed. 'Well,

Jim—he's one of the ostlers—says there's a chap who's suddenly become a regular at the Bird.'

Martin blinked, shot a glance at Will to see his reaction.

Nothing.

Kit, however, spoke as she unconcernedly cracked a nut and ate it. 'He means the Bird of Paradise,' she supplied without the trace of a blush. 'It's the—'

'Brothel around the corner. Yes, I know.' He was having a hard time not blushing himself.

Kit's expression turned angelic. 'Madame Mireille is a customer. She came to the funeral.'

'Mireille?'

Kit laughed. 'It's not her real name. She's not even French.' She chose another nut. 'She asked Ignatius years ago to suggest a pretty name for a Frenchwoman.'

'Why on earth does she want people to think she's French?' he asked.

Kit shrugged as she cracked the nut. 'It's like dressmakers—everyone assumes Frenchwomen have mysterious skills. She thought it would be good for business.' She popped the nut in her mouth, crunched.

'You're going to make them blush, Kit.'

The slight tremor in Psyché's voice got a grin from Will. 'Not me. I've given up on blushing around you two.'

Martin, desperately attempting to banish the

idea of mysterious French skills, cleared his throat. 'Caleb, what else did your friend tell you about this fellow?'

Caleb grinned, swallowing more ale. 'Well, the chap asks a lot of questions. Questions about the shops roundabout in general, but Anna...' he cleared his own throat '...she's the girl he, er, sees—she has what you might call a private arrangement with Jim—she reckons he asks the most questions about Selbourne's. Keeps on that it's unnatural, a "young girl"—his words—living there all by herself and she must be lonely.'

Martin's blood iced. It sounded as though the blighter was fishing for information.

Will spoke. 'What did Anna think of that?'

Caleb frowned. 'Jim reckons she thought he was just a chap on the prowl for a woman he didn't have to pay.' He looked at Kit apologetically. 'Sorry. She didn't much like it—told him he'd catch cold at that because if the dog didn't take him apart there was others who would.'

Kit looked thoughtful. 'Nothing about Lord Martin's presence, though?'

Caleb shook his head. 'No. And Jim said nothing about that. He told me because Anna thought Mr Will and Miss Psyché should know.' He fiddled with his napkin. 'And you, of course, Miss Kit, but he didn't say anything about his lordship.'

He glanced back to Martin. 'I'd say he doesn't know you're here, sir.'

Martin nodded, thinking furiously. 'I think you're right about that. We need a description of this curious gentleman. Directly from Anna would be best.' And he was damned if he was sending a seventeen-year-old boy into a brothel to interview a—his mind tripped over the word *whore*. The girl had deliberately taken steps to warn Kit—who the hell was he to judge her when it was largely men of his own class who kept her in business?

Will cleared his throat. 'One of us will have to go, Lacy. I can—'

'Not you.' Martin said sharply. 'I'll do it.' For one thing, it was his responsibility. For another, Will was married and well known in the area. If he visited the Bird, it would be all over Soho within hours.

Caleb coughed. 'Yeah, so I cut it short with Jim and went over to the Bird to speak to Anna myself.'

Psyché leaned forward. '*That's* why you were late back from your break?'

'Yeah. Then we were busy this afternoon, so I reckoned I'd tell everyone all at once.' He drummed his fingers on the table. 'Anna says he's not a gent for one thing. Clothes aren't right and he doesn't talk like it. The Bird gets plenty of that sort, so she knows. She thinks he works with horses because he smells of horse a bit. She poked at him a bit about where he lives—said for special customers Mireille lets girls go to the house—but he clammed up. Always arrives on foot, too. Got that from the porter.'

Kit's brow furrowed. 'He must have money, though. I mean, if he's visiting the Bird of Paradise regularly—it's not cheap and Mireille doesn't allow credit to newcomers any more than Ignatius did.'

'Good point.' Martin had never really thought about the business side of running a brothel, or considered the parallels with other businesses, but trust Kit to know and consider it logically. 'Which makes it likely that he's employed to spy by someone who doesn't want to be seen.'

He turned to Caleb. 'You've done extremely well. How did she describe him?'

Caleb blew out a breath. 'Forties. Solid, not fat but solid, well-muscled, she said. Ordinary looking. About five ten or eleven, brown hair cut short, brown eyes. No jewellery or anything fancy, but good boots.'

Nondescript. A fellow who wouldn't stand out—but Martin could think of one man who answered that description. And he didn't like it.

'Caleb...' Kit's voice shook. 'Do you think it's that—?'

'Bragg.' Caleb almost spat it out. 'It sounds like that Bragg fellow.'

In his office the following morning Martin wrote up the oral report he had given Holford on the previous night's development.

Holford had spoken about their progress with Lady Beechworth. 'She has agreed to come up to London, but she refuses to come until her brother and sister-in-law arrive to take charge of her children.' He scowled. 'Can't fault her concern, not after Sir John was murdered. And of course, now she knows how high the investigation has gone, she's even more frightened.'

Martin signed and dated his report. Holford had let something else slip. Or mentioned it deliberately more like. Huntercombe and his family had taken up residence in Grosvenor Square for the Season. So Martin had screwed his courage to the sticking point and penned a brief note to the marquess, asking when it would be convenient to call and suggesting that he send the reply via Will Barclay. He'd sent the note off by messenger a few minutes ago.

The knock on his door pulled him out of his thoughts.

'Come in.' Holford again likely, or a message from him…

The door opened to admit if not the last person Martin had expected to see, certainly someone low on his list of probabilities.

'I hope this is not an inconvenient moment, Lacy.'

'Not at all, sir, but you can't have received my note already.'

He'd heard stories about Huntercombe's omniscience, his uncanny ability to show up when you least expected him and when it was least welcome. Not that Huntercombe was unwelcome precisely, but how in Hades had the marquess known where to find him?

'I'm afraid not.'

Martin gestured to the visitor's chair. 'Please, sit down. How did you know where to find me?'

'I didn't.' Huntercombe sat down. 'I came to ask Holford where to find you.'

Holford. He'd known where to find *Holford*? Martin wasn't entirely sure that Lady Holford knew where to find her husband. But if Holford still used the marquess and his connections on occasion, perhaps it wasn't too surprising.

'I believe we need to talk, Lacy.'

Martin braced himself. Huntercombe's voice might be mild, but he'd heard that when the marquess spoke the most softly he was the most dangerous.

'Sir.' He reminded himself of the value of holding his tongue and looking expectant. Even if Huntercombe had received his note, there was no way that he could possibly have divined *why* Martin had requested a meeting.

'Holford has already told me what you believe is going on. Is that why you sent me a note?'

Sometimes it was best to leap straight in.

'That's part of it, but I wished to request your blessing.'

'My blessing. Then you intend to marry Kit?' His face remained unreadable. 'Is this merely because of her reputation?'

Merely?

'Sir, if not for Carshalton and my mother's plots, Kit and I would have been married for over a year now. You know why I didn't marry her then. And it still concerns us, but—'

Huntercombe's brows rose. 'I know why you *thought* you couldn't marry her. She said much the same at the time. To protect Harry and I dare say you were both right then, but I think that particular risk is gone. Carshalton has long since realised that, duke or not, you would have been the son-in-law from hell.'

A startled laugh escaped Martin. 'That's putting it mildly.'

'Precisely.' Huntercombe's smile was lethal. 'He knows he can't control you. That if he tried to implicate you in Harry's death and rule you by blackmail, you'd tell him to go to hell. Besides, from what Holford tells me, Carshalton stands on the brink of scandal and a possible accusation of a political assassination as well as the further murder of a well-liked and highly respected man. Therefore Harry is safe.'

'We hope.'

Huntercombe nodded. 'Yes, but his only reason to try again is revenge. He has nothing to gain from it and everything to lose. When he came up with that plot he was looking to control your father's dukedom and its political power. I suspect all he knew of you was what your mother had told him.'

His mother. Now confined by his father's orders to a small manor near Carlisle in Cumbria. She was at liberty to visit neighbours, but the servants assigned to her were extremely well paid by the duke and had extremely strict orders. A lawyer in Carlisle ensured those orders were carried out to the letter and the duchess's correspondence was watched.

'Have you seen her?' Huntercombe's question was painfully gentle.

'My mother? No. Not since—not since that day.'

He swallowed. Not since the day Huntercombe had uncovered the plot to murder Harry.

'You confronted them. Your parents.'

'Of course I did!' Martin flung at him. 'That night. I had no idea if my father was involved as well. I… I told them I was leaving. That I was going abroad and that I probably wouldn't be back.'

'But your father wasn't involved in the plot against Harry.'

'No, thank God.' Martin let out a breath, remembering the searing horror and grief as he had driven back to London, believing both his parents had connived at Harry's murder. And at Beck's. 'I knew it then. His face when I told him what had happened—when he understood why Beck had died.' It still sickened him. 'Beck was never going to marry. We all knew that he was indifferent to women sexually, that he preferred men. My father didn't mind as long as he was discreet, but—'

'But Carshalton approached him about a match with Kit—'

Martin nodded. 'Yes. He told Carshalton that Beck would never marry. But he didn't, thank God, say anything about Harry.'

Huntercombe's expression was grim. 'Quite. Otherwise I think Harry might have been disposed of first. As it was—'

'Carshalton found out that my mother was obsessed with the notion *I* should one day inherit. Yes. He pretended that he simply wanted the alliance with my family and I would do if Beck wasn't interested. When he did find out about Harry, he was going to leave it to my mother to solve that problem and then you married Emma.' He stopped as his mind tripped over something Huntercombe had said. 'How did you know Carshalton approached him about Beck marrying Kit?'

'I called on your father, too. Before I left for Cornwall that December.' Huntercombe's face was grim. 'I had to know what he was going to do about your mother.'

'You never thought he was involved.'

Huntercombe grimaced. 'I thought it unlikely. After I saw him, like you, I knew he was not. He's bull-headed and arrogant, but murder? And of a child? No. You came back to London because of him.'

Martin nodded. 'He'd lost all three of us. Beck, Peter, myself. All his sons and even his grandson—' At Huntercombe's raised brows, Martin flung up one hand. 'My apologies, I didn't mean... I don't blame you and Emma for being cautious—'

'It's not us, Lacy. It's Harry himself.' Huntercombe crossed one booted ankle over the other. 'One of the reasons I wished to see you. Harry refuses to see his grandfather because he believes Keswick will attempt to take him from us.'

Martin nodded slowly. 'As he did before.' He met Huntercombe's eyes. 'And I helped him. For what it's worth, I believe my father regrets that as much as I do. I'm sorry.'

'You believed you were doing the right thing.'

Martin snorted. 'You were still on the verge of slapping a glove in my face at the time, Huntercombe. Very likely with your fist still in it.'

Huntercombe smiled. 'True. Martin—may I call you that?'

Martin nodded.

Huntercombe continued. 'Martin, why are you asking my blessing to marry Kit?'

Martin centred the report he'd been re-reading very precisely on his desk. 'Originally I wasn't planning to marry Kit until Carshalton is no longer in a position to cause trouble for anyone except the devil.'

Huntercombe scratched his jaw. 'Ah. That solution did occur to me and I agree he must be stopped, but I think for your current situation it's not necessary. Except—'

He paused. Eyed Martin thoughtfully. 'From your report of Kit's confrontation with him the other day, he still intends her to marry Staverton.'

'Yes.' He couldn't help the hard, clipped tone in his voice. 'That's not happening.'

Huntercombe's smile flickered. 'Certainly not. But I suggest that you don't play that card in any attempt to persuade Kit to marry you. She would very likely decide that marrying her would endanger *you*.'

Martin stared. That Kit might refuse marriage to protect him hadn't even crossed his mind.

That kindly smile came again. 'Now to the reason I wished to speak to you this afternoon, Martin. I require your help. Not just in keeping Kit safe, but with Harry and your father.' Huntercombe leaned forward, resting his elbows on the desk. 'I can prepare the boy for the title in general terms, the responsibility, management of his lands, investments and so on. But he needs to know Keswick's people—the tenants, the land, the details of his holdings which are very different to mine.'

He could see that. The bulk of Huntercombe's land, including his principal seat, was in Cornwall. Keswick's holdings were in Cumbria. It might as well have been a different country up there. In many ways it was.

Huntercombe spoke again. 'The title aside, Harry should know his grandfather. So should Georgie. And they should know their uncle—you gave the children that portrait of their father, Lacy. They both want to know you. Emma wants them to know you.'

He swallowed. 'She's very gracious.'

The chance to make amends, to put right the relationship between his father and Harry, was before him.

'What do you suggest, Huntercombe?'

After Huntercombe had explained, he rose. 'You should discuss this with Kit. Send me a letter via Grosvenor Square. I'm remaining in town for now. Good day to you.'

Martin got up from his desk, his brain reeling. 'Good day, sir. I'll let you know when would suit.'

'Do that.' He was at the door, reaching for the handle. 'Oh, Harry tells me that he offered you one of the pups from the litter his and Georgie's bitch is expecting?'

'Er, yes, but—'

'Do you really want one, or were you assuming I'd veto it?'

Martin grinned. 'Yes, I do want the pup. Otherwise I'd have told Harry I didn't have time for a dog.'

Huntercombe's smile turned wicked. 'Good.

When Holford complains, remind him that one of Fergus's predecessors slept under my desk without incident for several years. A male? No point upsetting Moth with a bitch.'

'None at all.'

'Ah, one other thing, Martin. You thought the other day that I was concerned about the possibility of your taking advantage of Kit.'

And he'd done exactly that.

'Yes, sir.'

He had the nasty feeling that Huntercombe's penetrating gaze saw a great deal more than he would have wished.

'I was somewhat more concerned that *she* might take advantage of *you*. She has some very radical notions on the subject of marriage.'

Martin felt his jaw drop. 'I had noticed that.'

The marquess nodded. 'I thought you might have. Give her time, Lacy. She'll come around as soon as she's noticed that she does indeed trust you in all ways.' He smiled. 'She's stubborn, but not terminally so.' With that, Huntercombe departed.

Martin stared at the door, concluding that the Marquess had clearly earned his reputation for omniscience, and might even have what his old nanny had called the Sight. He could only hope the man was right about Kit.

Chapter Nineteen

As dusk fell along with a steady downpour, Mireille sipped her tea by the fire and sneered at Kit over the rim of the cup. 'No.' Her usual exaggerated French accent in abeyance, Mireille set the cup and saucer down. 'If that's all, I'll be going.'

'Madame, please. It's important.'

The woman's dark eyes narrowed. 'Not so important you'll tell me what it's all about. I know how your sort views me and—'

'My sort?'

'A toff.' Mireille picked up her cup and saucer again, sipped. 'Turning your nose up at an honest working woman and her girls, while your fancy lover sneaks in each night.'

Kit set her own cup and saucer down with a rattle. 'That's not—' If Mireille knew *that*—

'Not my business?' The painted lip curled. 'Told my girls they weren't to gossip about it and when

Anna came to tell me about that fellow asking all his questions, I made sure it got back to you.'

Kit took a deep breath. 'You told Anna to get word to us? I didn't realise. Thank you.' She was making a complete mess of this. 'Lord Martin isn't here because he's my lover.'

She accepted the crack of laughter and went on. 'He's not. Mireille, you know what happened to Ignatius—'

'Aye, and I'm as sorry as I can be. He was a good man. Always raised his hat to me and my girls.' The woman rose, flicking out her skirts.

'Please wait,' Kit begged. Even if the woman left, she could not let her think she had been snubbed. 'You came to his funeral. You've been a good customer. One of the few to whom he would extend credit. That doesn't change with me running Selbourne's. Damn it! Why did you come to the back door? You've never done that before.'

By the time Mireille *had* knocked it was nudging on the time she was supposed to be at the Phoenix. Kit hoped to God Will or Psyché wouldn't come looking for her. This was something she would need to lead up to carefully.

Mireille sat down again, her cheeks slightly pink. 'Thought you might be going to tell me things *were* changing. Wouldn't blame you. I know, better than most, what it's like for a woman running a business. And I always came after closing even for Ignatius.'

'Yes, and I didn't rush upstairs clutching my smelling salts and pearls either.'

This time Mireille's laughter held genuine humour. 'No more you did. Look, fact is I can't do what you asked. I can't pass you off as a maid in there. I don't let my own maids on those floors when we're open for business of an evening.' Her lip curled. 'Too many men think any girl in a brothel is included in the price and I can't be everywhere.'

'Oh.' Kit let out a breath. 'I didn't think of that.' Ignatius had once said that as a brothel owner, Mireille was decent. She looked after her girls, insisted the customers used cundums and was known to ban men who were too rough with the girls.

Mireille frowned at her. 'Why are you so set on getting a look at this chap?'

She'd asked for a favour. Perhaps she had to give something first. Like trust. 'I told you Lord Martin isn't here because he's my lover—or not just because. He's protecting me.'

The finely plucked brows lifted. 'Right. I've heard it called that, but—wait. You mean really protecting? Because of what happened to Ignatius?'

'Yes.'

Mireille let out a low whistle. 'That's different then. You think this chap might've had something to do with that?'

'Maybe.' She asked the question that was bothering her. 'You said your girls know that Lord Martin is visiting here.'

Mireille shrugged. 'They're not blind. But they don't gossip about Ignatius and that covers you. For now.'

Kit breathed a sigh of relief. 'I'm grateful. Can any of them sketch? So we could see if we recognise this man?'

Pitying amusement accompanied the head shake. 'That's a lady's hobby, that is. I've a couple can pass as a young lady, but none are the genuine article.'

Kit blinked. 'I suppose not.' She forced a smile. The disappointment wasn't Mireille's fault. 'I'm sorry to have wasted your time. Shall we enjoy our tea? Afterwards I have some new volumes on the top shelf since last you visited. I'll fetch them down.'

Mireille cast a speculative glance at the upper shelf where the erotica was kept, then gave Kit a thoughtful look. 'Can you sketch?'

Kit smiled. 'My one lady-like accomplishment. Yes.'

Drumming her fingers on the table, Mireille pursed her lips. 'Might be I can work out a fix. You need to see his face long enough to make the sketch. There's a way to manage that. I'll have to talk to Anna and one of the other girls. Could be you'll see a few things you've not seen before, but that's the price of doing business.'

Kit nodded. 'I promise not to sketch them.'

Mireille roared with laughter. 'If you do and you're any good I could probably sell them for you.' She finished her tea. 'Let's be having a look at these famous books, and then I'd best get back to arrange things. He's coming tonight.'

'Tonight?'

'Aye. Booked himself in for ten o'clock. I'll send a lad around to the back door for you around half past nine.'

Mireille had barely departed—via the back door at her own insistence—when Martin knocked on the front door.

Kit let him in, rehearsing in her mind exactly how she might lead up to what she had to say…

'Who was that and why aren't you over at the Phoenix already?'

The level voice didn't fool her in the least: he was furious.

Reining back her own annoyance—they were lovers, yes, but she didn't answer to him—Kit said simply, 'I had a visitor. I could hardly throw her out.'

'A woman who came and went through the back door?'

She shut the door behind him with a bang. 'How do you—?'

'Know that? Because while we could see you with her, Psyché was fairly sure no one had come through the front door and we didn't see your visitor leave.'

Her annoyance kicked over the traces. 'I'm amazed you didn't come over to see who I was entertaining.'

'I would have. Psyché convinced me otherwise.'
Thank God for Psyché.

'Damn it, Kit! We had an agreement that you would go to the Phoenix at—'

'Closing time. Yes.' She dragged in a breath. Sometimes there was no point wrapping things up nicely. 'I asked Mireille to call and she arrived rather later than I expected.'

Observing Martin's dropped jaw, she clicked her fingers for Moth. 'Shall we go over now?'

'Mireille. From the Bird of Paradise. She—you *invited* her to call?'

At least she had the satisfaction of knowing that she'd shocked him. Time for the coup de grâce. 'Yes. I'll be returning the favour later this evening.'

'The hell you will.'

'For God's sake, Barclay! You can't possibly think this is a good idea!'

Damn it all, he'd counted on Barclay having his back in this. But all the man had done was suggest that he, Martin, might allay any concerns by acting as an escort. In fact, he'd thought Kit's insane notion positively brilliant.

'I'll warrant you wouldn't think it was a brilliant idea if *your* wife was planning to visit a brothel!'

Barclay raised his brows. 'One, Kit is not your wife. You can't actually stop her. Not unless you tie her up. Two, ask yourself how you'd feel about it if someone else—say, Caleb—had come up with this plan.'

'I can't draw,' Caleb said hurriedly.

'He's what, seventeen?' Martin scowled. 'I'd be just as—' He stopped as he met Will's disbelieving grin. 'Oh, very well. I wouldn't much like it, because he's only seventeen, but Kit's a female!'

'If you think it's only women who are sold in brothels you're a great deal more naive than I imagined,' Will said drily.

Caleb gave a muffled snort. 'The Bird isn't a molly house, Mr Will.'

'I know,' Will said with a grin. 'But for all Lacy knows it might be that as well. Which would make it just as dangerous for you as Kit.'

'There's her reputation, too.' He given Selbourne his promise that he'd protect Kit. 'If it is Bragg, I'd recognise him. If I went first—'

'And if it isn't, we wouldn't be any further forward,' Kit said, her pencil dancing over the book in front of her. What the hell was she doing? 'And that's assuming Mireille would agree to your being there.'

Psyché spoke up. 'Kit is the only one of us who can sketch a decent likeness.'

Martin clutched at that frail straw. '*How* decent?'

Kit passed her notebook across the table to him. 'You tell me.'

His own likeness scowled back at him from the book, along with a quick sketch of Psyché, a half-smile curving her lips. Both were instantly recognisable, even done roughly in pencil. If she used colour… Silently he handed the notebook back.

Against those sketches he didn't have a logical argument to advance.

He met Kit's gaze. 'Damn.'

Will spoke again. 'Don't for one minute imagine that I liked the scheme Psyché came up with last year for getting Kit out of here when Carshalton was hunting her. It was damn bloody dangerous and I tried everything I could to change her mind.' He gripped Martin's arm, gave it a friendly shake. 'It's the price we pay for having a woman who thinks for herself and expects to play her part.'

'Speaking of which…'

Will turned his head to eye his wife suspiciously. 'Speaking of what?'

'Thinking for ourselves,' Kit said. 'Psyché and I think we can refine this a little.'

Martin couldn't fault the wary expression on Barclay's face. 'Exactly what do you mean—*refine*?'

* * *

Kit gripped the case holding her sketch pad and pastels and followed the lad from the Bird of Paradise through the tangle of yards and lanes. The boy held a small lantern, but Kit didn't doubt that was more for her benefit than his. Martin brought up the rear, his pistol in his hand.

The boy, Tom, had scowled at Martin, telling Kit he'd only been told to bring her and not to go blaming him if *'Madame gives his nibs a flea in 'is lughole'.*

The yard behind the Bird of Paradise was small and surprisingly tidy. Kit wasn't quite sure what she'd expected, but it wasn't flowers growing in pots. Then she took a closer look and stifled a choke of laughter. The pots were full of Queen Anne's lace. How very practical!

Mireille herself greeted them at the backdoor. Her brows shot up when she saw Martin.

'I said *you* could come in, girl. Not him, lover or no.'

'Ain't my fault, missus,' Tom assured her. 'Told 'em, I did.'

Kit cursed mentally. 'I know. He—'

'Wouldn't agree otherwise,' Martin cut in. 'Not your boy's fault. Good evening, ma'am.'

Kit held her tongue as Mireille silently looked Martin over, apparently assessing him.

'Pretty manners pay no toll. So you think I'd

let her in if I thought she'd come to harm in my place?'

The woman's voice bit cold and Kit's heart sank. 'Mireille—'

'I might have.' Martin's voice was nearly as cool. 'You can't possibly have thought I'd like the idea of Miss Selbourne walking into a brothel unprotected.'

She shrugged. 'Thought you'd forbid it outright and that'd be that.'

The corner of Martin's mouth twitched. 'It has been forcibly pointed out to me this evening that I am not Miss Selbourne's husband and have no power to forbid her to do anything.'

Mireille snorted. 'Right. Well, since I want to know if this bloke had anything to do with Selbourne's death you can come in. Might be all for the best if you did. Means I can get back to the front rooms. Make sure it all goes off like I've arranged.'

'You were going to remain with her yourself?'

Kit couldn't blame Martin for sounding surprised. It hadn't occurred to her either.

'Said she'd be safe, didn't I? How else was I going to see to it? Since you've invited yourself along you may as well be useful. Come on. Time's wasting.'

Martin peered through the peephole into the gaudy and currently empty room. That a brothel had a room with a peephole wasn't exactly a surprise. A man without enough money to buy a woman for the night could, for a far lesser sum, buy time at the peep and take his pleasures vicariously.

'You'll want to be quiet,' Mireille said, her voice low. 'Wall here's thin because of the peeps.'

He blinked. 'More than one?'

She rolled her eyes. 'Not everyone wants a view got your height. Got a few, but only two open tonight.' She tapped Kit on the shoulder, indicated a much lower aperture with a chair pulled up to it. 'That one's for you. Usually use it for older gents. They'll pay extra for a seat.'

He grimaced. 'And the door?' There was one right beside the upper peephole.

'I keep my girls safe,' snapped Mireille. 'If there's a customer I think might get a bit rough with a girl, I keep an eye on things. That door means I don't have to get all the way around to the main door before I can put a stop to it. Plus there's sometimes a customer needs to leave the back way. Don't worry. It's locked. Anna's got the key.'

He nodded. 'I see.' He wasn't sure that he did.

She hesitated. 'Look. I've got one of the other girls going in with Anna. They're going to put on a little show for your bloke.' She jerked her thumb at Kit. 'Keep him looking this way an' give you a better look at his face before they get down to business. That's what you need, isn't it?'

'Oh. Yes. I… I suppose so.'

Kit sounded to Martin as though she were thinking her way through that. He could interpret it only too well. If their spy had got straight down to 'business', she would have seen very little of his face.

Settling in the chair, Kit opened a small satchel. 'Thank you, Mireille. I hadn't thought about that.'

The woman shrugged. 'Didn't think you had and I don't doubt his lordship would rather you didn't see any of this, but we don't always get what we want. Best I can do.'

Martin stared at the woman. She hadn't known he would be coming. As far as she had known only Kit was supposed to have arrived. Which meant she hadn't arranged this for his benefit at all.

She'd done it for Kit. And for Selbourne.

'Thank you, ma'am.'

She raised her brows and inclined her head. 'And welcome. Take yourselves out the same way when you're done. Tom will be waiting to guide you back.'

'If it's the man we suspect it is, that will be sooner rather than later.'

Mireille nodded. 'No skin off mine.'

Hoping the dim light hid her blushes from Martin, Kit concentrated on getting out what she needed. She looked through the peep. Blinked. The room was reasonably well lit, lamps glow-ing on tables, the light glinting off a large, gilded bed with crimson hangings on the adjacent wall. Beside it stood a gilded sofa, also upholstered in crimson. Directly before the peep there looked to be a sort of dais or stage.

She opened her mouth to ask Martin what the stage was for and the door of the room opened.

She recognised Anna at once. Mireille's girls often strolled around the streets, prettily dressed, and she had seen her chatting to Bert at the Lion. The man... She heard Martin's sharp intake of breath and knew what he'd seen. It wasn't Bragg, but the resemblance was there.

She pushed that out of her mind, focused on her subject...surely she had seen him before... It wasn't just that he reminded her of Staverton's coachman.

Anna led him further into the room, into the light. Kit focused on his face. Nondescript brown hair, greying, she thought, about the temples. A heavy jaw and the eyes slightly wide—over a broad nose.

'What's all this about then?' Suspicion roughened his voice. 'I'm not paying for fancy. A plain poke's what I'm after.'

Kit's breath caught. Even the voice raised an echo in her memory, the timbre, the inflections, although not the accent...

Anna smiled. 'Oh, you'll get that all right and tight.' She swivelled her hips, leaning back on the end of the sofa and languidly tugging at a bright red ribbon between her breasts, so that her gown opened revealing ripe curves. 'A little *quelque chose* on the house. For being a good boy.'

Pushing all speculation out of her head, Kit started drawing.

'Yeah?'

He seemed to settle a bit and approached Anna.

Not seeming to hurry, she eased along the sofa, keeping her distance. 'That's right. Got a bit more...'

The door opened again, and another girl strolled in wearing what appeared to be nothing more than a few artfully placed scarves that fluttered as she walked.

'What the hell?'

Anna's smile slid towards sultry as she stroked her breasts. 'You got two of us tonight, big boy. Think you're up for it?'

'Reckon I am. Get on the bed.'

His voice was hoarse now. Kit heard the lust in it as her fingers flew over the page.

Don't think about it. Draw what you see, what's in front of you.

'Someone's in a hurry,' purred the new girl.

She sauntered across the room, scarves dancing, and patted the sofa. 'How about you sit down here and Annie and me'll get you nice an' hot. I'm Gabby, by the way.' She blew him a kiss. 'Got the gift of the gab, I do. Real good with my mouth, you might say.'

'Might I? Here!' He grabbed her wrist as she headed for the dais. 'Where are you going?'

Anna rose from the sofa, all fluid grace and her gown slipped from one shoulder. 'Now, now. Don't be impatient. You're getting the works tonight. No need to rush. We got a little show for you.'

Together the girls mounted the dais and Kit sketched rapidly. She had him full face now, the lamplight falling perfectly. The medium brown hair—she indicated that with pastels, but stayed focused on the features…nose, shape of the mouth, cheekbones…and she had to be careful to make sure she drew *this* man, that she didn't allow any hint of resemblance to Bragg to blind her to what she was seeing in the now. Eye colour, impossible at that distance and in that light, but she could get the skin tone well enough—and Caleb had said brown.

Meanwhile Anna and Gabby had draped their arms about each other and a couple of the latter's scarves had drifted to the floor. Impossible not to see that Anna's gown now hung about her waist and that the pair of them were stroking each other's breasts as they swayed.

'Pretty, aren't they?' Gabby said huskily. Hips undulated, another scarf fell, and Anna's gown slid right to the floor. She stepped out of it and nudged it aside.

'Yeah. Give 'em a squeeze.' The man's hand was at his groin now, rubbing, shoving his breeches down.

Kit hurriedly focused back on his face, cheeks burning, starting to understand exactly why Martin had objected to her plan.

'Like it, don't you?' Anna's low purr rippled seductively.

'Yeah. I like it. Go on, bitch. Touch her up proper. Down there. Then I'll show you both what I got for you. See if your friend speaks a little French, maybe.'

Gabby laughed. 'Oh, I think I could muster up a little French for you, *monsewer*.' She strolled towards him, hips swaying.

Martin felt soiled, sickened on his own behalf, let alone that Kit was watching this. Not so much by what the girls were doing, but by the naked lust on the man's face as he watched them, issued demands. As if they were little more than animals to be ordered about.

He shifted from the peep. Surely Kit had a likeness by now?

'Oy! What's that?'

Martin froze.

'That's my tit, cully.'

'The light. What's that light there on the wall?'

Heavy footsteps. 'You bitches got a peephole!'

Kit's wide eyes met his, then she snapped her

book shut and shoved it back in the satchel along with her pastels and the charcoal.

'Now, now. No need to get all huffy.' Anna's voice soothed. 'Madame said she might take a look, being as how Gabby's new here, an' I'm s'posed to be training her. You'll get your money's worth all right.'

'Not before I've taken a look out that door I ain't.'

Martin grabbed Kit's hand as she slung the satchel over her shoulder and hurried her away.

Chapter Twenty

By the time Martin shoved her through the back door of her own shop, Kit was breathless at the pace they'd made following Tom's lantern.

'For heaven's sake, Martin!' She kept her voice low as he made to slam the door. 'At least let me give the child a shilling for his efforts.'

Tom looked up affronted from dousing the lantern. 'Ain't no child!' But he brightened at the sight of the coin and tucked it away safely. 'Thanking you all the same, Miss.' He gave Martin a wary look. 'Night, Guv.'

'Goodnight, Tom. And thank you.'

To Kit's amusement, Martin produced a second shilling. 'Please thank your mistress again and assure her that I owe her a very great favour. Also, warn her if that particular customer returns, she would be wise to fob him off.'

Tom touched his cap and melted away into the shadows as Martin shut the door and secured it.

The curtain into the shop drew back to reveal Will and Psyché.

'Well?' Psyché smiled at Kit. 'Let's see the sketch.'

She pulled out the book, opened it and handed it over. 'It's not Bragg. But—' All along as she sketched she'd seen the familiarity. And wondered.

Martin spoke up. 'They could be brothers. Is everything else in train?'

Will nodded. 'Caleb is watching. I'll go and join him now.'

'Wait.' Kit spoke slowly. 'I think I've seen him before.'

'What? Where?' Martin demanded.

'Here. In the shop. It's hard to be certain because I was up one of the ladders much of the time tidying—' She frowned. 'Biblical commentaries, I think. It was the day Ignatius was killed. He used the slope and it was after that that Mr Daly knocked it off the table.'

Martin drew in an audible breath. 'If he was the one to plant the letter, then he knew exactly where it ought to be. If we can find out where he goes—'

'I'll be on my way.'

Psyché gripped Will's hands. 'You'll be careful?'

He bent to kiss her cheek. 'Depend on it.'

'Barclay, I still think—'

'No.' Will shook his head. 'You stay here, Lacy. Your task is keeping Kit safe. Caleb and I will follow our spy.'

* * *

Martin locked the front door behind Will and Psyché and set the bolts and bar. Kit had already gone upstairs.

He found her in the parlour pouring a glass of brandy.

She held it out. 'I thought you might want this.'

Her voice, so tentative and uncertain, and the little worry lines, made him long to hold her, but if he did that, he'd lose track of what he needed to say.

He took the brandy. 'Thank you.' How to say it? He wasn't entirely sure he understood what he was thinking, let alone how to explain it.

'We need to talk.'

She nodded, biting her lip. 'Yes. Martin, I'm—'

'I owe you an apology.'

'What?' She picked up the decanter, poured another glass. 'Whatever for?'

He took a swallow. 'I broke trust with you. I tried to stop you going to the Bird. I didn't mean it like that, but that was what it was.'

She stared. 'I thought perhaps by going, by watching that, I had disgusted you—I was going to apologise.'

He shook his head. 'Terrified me, yes. Kit, I know I overstepped. Will had it right—I'm not your husband and I know the idea of a husband wielding that sort of authority horrifies you. The problem is that I want—*need*—to protect you. Not because you're *a* woman, but because you're *my* woman. The woman I love.'

He let out a frustrated breath. 'It wasn't because I see you as *less* in any way.'

'So you came with me.' She sipped her brandy.

'Yes. To stand with you, not in front of you. Not blocking your choice to act.' She said nothing, so he floundered on. 'Sweetheart, I understand your need to trust that I wouldn't exercise that sort of authority—'

She shut her eyes and his world rocked, nearly broke.

'Then—' her voice was very soft '—I owe you an apology. Because that's exactly what I've done to you. Blocked your choice. That isn't why I hesitated to marry you.'

He frowned. 'You said—'

'That's why I wouldn't marry anyone else. But I allowed you to think that was my reason for not marrying *you*. It wasn't.'

The world steadied. 'Go on.'

She swallowed, met his eyes. 'I tried once to protect you from knowing what your mother had done. This was just as stupid.'

'Carshalton,' he said quietly. 'You realised that if we married, he might decide I was an obstacle to his plans for you.'

'You knew?'

He tossed off the rest of his brandy and went to her, taking her hands in a strong clasp. 'I knew he might try it. Huntercombe pointed out to me that it would be a stumbling block for you.'

'I'm sorry,' she whispered. 'I was so set on my own independence and choices that I didn't see I was trampling on yours. Standing in front of you.'

He raised her hands to his lips, kissed them. 'Kit, does this mean you'll marry me?'

Tears in her eyes, she nodded. 'I just took you to a brothel. I suppose I should do the right thing by you.'

He drew her into his arms, just held her, his cheek resting on her curls. 'Damn right you should.'

Her arms tightened about him. 'I realised something in there. It was different to…to what we do. In bed. I mean, I don't suppose what they actually *do* is all that different, but it *felt* different, as though something was missing. He…he didn't even seem to see those girls as human. Just as *things* he'd bought for the night.' She huffed out a frustrated breath. 'I'm not making sense.'

He brushed a kiss to her temple. 'Yes, you are. We've been making love. Gabby and Anna put on a very pretty seduction, mind you, but it wasn't love.'

'Oh.' She pressed a little closer. 'Speaking of seduction, there was something Gabby said— something about speaking French. Was that… er…a euphemism?'

Laughter shook him even as heat burned

through him. 'More like a *double entendre*,' he said. 'Come to bed and seduce me and I'll explain.'

'Not show me?'

'That, too,' he promised. 'Believe me, the dragon is starving tonight.'

Kit thought about that and heat tingled under her skin along with a frisson of nerves. 'Most self-respecting dragons eat maidens.'

His smile dawned, slow and wicked. 'We do indeed.'

Fifteen minutes later Kit cried out in shock as Martin found her wet, aching core with his mouth. Dark pleasure speared her, melted every possible thought in the heat of passion as she broke under the onslaught of sensation. She was lost, helpless, as he surged up her body and plunged into her, deep and sure.

The rhythm sang in her, finding its answer, its pulse, in the heart of love.

Lying in his arms afterwards, her body lax and warm, a memory stirred. 'You saw Huntercombe.'

'Mmm… He came to see me.'

'Not about *this*?'

Laughter shook Martin. 'Not exactly. I think he knew, but he asked a favour of me. Of us actually. Let's leave that for the morning.' His arms tightened. 'Your dragon is nearly asleep.'

Her dragon. She liked that much better than being rescued from one.

* * *

Caleb frowned as their quarry mounted the front steps of the Bloomsbury mansion. 'Bit odd, isn't it? Reckon his sort would be going around to the back, not in through the front door.'

Will nodded, easing back around the corner and taking Caleb with him. 'That's the least of our worries. Come on. We need to get back.'

'Who lives there, Mr Will?'

Will glanced at him, as they hurried along Hart Street. 'Kit's father. Our man reported directly to Carshalton.'

Carshalton drummed his fingers on the desk as he stared at his henchman. 'What the devil do you mean, a *spy*?'

'I saw the light as someone shifted from the spyhole, sir. Knew what it was at once. I made 'em open the door out to the back. Right beside the peep it was and locked to boot.'

Carshalton shrugged. 'Mireille's fussy, I'm told. Won't let the customers knock the whores around even when they deserve it—one of the guards, no doubt.'

His man shook his head. 'That's what the whores reckoned. Or the bitch who runs the place checking all was shipshape, but—' He reached into his pocket. 'I found these on the floor out there. Right under one of the holes.'

Carshalton frowned at what he held out. A cou-

ple of pastels—pale, pinkish creams. *Flesh tones.*
And a stick of charcoal. 'I see.'

He set them on his desk. Someone had been
sketching.

Chapter Twenty-One

Keswick House on the Strand had stood in one form or another since before the days of the Restoration. The Great Fire had destroyed the original house, but the duke of the day had rebuilt it, grander than ever. Now the current duke lived in it alone, almost a recluse.

But today carriages drew up before the great portico added by Martin's grandfather. The first of the carriages was the gig from the Red Lion.

Martin handed Kit down and passed off the reins to a groom. 'I'll be glad when all this is over.' He had received a note from Holbrook early that morning. Staverton had been 'detained'—a polite word for house arrest. He was talking frantically. The man in the brothel had been arrested. He had turned out to be Bragg's brother. Unlike Staverton, both Braggs were so far keeping their mouths firmly shut.

She squeezed his hand. 'But hopefully it will be over. If it's not—'

'Kit, we're getting married. Regardless.'

'But what if he isn't stopped and he comes after—'

'I can look after myself. And your father can go to hell.' He could only hope he had a hand in that.

A closed carriage pulled up behind them. A footman leapt down but the door opened before he could reach it and Harry Lacy and his sister Georgie leaped down without waiting for the stairs.

'Uncle Martin. Kit! We're here!'

'So I see.' Martin held out his hand to Harry with a grin. 'You're looking well. And here's Georgie.'

His small niece subjected him to an inspection that would have done credit to an archduchess. 'You didn't come to see us.'

'*Mea culpa.* Are you going to forgive me?'

Georgie sniffed. 'Yes.' She turned to Kit. 'I'm very sorry about Mr Selbourne. Mama says you're very sad. Are you too sad to come and stay with us again this summer?'

Kit bent down to hug the child. 'Not too sad for that, Georgie. And here are your Mama and Uncle Hunt. Oh, and here's Mr Barclay.'

Will had ridden in as the marquess and marchioness, having waited politely for their footman to let down the steps, came over arm in arm.

Lady Huntercombe held out her arms to Martin, her face alight. 'Wretched man! If I'd known it would do the trick we would have invited ourselves to Keswick House months ago.'

Every doubt and defence shattered in the warmth of her welcome. 'Ma'am.' He caught her raised brows. 'Emma,' he said and hugged her. His eyes stung. 'You've forgiven me.'

'Long ago,' she assured him and released him. 'And Hunt says that you may have some happy news for us.' She smiled. 'I'm so glad. Now come and reassure poor Harry that the duke isn't going to eat any of us or keep him here.'

Keswick received them in the drawing room. He sat alone in the enormous room by the fire that Martin knew from bitter experience barely gave out enough heat to take the Arctic chill off the room. Keswick, used to this, was dressed warmly including a heavy silk brocade banyan. He had one foot propped up on a footstool and clutched a walking stick as they approached.

'Come in. Come in. You, there.' He waved the walking stick at one of the footmen. 'Let them know below stairs that the refreshments should be brought in.'

'Yes, Your Grace.'

Keswick scowled around at them. 'Well, I've some uncomfortable words to say—uncomfortable for me, that is—so I'll say them and be done.'

He beckoned to Harry. 'Come here, boy. I'll start with you.'

With a nervous glance at Huntercombe and Emma, Harry walked to stand in front of the old man who scowled even more ferociously.

'I owe you an apology, boy. Because I didn't like your other grandfather—still don't for that matter—I was an old fool and behaved very badly when your father and mother married. And I kept right on behaving badly, so you and your sister, and your mother suffered for it. It was wrong and I apologise. Worse, it spawned a situation that put you in danger along with your mother and sister.' He glared at Harry.

Harry scowled right back. 'Does that mean you aren't going to be rude to Mama any longer?'

Keswick pursed his lips. 'And if I was?'

'Then I should have to tell you, politely, that Mama is my mother and you aren't allowed to.'

Some of the wrinkles chased themselves around Keswick's face into a faint smile. 'Going to call me out, are you?'

'No, Your Grace. Uncle Hunt said you're too old.'

Huntercombe shut his eyes.

Martin grinned.

The old man's shoulders shook. 'Very true. Well, pull up that stool, and I dare say my staff will find some lemonade and cake for you and your sister. I think I'll stick to brandy. Where's the girl? Georgiana, isn't it?'

Prodded by Emma, Georgie went to him. He looked her over. 'I'll warrant you're a rare handful.'

'Yes, Your Grace.'

His eyes widened. 'Yes?'

'Mama says it's polite to agree with older people.'

Keswick swivelled in his chair to look at Emma. 'As I said: an old fool. Peter would have been proud of them.'

The rheumy old eyes fell on Kit. 'Martin said you were coming. Can't say I ever had much time for his politics, but that uncle of yours was a good, honest man. I'm sorry he's gone.'

'Thank you, Your Grace.'

'Sir.' Martin took Kit's hand. This seemed as good a moment as any. 'I should tell you that Miss Selbourne—Kit—has agreed to marry me.'

Keswick narrowed his eyes. 'Asking my permission, are you, boy?'

Martin shook his head. 'No. Absolutely not. I'm telling you. Your blessing will be welcome, but not indispensable.'

Keswick's snort was that of an elderly dragon. 'Someone better ask them to send up champagne.'

Under cover of the general conversation and congratulations, Will spoke softly to Martin. 'Congratulations. You're a lucky man. So, something you might find of personal interest under the circumstances. The property next door to Selbourne's—the draper.'

'Yes.'

'The lease expires shortly. Let me explain.' He drew Martin aside.

The party was in full swing, when one of the footmen came in and spoke quietly to Martin. 'My lord, Lord Holford and Lady Beechworth have arrived. They have been escorted to the library as you instructed.'

'Thank you, Samuel. I'll be along immediately.'

He glanced around. Harry was still sitting beside Keswick, munching on a slice of cake, and listening to the old man who actually had a smile on his face as he told some tale. Huntercombe and Emma stood nearby chatting to Kit, while Will had been cornered by Georgie and was playing backgammon with her.

He went to Kit and spoke softly. 'Holford has arrived. I've been thinking. Will you accompany me?'

'Me?' She frowned. 'Why? Surely Lord Holford won't—'

'You'd be surprised,' Huntercombe said. 'Holford's a wily old fox. And Selbourne trained him.'

'Oh.' She looked uncertain. 'Martin, do you really think—'

Emma laid a hand on Kit's arm. 'I think it might be a little easier for Lady Beechworth to have another woman there, Kit dear. A woman who has also lost someone she loves because of this mess.'

Kit swallowed. 'Very well.'

Holford rose at once as Martin escorted Kit into the library.

'Lady Beechworth, may I present Lord Martin Lacy? He has been conducting the investigation into Sir John's death. And Miss Selbourne who has, I believe, assisted him most materially.'

The tired-looking woman in black stood up. 'My lord. Miss Selbourne. I hope that some of this can be resolved this afternoon. I need to know why my husband died. Bad enough when we believed it was a random act of violence, but—' She pressed a hand to her lips.

'Will you not be seated again, Lady Beechworth?'

Kit knew that gentle voice. Knew his kindness and knew the woman's grief. She took a seat at a small desk a little distance away and waited.

Lady Beechworth resumed her own seat. 'Will you tell me, Lord Martin, what it is that you need to know?'

He sat. 'Ma'am, I understand that your husband had a visitor a day or so before his death. A visitor with whom he quarrelled. Can you tell us what that was all about?'

Lady Beechworth gripped her hands together. 'First, you must understand that we are not very well off. Sir John had experienced some financial reverses a few years ago—the banking crisis, you see.'

'Yes, ma'am.'

'Well, this gentleman, Mr Canterbury—' Kit breathed in sharply, but said nothing as Lady Beechworth continued '—wrote to Sir John, claiming to know something about all that and saying he could help set it right. He asked if he could call. Sir John discussed it with me and we decided that speaking to the man could do no harm.'

Kit found pencil and paper in the desk and began to draw.

'And he came?'

'Yes. Sir John saw him alone, but—' She twisted her hands together. 'I was outside in the garden with the children and the window was open. They argued. I could hear angry voices.'

'And afterwards?'

'Sir John said that Mr Canterbury was a wrong 'un. Those words exactly. He had been offered a bribe. A bribe to call a halt to our work for the Abolition movement.' Anger flared in her eyes. 'You must know that we are collecting signatures for a petition calling for an end to the slave trade and so far we have several hundred names. We also have a list of subscribers.'

Kit drew furiously, despite shaking hands, as Lady Beechworth spoke of her husband's anger.

'Can you describe this Mr Canterbury, ma'am?'

Kit stood up and walked over to them, her throat aching. 'Is this the man?' She handed her sketch to Lady Beechworth.

The shocked gasp and hand to the mouth gave her the answer.

Lady Beechworth looked up at her in wonder. 'How did you know?'

Martin stared at the sketch. 'Kit—what made you think of him?'

She looked down at her father's face, her world reeling. 'He was born in Canterbury. He used that name sometimes when he wanted to trade anonymously. His first ship was called the *Canterbury*.'

Holford rose. 'Lady Beechworth, my people will see you safely back to my house. Thank you.' He turned to Martin. 'You remain here, see Miss Selbourne safely home. We've got enough. I'll see to this personally. Perhaps you might ask Barclay to come along. Since he stopped a bullet fired by our "Mr Canterbury" a year ago, I've no doubt he'd like to be a witness.'

Blindly, Kit left the room.

Martin found her in one of the small salons near the library.

She sat by the window, staring out into the great courtyard.

'Sweetheart?'

She turned and the tear tracks on her cheeks tore at his heart.

'Martin, I…we can't. I mustn't.'

He thought his heart might stop beating. She was going to refuse to marry him.

'Mustn't what?' He went to her, gripped her hands. 'Let him destroy our lives?'

'Martin, what he's done. Seeing that poor woman—it brought it all home to me.'

She tugged at her hands, but he held on. 'What about Staverton? What he's done? Will you condemn Lady Harbury for that? Psyché?'

'What? No! Of course not.'

'Then don't condemn yourself.' He held her shocked gaze. 'Or me. What about what you've done? You've done your part in stopping him. You've tried to set things not right, they can't be set right, but straight. In helping to find justice you've done something to balance the books.'

'It's not enough.'

'Maybe not, but it's what can be.' He drew her unresisting into his arms and held her, his cheek resting on her soft curls. 'He's not going to ruin two more lives, Kit. Not even if I have to drag you to the altar.'

'Drag me?'

He heard the edge in her voice and pressed a kiss into her curls. 'Don't think for a moment that I wouldn't do it, sweetheart. Damned if I'm going to be seduced and abandoned like a virgin in a melodrama.'

She gave a choked laugh and then she wept.

* * *

Kit leaned against Martin's shoulder as he drove the gig back into Soho as dusk fell. Exhaustion gripped her. It was over. By now Carshalton would have been arrested. Staverton would be disgraced—Holford seemed to think trying to keep things quiet was a waste of time.

Something will get out no matter what we do. The important thing is for us to choose what *gets out.*

Psyché would be relieved. Harbury had named Staverton as guardian for his children in his will and Staverton, according to Huntercombe, had been threatening to remove the children if Lady Harbury did not dance to his tune.

As one of the trustees for Lady Harbury, Huntercombe thought it would be possible to have the guardianship transferred to himself. Not that he planned to interfere with Lady Harbury. Quite the opposite.

She scowled a little. The guardianship laws were deeply unjust, and…she laughed at herself. No point tilting at windmills today. Today, and tonight, she was going to be happy.

'Something funny?'

She nestled against him. 'Something silly. I'm happy, that's all.'

He flashed her a smile. 'Good. I'm happy, too. Huntercombe asked when we intended to marry. I told him as soon as possible.' He slowed near the

Phoenix. 'Shall I let you down here? You can collect Moth from Psyché and wait there while I take the gig back to the Lion.'

'I'll walk up with you.'

The ostlers took the gig and Martin's horse and before long they were walking back towards the Phoenix. It had closed, but the shutters were still open, and Martin could see Psyché and Caleb and the rest of the wait staff pushing tables back and stacking chairs on them.

Kit slid her hand from his arm. 'Do you want to go across? I need to speak to Psyché. She was so worried about her cousin losing the children to Staverton. I want to tell her what Huntercombe said.'

Martin hesitated. And mentally shook himself. It was over. Kit would be perfectly safe crossing the road by herself with the dog. 'Very well. But you aren't to set the bar on the front door. Promise? I'll come down and do it later.'

He knew she *could* do it, but he couldn't bring himself to leave a heavy load like that to a female. He didn't care how strong she might be.

'Oh, very well.' She smiled up at him. 'I won't be long.'

'Don't rush.' He feathered a kiss over her lips. 'I'll have time to set the fire.'

He saw her into the shop, saw Psyché set down a tray loaded with empty coffee cups and come towards her. Moth appeared from the direction of the fireplace, tail wagging.

Smiling, he turned away. Everything right now seemed absolutely perfect.

Crossing the road to the bookshop, he looked at the building beside it. Like the building that housed the Phoenix, it belonged to Huntercombe and, according to Will that afternoon, the lease would be up in two months. Andrews, who ran a draper's business from it, had decided to retire.

Possibilities whirled in his head as he let himself into the shop, bell jangling, and locked the door behind him. Used to the dimness in the shop, he crossed to the hearth and lit a candle from the tinderbox on the chimneypiece. He hesitated. Leaving candles burning in a bookshop was never a good idea, but Kit would only be a few minutes. He lit a second candle and left it burning ready for her in the hearth.

Odd the cat hadn't come down to greet him. He climbed the stairs swiftly, whistling softly to himself, considering how best to suggest to Kit that she think about hiring an assistant she could train as a manager. Maitland, his brother's old secretary, was looking for a position. Then perhaps they could take a short holiday in the summer, pay that visit to Huntercombe's family at Isleworth.

He smiled to himself. Harry and Georgie would approve of that. He wondered if Kit remembered her long-ago promise to Georgie that she could carry flowers at their wedding. At long last that promise would be kept.

He opened the door to the shadowy parlour, stepped in and with a yowl the cat shot out the door between his legs. Martin cursed, lost his balance, nearly dropped the candle and remembered—

We left the door open for Hodge...

Sensing movement behind him, he turned sharply as something crashed down, glancing off the back of his head and striking his shoulder.

With Moth at her heels, Kit dashed across the road. She looked up as she reached the opposite pavement, expecting to see light in the parlour. He would have lit a lamp, the fire would be—

She frowned. Odd, the parlour windows were still dark. He might have gone into the bedroom—*their* bedroom, to light that fire first. Every fibre dancing and fizzing with joy at the day, she unlocked the front door and saw, as she walked in and the bell jangled above her, the candle left for her in the hearth.

Her heart gave a little sigh of pleasure. Such a small thing, a candle left burning when you came home. But it spoke of exactly that. Home. Belonging. Someone thinking of you. Like not wanting you to lift a heavy bar.

The yowl from under the desk made her jump. 'Hodge?'

The cat came out, fluffed to twice his normal

size, and yowled again, the sound rumbling up from his chest. The same sound he'd made the night they had found Ignatius—

Something was wrong. Kit took a deep breath to call out to Martin and froze. It was faint, very faint, but surely she could smell—

Moth lifted her head, growled softly and her hackles rose.

Sandalwood, the faintest drift of it in the air.

Hooves clattered in the street. Chilled to the marrow, she looked out the window. Will dismounted from his horse, lashed the rein around a post and ran into the Phoenix. They'd help her. She could run out, back to the Phoenix…

And if she did the doorbell would let him know that she'd run for help, he'd be able to see her go from the parlour windows. Somehow Carshalton had slipped through the net and she was going to have to stop him.

His head ached like an anvil with a thousand hammers pounding inside it. He floated, confused, disoriented, nauseated by a faint odour…

Kit had been nauseated, too…

Sandalwood. Even before he cracked open his eyes Martin knew who had hit him.

Kit was walking into a trap.

Struggling to breathe through the dizzying sickness, he heard her light voice, faint through the closed door. She was coming up and Carshalton stood waiting, ready for her. His brain wouldn't work. Pistol. Carshalton had a pistol, but wouldn't use it unless he had no choice. A shot would bring someone. Last thing the bastard wanted.

Force him to use the pistol.

He was lying in front of the fireplace, between the wingchairs, in full view of the door.

His head spun and his stomach rolled, but he sat up. Yelled a warning.

What came out was a barely audible wheeze. Something sticky trickled down his neck and even with his wavering vision he saw the door handle turn. She'd see him the moment she walked in. See him hurt. Run to him and—he shut his eyes in despair.

Carshalton spoke coldly from the side of the room, well clear of the door this time. 'Leave the dog outside, Catherine. I'll shoot it if it comes through the door. Then a knife for you and Lacy. Run and I'll shoot Lacy where he lies.'

'Kit!' His voice came out this time. 'Run!'

The door opened only enough to admit her and she closed it behind her immediately as the dog started barking.

'Leave him alone, Carshalton. I'll come with you if that's what you want.'

Carshalton uttered a harsh laugh. 'Take you with me? After you've ruined me? No. I've a ship waiting. And not where they'll expect. I've enough to see me through for now.'

'Then why did you come?'

She came in a little further and Martin struggled to his knees. If he could get to Carshalton, then—

Kit had her muff. And not merely carrying it. She had her hands in it. His brain cleared a little... surely her pistol was in a drawer in the desk here.

'To make sure I ruined everything for you before I leave. You won't get a damn thing, you know. Even if I hadn't disinherited you, that weasel Holford will make sure the Crown gets everything. This bloody fool first, then I've a knife for you.'

Distract him.

'How'd you get away, Carshalton?' Better, his voice was stronger.

The man snorted. 'Whoever sketched Bragg senior in that damn brothel dropped their pastels. So I knew.'

Carshalton raised his pistol. The click echoed.

'Carshalton.'

Kit's cold, clear voice got Carshalton's attention.

He turned towards her as she raised the muff. There was a muffled click. 'What—? You *wouldn't.*'

'I would. Put your pistol down and leave.'

Dizzy, head throbbing, Martin fought to his feet, as Carshalton swore and brought his pistol to bear on Kit.

Martin hurled himself at the man as a pistol roared.

They crashed to the floor together and there was another, muffled, shot. Under him, Carshalton jerked convulsively, then went limp.

The world lurched. *Kit.* If he'd shot Kit—

'Martin!'

His head pounding, Martin registered her voice, but concentrated on keeping his weight on Carshalton. 'Kit, stay back.'

She ignored him. 'I… I think he's dead.'

And now Martin could smell it. The blood and the voiding in death. Outside the door Moth barked furiously.

He rolled off the body and struggled up to wrap his arms around Kit, shaking. 'My God. I thought he'd shot you—how the hell did you get your pistol?'

'This one belonged to Ignatius. He kept it in his desk downstairs. I… I had to stop him. Stop him killing you.'

There was another crash as someone broke through the front door and footsteps pounded up the stairs.

'Kit! Lacy!'

'Will!' Kit called out. 'In here! We're safe.'

Will burst through the door with the dog and stopped, his face white.

He stared at them, saw Carshalton. 'You call this *safe*?' He strode to the window, unlatched it and flung up the sash. 'It's all right, love. They're safe. Ah, a pistol discharged. Kit forgot to unload it. You might bring a bandage. Lacy bumped his head.'

He turned back to the room. 'No point making the entire street a present of this.'

He rolled the body over. Blood stained darkly, either side of the chest. Will frowned. 'You both shot him?'

Kit shook her head. 'Me. His…his own pistol must have discharged, too. When he fell.'

Will looked at Martin. 'They're going to prefer it if officially *you* shot him. There's already a warrant for his arrest, but if it's known Kit shot him it might muddy the waters.'

Martin nodded. He didn't care. He held on to Kit as the dog whined and snuffed at them.

Will looked at them. 'I'll be back. I need to send a message to Huntercombe.'

'Holford,' Martin said, his brain re-emerging. 'Let him know.'

Will nodded. 'Count on it.' He frowned. 'Let's get you down to the shop. You can't stay up here with that.'

Martin managed the stairs with Will and Kit's help and found himself ensconced before the fire, which Will took the time to stir up before leaving on his errands. Psyché came with hot soup and coffee, helping Kit with Martin's head wound before leaving them alone.

Kit had pulled a footstool close to the fire and

sat on it. 'I killed him, Martin.' Her voice was a shattered whisper. 'My own—'

'No. He wasn't. Not in any way that matters.' He said it steadily, through the lessening ache of his head. 'You saved our lives. Don't let him get between us now.' He leaned forward, gripped her hands and held her gaze. 'You heard him—he was going to kill both of us. The Furies aren't going to haunt you for this night's work.'

A breath shuddered through her. 'No. I was going to say I didn't care. But still—I... I shot him.'

'It's not meant to be easy—killing,' he said quietly. He released one hand to cradle her cheek. 'If it was, you'd be as bad as he was. Would you blame me if I'd shot him? Because, believe me, I would have, even knowing I'd feel the horror of ending a life.'

A steadier breath this time. 'No. God, no.'

'Then don't blame yourself.'

'No.' Even steadier. 'You're safe.' Trembling fingers touched his face as if to make sure. '*We're* safe. Ignatius is safe, too.'

The cat reappeared and leapt into his lap, settled down. Automatically he stroked it, felt the beginnings of a purr. They were safe because Ignatius Selbourne had kept a cat and taught his great-niece to think and handle a pistol.

He could live with that.

Epilogue

Early October 1805

The sharp autumn breeze nipped at Martin as he walked home through Soho in the softness of twilight. The day had held its bright promise and he'd elected to walk from Whitehall rather than taking a hackney.

'I had no idea it could be like this, you know?'

He glanced down and the young spaniel, Dash, wagged his tail appreciatively.

His life was a far cry from the bleak affair it had been last spring. Then despite the satisfaction and challenge of his work, he had been lost, drifting, all the stars hidden from him. Kit had changed all that, bringing a joy he had never imagined, even when he first fell in love with her.

Along the street shops were shuttered for the night, lamps and candles shone in upper windows. Over the way the Phoenix was shut for the night and a light showed in the apartment above where Caleb now made his home. Psyché and Will had taken a house further up the street where their daughter had been born a month ago. More joy there.

At the expanded Selbourne's Books the shutters remained open and lamps glowed in the shop. Next door, in what had been the draper's, Kit had added a circulating library entered through an archway cut between the two buildings. For two nights a week she taught reading and writing in there to several women who hoped to better their situation. One of them was Gabrielle from the Bird.

Martin entered the shop and as Dash made a charge for the stairs to the apartment, the fair-haired man in his late thirties behind the desk looked up with a smile.

'Evening, Lacy.'

'Maitland, good to see you back. How was the buying trip?'

Maitland grinned. 'Kit is ecstatic. Rumford was so eager to sell off his father's library that I got it for half what she was prepared to pay.'

Martin interpreted that to mean Maitland had haggled like a fishwife at a Friday market. His brother's one-time secretary had turned out to have not just a love of books, but a talent for the book trade.

Maitland rose. 'I'll be off now you're here. Kit's

upstairs.' He laughed. 'Gloating over her booty, you might say.'

'Oh?'

'I'll let her tell you. Several gems and one—well, she says Huntercombe will want it, but between you and me, the man may have to wrest it from her cold, dead hands.'

Martin was still chuckling off and on at that after locking and barring the door behind Maitland. Dousing all the lamps bar one, he picked it up and started upstairs. Dash by now would be curled up all but on top of Moth by the fire.

On the landing at the top of the stairs he stopped to hang his coat on the rack and lay his hat and gloves on the small table there, along with his thankfully empty satchel. Their expansion into next door meant that as well as the parlour there was now a dining parlour and two small studies, one for each of them. He still wasn't sure how Kit had persuaded him to line the dining parlour with bookshelves. He was damn sure it was the only dining parlour-cum-library in London.

Since the door to Kit's study stood open and no light showed he opened the door to the parlour. The glow of lamplight greeted him. The dogs lay curled by the fire, Dash half lying on Moth. She heaved him off unceremoniously and came to greet Martin, wagging her tail.

Kit looked up from the book she was examining at the tea table. 'Martin! You'll never guess!'

Having rubbed Moth's ears, he walked over, kissed his wife thoroughly. 'That Maitland got the Rumford collection at a discount?'

She positively glowed. 'He's a wonder. I'm glad you told me about him. But he didn't tell you the best part.'

'The mysterious item that poor Huntercombe will have to pry from your cold, dead hands?'

Kit snorted. 'Well, maybe.' She held up the folio volume in gloved hands. 'The rest of the collection is being packed up for the carrier, but he knew I'd want to see this at once. I had no idea Rumford had a copy. Ignatius would have been thrilled. It's the first edition of—here, look for yourself.'

Martin knew better than to take the volume and read the title page over her shoulder.

The whole works of Homer...in his Iliads, and Odyssey. Translated according to the Greeke, by Geo. Chapman. London: At London printed for Nathaniell Butter.

'I've never even seen a copy of this edition,' she said softly. She closed it gently, laid it reverently on the table.

'Will you keep it then?' he asked. 'A special treasure?'

She let out a sigh. 'Tempting. But it's like what Huntercombe told Georgie at our wedding about puppies. You can't keep them all. Some of them have to go out into the world. And I'm running a business here.' She nudged the book away. 'Besides…' she rose and went into his arms '… I have my treasure. Right here. Not even Chapman's *Homer* compares to this.'

Martin drew her closer, kissing her deeply. He had no idea how other men might feel about being rated higher than a dusty, somewhat battered old book. He was just fine with it.

* * * * *

COMING SOON!

We really hope you enjoyed reading this book.
If you're looking for more romance, be sure to
head to the shops when new books are
available on

Thursday 19th January

To see which titles are coming soon, please visit

millsandboon.co.uk/nextmonth